A Dancer in Darkness

by David Stacton

A
Dancer
in Darkness

David Stacton

Pantheon Books

c.1

© 1960 David Derek Stacton
First American Edition 1962
Published by Pantheon Books, a Division of Random House, Inc.
Library of Congress Catalog Card Number: 62-14265
Manufactured in the U.S.A.

For Madeline in small token
of a very long friendship;
and Harrison Ainsworth;
and Antony Hope; and Ouida;
with apologies

Antonio, Antonio,
our lives are only other men's means.
Thus fall Emperors and Queens
to grease the kindling of another's fire
with the rancid renders of their own desire.
There is no song
soothes its listeners for long,
except, escape with me.

ONE

Bosola was on his way to see his sister, a woman he had not seen for ten years. He had seen no woman for ten years. The reason for that was that he had lost his footing, his patron had disowned him, his presence had proved inconvenient, and so he had spent the decade in the galleys. The Dominicans arrived once a week to haul their charnel cart from the galley barracks to potter's field. He had escaped in that.

He was no longer young. He no longer had that fire. He had become a dancer in darkness, a man who is free only when the lights are out and the audience has gone. He had been burnt to a cinder. But grace he had, and style. He would still be a gentleman, if he could. He meant to clamber back to that position, despite the galleys of Puteoli.

In the back streets of Naples he struck down a *lazzarone*, one of the colourful rabble of that town, and switched clothes with him. Ten minutes later, dressed in skin-tight yellow hose, soft leather boots, and a jerkin, with a stocking cap on his head, and even a little money, he sauntered about in the belief that he was a free man. And perhaps he was right. His boots rang against the cobbles, and he liked the sound. He had learned his lesson. A poor gentleman is down for good. It is the poor themselves, in a bad age, who have the art of growing rich. And that is freedom.

As for his sister, she was a dancer in light, and meant to stay there. She had a horror of the dark. Therefore blackmail would appeal to her more than a plea to her goodness. She passed these days for a future saint, but she knew best by what means she had achieved that sanctity, and so goodness seemed to her irrelevant.

His sister was Sor Juana, the famous Sor Juana, that Sor Juana whom all the world, so said part of it, except himself, conspired to adore. But in ten years she, too, had had the time to grow tired.

She paused now at the top of the landing, slightly out of breath, and glad to reach her own rooms, for her fellow nuns fatigued her, as they always did these days. Often, in her heart, she had wanted to laugh at them. But that she dared to do only at night, over her writing desk.

It was the writing desk that had made her a nun. And even to reach the writing desk, she had had to come a long way.

Over fifteen years ago, one dusty morning in 1584, a barefoot girl of nine had come down from a village behind Sorrento. The shores of Vesuvius were then an arid plain. In the distance lay Naples, and Naples was her goal.

Her name was Juana dal Nagro. Her face had an almost transparent beauty, but beauty, after all, is not so rare. The one quality that really set her apart was genius.

Knowledge she absorbed as a blotter does ink. When she was saturated with it, she poured it all out again in a flood of clever, pious, erotic, or sophisticated verse. At the inquiry attendant upon her subsequent canonization, it was claimed that no child could be so brilliant without God's grace. But God's grace had nothing to do with it. You could tell that instantly, from the way she held her tongue between her teeth.

The Court took her up. Dwarfs they had had. The Spanish always have dwarfs. But children of genius were something new. She charmed them. She amused them. She was a novelty. And so she prospered.

At ten she knew Latin, Greek, three modern languages, and a smattering of Hebrew. Her portraits show a girlish face, but a girlish face without a hint of innocence. It is a face that willed to be pre-eminent at any price, a professional face, the face of a woman whose profession was herself.

She knew she was nothing better than a clever animal in the eyes of those who petted her. She had not the family or the dot to make a good marriage. Only one course was open to her. She became a nun, at the cloister of San Severo.

Now, on this May morning of 1611, she had been a nun for fifteen years. Her cell was fitted up as a library and the view from her window was excellent. It was rather like having a desirable chair at the University of Bologna, except that she could not leave. She received the fashionable and the great every Tuesday and Thursday afternoon. The mother superior hated her. She was being taken up by the Cardinal. Her future was assured. She was twenty-nine.

She also had the restless hands of a child and the face of a matriarch. Others had founded great convents. Why not she?

She crossed the landing towards her room, shaping her thoughts to fit her pen, and went immediately to her writing stand, a Spanish travelling chest whose bronze and velvet front let down over a double trestle. Beyond lay the window, and beyond the window the soft scented murmurs of the night and the metrical insistence of the cloister fountain.

Her cell was not one room, but two, for opening off it was a small private oratory stuccoed with columns and floral swags. She turned to it automatically, but took no more than a first step, for leaning against the doorway was a *lazzarone* dressed in yellow, with a young body, an old face, and a black beard. He lolled there, with one leg crossed over the other, at his ease. She blinked, but he was still there.

It did not occur to her to cry out for help. She was not the sort of woman who would cry out for help. But her eyes grew solemn.

Bosola stood with his feet planted wide apart and his arms crossed, looking down at her. "Sister, you do not know me," he said dryly, and swaggered a little in his latest disguise.

Sor Juana started, peered at him more closely, and then sat down in her field chair. "You escaped."

"I died," he told her. "It was so much easier." He looked around the austere security of her room and lost none of its prosperity. "The guards sold the dead to the anatomy school. They grow rich that way. It wasn't difficult." He felt suddenly tired and leaned once more against the wall.

He knew any preliminaries with her would be useless. "You

11

know the Cardinal," he said. "I want you to write me a letter to him. A safe conduct, if you like."

"I have no power with him."

"I am your brother. Or don't you wish that known?" He stood up, strode to her desk, and stood over her. "Write," he said. "Write."

She wrote.

When she had finished, for he did not trust her, he read the note before it was sealed. It was noncommittal and served to introduce one Niccolò Ferrante, which was the name he had told her to use.

"Sleep well, sister," he said.

She bit her lip, opened one of the drawers in her desk, and threw him a small sack. It chinked in the air. "You will need money," she said dryly.

He did not need it, but he took it. If this was the only way she could show kindness, it was at least better than none. On the other hand, it was probably a bribe. Putting the bag in his jerkin, he turned and left the room.

Sor Juano did not intend to be hampered by her brother. Once he had gone, she began to make certain plans.

III

The Cardinal and his brother the Duke were at Castel del Mare, at the Sanducci Palace. Their sister was recently a widow. They had come there for the funeral.

The appearance of a new *lazzarone* in their midst occasioned no comment, for the Cardinal kept about him a gang of soldiers, executioners, and toughs. They were, he said, his nightingales; and to his nightingales were added the unruly suite of his brother, who sang a deeper note in the same scale. The worst of these toughs was a man called Marcantonio.

As Bosola rode across the *piazza* towards the palace, on a horse bought with Sor Juana's money, and still in his *lazzarone* costume, he saw that some common street players had set up a platform before the palace gate.

A woman stood on the platform, yowling her lungs out. Her

12

voice was four-fifths gravel, and her fingers clicked like pistols missing fire. Bosola drew rein to watch.

The other players capered around her, throwing their scrawny limbs into the wind. Signor Bombard held his bottom and threw out his legs to the attacks of Sganarelle with a three-foot syringe. The woman had a weary face. Her caterwauling aroused the soldiers loitering around her. They threw her money. The singer gathered up her skirts and began to dance.

A tall guard made a lunge for her. She slapped him, and went on singing. Then the other guards closed in on her. The players capered themselves to the safety of the wall.

The woman burst out from among the soldiers, her bodice torn, righted herself, and ran towards Bosola. The yellow guardsmen streamed after her.

Bosola reached down, scooped her up to the saddle, and wheeled his horse. The woman made no sound. He cursed himself for a fool, and dug his rowels into the scarred body of the horse. A crowd was jammed in the far opening of the street, where it opened out into a small square.

There was nothing to do but jump. The horse's hooves caught on a basket a woman had on her head, sending bright slimy squid flying through the air. The horse stumbled on the cobbles on the other side, and its hind quarters went down. There was no time to worry about the horse. Bosola grabbed the woman, and ran for the portal of the church at the far end of the square.

The church was draped with long black streamers over the façade. Bosola shoved the woman through the portal and ran into the nave. The woman sobbed and followed him. They were fortunate that the church was draped for a funeral: the crowds were superstitious, and would remain outside.

He peered round the quiet darkness of the nave, and moved forward towards the catafalque which dominated it.

"What's your name?" he asked.

"Rosina."

"You should know better than to provoke soldiers."

She shrugged. "I must earn my living, and some are not bad." She sat down on a chair, untied her skirt, and took money out of it, counting.

13

"Then why run?" he asked contemptuously.

"I am six months with child."

Bosola grunted and went to inspect the catafalque.

The church dated from Norman times, and it had the Norman gloom. The catafalque hid the High Altar, whose flicker was dimmed by the giant candles which stood at the head and foot of the sarcophagus. He jumped on a reed chair, to look on the bier.

A little man lay up there, like the abandoned chrysalis of a butterfly. He had been small in life, and death had made him smaller. He was dressed in engraved pageant armour whose helmet was four times the size of his head. It stood at the top, its plumes nodding in the breath from the candles. The man had a grey beard and a pinched, mean, haughty face. Over his body was flung the scarlet cloak of the Knights of Malta.

Bosola jumped down from his reed stool and caught the superstitious eyes of the woman.

"Who is he?"

"My Lord Piccolomini, Duke of Amalfi. That is why they are all here. The Duchess is a widow with a three-year-old son."

"The Duchess?" That would be the Cardinal's sister. "She cannot be more than twenty."

Rosina dusted off her skirts and pulled her bodice into place. She was such a huge woman that her pregnancy was scarcely visible. "They must marry her off again, so they all come here. Poor thing, they say she's beautiful," she added wistfully, in that way that the poor have of pitying their betters.

When he had last seen the Duchess, she had been seven. Bosola jumped on the stool to look at the catafalque again. Then he drew the dagger in his boot and tossed it in the air thoughtfully. If the whole brood were here, his chances would be the better, but he scarcely knew which he was after, preferment or revenge.

TWO

In the ten years since Bosola had been sent to the galleys, the
Sanducci had climbed far. This palace was what they had come
from, provincial nobles with one horse, who had ridden the
Spanish coat-tails into power. Bosola looked round the courtyard. He knew the place well.

Ferdinand, it was true, was sixth count and second Duke of
Bracciano, but Bracciano was a sterile vineyard in the hills,
with a strawberry patch down by the lake. Now there was Capel-
monte, Astri, the fief of Erculano, Calabria (but Calabria did not
recognize the fact), and Papal lands for all. In power or out, the
Spanish had made them rich. Bosola was only one of many they
had trampled underfoot in their greedy scamper after power.

Unobserved, Bosola mounted the stairs and made his way
into the palace. That was the advantage of his dress. If he had
been tricked out as a gentleman the world would have wanted
to know his business. As it was, they assumed he was on some
errand the nature of which it would be better for them not to
know.

He made his way up the state staircase to the loggia above.
and found himself walking warily, on the balls of his feet, and
hugging the wall. It was in a corridor such as this that he had
murdered the man for whose death he had gone to the galleys.
He smiled grimly, wondering what the Cardinal would make of
his resurrection.

The light grew dimmer. He was now in the oldest part of the
palace. Dust lay heavy on the floors. When she was a child,
these rooms had been the Duchess's. She had lived here almost
alone and almost unseen, ignored in a stone cul-de-sac, until
she was old enough for her brothers to marry her off.

A door opened ahead of him, and he had just time to draw

into shadow. A large buxom woman came into view, holding in her arms an enormous pile of stuff whose silver threads caught the light. She could not see him. He could see her.

It was Cariola, the Duchess's nurse, and now her gentlewoman. She was a heavy-skinned woman of forty, and her eyes glittered with a coquettishness gone sour. She scurried down the corridor and despite himself he was upset. She might prove difficult.

When she had gone down the corridor a little way, he stepped out of the shadow and followed her.

She looked over her shoulder. Light from the window hit him, lighting up only his hose and boots. She stopped. He had seen that look of listening attention in frightened birds. He did not move. From a distance of thirty feet they peered at each other in the tricky light, then she went into a room at the end of the hall and closed the door.

He did not think he had been recognized. He walked on and stopped before the door she had entered. The light was very bright here. He heard Cariola's voice raised loudly and grinned. That voice had lost none of its peculiar mixture of cloying sweetness and the nag. That was what came of being a gentlewoman in reduced circumstances.

Then he heard the other voice. It was a voice of a curious silvery lightness. The Duchess, who had been Aemelia Sanducci, had none of her brothers' cruel Spanish tastes. Yet the voice had authority. It was as though she would not be put down. Her will was taut as wire.

The two women went on talking and he could not make out the words. There was nothing more for him to learn here. He went in search of her brothers.

II

Ferdinand was not hard to find. He was in the courtyard.

The courtyard of the palace was its one pleasant feature. On two sides there were open second-floor galleries, and the third had double casement windows. The fourth was a wall. A crowd was gathered there when Bosola entered. He was a short man and the crowd hemmed him in, but he could just catch a glimpse of what was going on.

Ferdinand must now be thirty-three. He moved through life jerkily, and it probably never even occurred to him that his elder brother, the Cardinal, pulled the strings. He was little more than a young tough with a title.

Because they were poor and preferment had only been available to them through the Church, Duke Sanducci had become Cardinal Sanducci, and left the title to his younger brother. Thus, as they began to rise, it was Ferdinand who reaped the pomps. His brother the Cardinal kept only the power.

Now Ferdinand swaggered down below. It could not be denied that he swaggered well. He had a certain blind phallic ardour. Bosola peered at him scornfully.

The Commedia del Arte players had come into the courtyard, and Rosina was back with them, looking none the worse for her experience. Ferdinand had had chairs set up to watch them. He sat clicking his fingers clumsily. Bosola forced his way to the front of the crowd, folded his arms, squinted in the sun, and watched Ferdinand.

Ferdinand was either drunk or tipsy with his own importance. He got up from his chair, swept Captain Bombard aside with his arm, and began to prance around Rosina. Rosina looked startled and then gave him a smile reserved for the quality. Ferdinand flung off his hat and stamped up and down, throwing out his arms and shouting. After an instant of hesitation, the other players capered around them both.

Rosina wanted to stop. She looked worried about her belly. Ferdinand would not let her stop. His face was flushed with that maddened blindness only Spanish dancers seem to feel. Sganarelle was still carrying the two-foot syringe which he used to squirt Bombard's behind. He aimed it at Ferdinand and rammed down the plunger. The air blew against Ferdinand's rump. He reached out a leg and kicked Sganarelle in the face.

The musicians scraped faster and faster. It was a jota. Ferdinand snapped his fingers and reared up on his toes over Rosina. It was clear he was proud of the slim arc of his body.

17

At this point in the dance Rosina was supposed to twirl rapidly, banging a tambourine against her folded wrist. Instead she fainted.

There was a sudden silence. Only the musicians scraped on. Ferdinand stopped, looked down at her, shrugged his shoulders, and threw a handful of coins at the players.

Among the recent gifts to the court had been a procession of dwarfs. The little men were dressed in saffron, the Sanducci livery. The Spanish, being a people well swathed in their own pride, enjoyed imitations of themselves. The dwarfs, being Spanish, decided to oblige.

They swept out across the courtyard, imitating the commedia players. Then one who had loitered behind scuttled haughtily forward, his little voice squeaking imperiously, and began to posture in imitation of Ferdinand.

Bosola had never seen the little men before. He watched avidly. So did Ferdinand. Rosina lay where she was.

None of the dwarfs was taller than three feet eight. This gave their movements the bound jerkiness of children. The tambourines rattled and shook in the air. There was no other sound. The crowd seemed to be watching the approach of something inevitable. Ferdinand stood and glowered.

Suddenly the dwarf impersonating Rosina screamed and fell down. Another dwarf rattled a tambourine, as though for attention. The dwarf parodying Ferdinand kicked the fallen one. Another roll on the tambourine. The dwarf mimicking Ferdinand reached into his jacket and gravely threw a handful of straw to the company. Then he took off his cap and bowed, bursting into a peal of silvery giggles. His eyes were scornful and his face old.

It was more than Ferdinand could stand. He leaped forward, picked up the dwarf, and hurled him against the courtyard wall. Then he fled from the court.

Involuntarily Bosola looked up and saw lurking behind one of the windows a figure he recognized as the Cardinal. Nothing ever stirred in that watchful face. The Cardinal withdrew.

The other dwarfs had gathered round their companion, who still lay by the wall. His spine was broken. They picked him up sorrowfully and carried him away.

18

The Cardinal had not recognized Bosola, but he had recognized something, and he hated anyone he could not instantly place, for he set great store by his memory. It had served him well.

His Eminence was a bland man, but certain things about him were peculiar. The most noticeable of these was his leg. No matter how he might parade as a Prince of the Church, there always emerged from his heavy scented robes that telltale leg. It was a supple leg; a pleasure-loving leg, a knowledgeable leg, and a leg that carried him lightly over any opposition he wished to crush.

For woebetide those who get in the way of a man whose ambitions have been thwarted, and the Cardinal had wanted to be a ruling Prince. That being impossible, he had become a Prince of the Church instead. Within the cage of his unwanted eminence, the Cardinal's ambition flung itself about like a wild animal, and when he slept at night, and had bad dreams, the noise that animal made was truly terrible.

In his mind he docketed everyone as useful, dangerous, or meaningless, and the man he had seen in the courtyard was all of those. The question was: Who was he?

He shrugged the problem off for the moment. He had other matters to attend to, and those soon. The first of these was his sister and his sister's lands, which meant, ultimately, his sister's son.

The only illusion he had about his sister is that he had no illusions about her at all. His sister, he knew from the spies he had carefully placed about her, had no lover. Therefore that shrivelled up little man lying dead in the cathedral had produced a legitimate heir. In some ways it could be an advantage to have a boy so far from his majority.

And Amalfi, though a poor enough place, was still a place worth having.

He paced up and down his study, irritably kicking aside the skirts of his robes. He had risen to power on the backs of servants he had been too wise to crush, yet one or two had escaped him. That was why the *lazzarone* in the courtyard had disturbed him. He had the feeling the man was someone who had slipped through his net.

He stopped at a tabouret on which a chess-board had been set up, and reached with a spidery hand towards the pieces, his amethyst ring upsetting a knight. He righted it thoughtfully, regretting that there was no piece on the board called the dupe. Yet the object of the game was to make all the pieces equally the dupe. That was an important thing to remember.

As he moved about the room, mirrors seemed to wait for him. The Cardinal was a handsome man, with bones so prominent and flesh so tight, that firelight always seemed to be flickering over his features. He was patrician. He had the grey, thoughtful eyes of a bust by Donatello. Yet, like those busts, his eyes were of no colour. It was only his character that made them seem grey.

He paused at the window. The dwarfs had been the Cardinal's gift to Ferdinand. Ferdinand could not refrain from bullying anything smaller than himself, and dwarfs are vengeful creatures. There could be use in that quality. He took a bell from a table and gave it an impatient shake. The door opened and his secretary came in.

"Send my chaplain down to the courtyard. Say that I sent him. One of the dwarfs is dying." He hesitated for a moment and then went on. "There is a man here, dressed as a *lazzarone*. I want to know who he is."

The secretary turned and sauntered out, his buttocks wriggling beneath his short jacket. The Cardinal waited until he had left. Then, gathering his robes about him, he swept out through the ante-chambers and towards his sister's apartments.

When he returned he was carrying a small bundle. The palace had a side door, very private in the street wall, and there his carriage was waiting.

THREE

By ten at night, the convent of San Severo was silent, except for the light in Sor Juana's cell. She was uneasy. Her rooms were too removed from the rest of the building, so that it was difficult for her to know what was going on. Intrigue was centred in the kitchens and the porter's lodge. She could not very well go down there herself.

In truth a convent was little better than a prison. It had the same pleasures, the same excitements, and the same alarms. But even the most coddled prisoner is still a prisoner. No matter how fine his condition, he still has the same limitation. He cannot move freely in the world.

She was fearful of Bosola, and the sirocco had begun. And the sirocco is not merely an evil wind. It is a branch of pathology, an ailment as seasonal but as severe as cholera or the plague.

Sor Juana had retired to her rooms as soon as she could. The wind made everything stir with invisible tension. Suddenly a pane of glass might shatter, or a bowl of flowers fall to the floor. Otherwise the wind rattled nothing. What it did was to make people itch, as though something were crawling all over them.

She could not concentrate. As the church bell began to toll, and as the moon slid about in a welter of slippery clouds, she got up and went into the corridor. She did not know what she expected to see there, but to see anyone at all was a shock. Someone was mounting the stairs.

It was the Cardinal. He had finished his business and was ready to enjoy himself. He always relaxed with Sor Juana, for he knew she was impotent to do him any harm. He reached the landing and came down towards her rooms in a swirl of important robes. He had never visited her so late before.

She led him into her rooms.

He tucked his little feet on a footstool and wondered just how much of her had remained naïve enough to be cheated. She had a lovely, unreal face, but her eyes had a crackle that belied her appearance. He could never be sure.

In the security of these rooms she was a gifted woman of letters, and he a Prince of the Church. It was necessary that they exchange a few professional compliments on both sides. He looked at her new verses.

"Admirable, admirable," he said. Perhaps he meant it. She waited, and he passed on easily to convent affairs. He suggested she must find the life a trifle confining. In former days women of her ability had founded convents, not lived in them.

And the need for convents was certainly great. One at Amalfi or Sorello, for instance, would do immense good.

Sor Juana was puzzled, but at the mention of Amalfi she listened more earnestly. She said she doubted she was a suitable instrument for such work, and waited for him to go on.

He did not go on. He merely smiled and said these things were not done in a day. He glanced around her cell and rose to leave, extending his hand, so she might kiss his ring, and watching the top of her bowed head with pleasure. He found her restful.

"I have brought you a foundling," he said. "His name is Raimondo, and there is no need to say that I brought him. He is heir to considerable estates. You might see that he is well taken care of, from time to time."

He glanced at her benignly, but if she had guessed who the boy was, she gave no sign. But then she would not. He gave a grunt of satisfaction and left the room.

Rather thoughtfully Sor Juana went to bed. It was the chance she had been waiting for, but what was the prize?

II

The palace retired much later than the convent, and indeed part of it could not be said to retire at all. The Cardinal returned unobserved, and stood for a while in the gallery above the great hall, looking down. He saw no signs of the *lazzarone*

22

in yellow, but Ferdinand was at his usual amusements, and very drunk.

Half an hour later he slipped into the corridor, motioned back the guard, and moved towards the Duchess's rooms. As he reached the turn of the corridor, he saw Cariola come out of the room he had entered earlier, with a blank look on her face, and hurry down towards the Duchess's chamber. He smiled quietly to himself and slipped into the room she had left.

The room was high and shadowy, and did not get much light. There were a few rugs, and a thick candle burned in a high sconce. He had not long to wait.

Cariola entered first. She looked as though she had been shocked by something else, that bothered her far more than this did. She was carrying a lamp. The Duchess followed immediately behind her.

The Cardinal looked at his sister with surprise and some pleasure. She had changed for the night into a soft, clinging robe, and her feet were bare. She was, after all, only a girl. She had small, enticing feet.

The two women bent over the massive cradle that stood near the sconce. No doubt the servant girl they had had to watch it had fled as soon as he had dealt with her. As the Duchess bent over, the robe flowed smoothly around her buttocks, and the satin skin beneath twinkled and glittered in the light. He thought her charming.

The two women whispered angrily. He was the more interested in Cariola. Something had happened to her, and he must find out what. He stepped forward, his silks rustling slightly.

"Good evening, sister," he said.

The two women straightened up. The Duchess instinctively drew closer to Cariola, and then, as though recollecting that she was afraid of nothing, stood alone.

"What do you know of this?" she demanded.

The Cardinal shrugged. "Send the woman away." In the cradle the blankets and sheets were turned back as he had left them.

The Duchess stepped off the rugs on to the cold floor and then back again. Her toes were agile and pink.

Reluctantly Cariola moved towards the door, still carrying

23

the lamp. They both watched the door close behind her.

Imperceptibly the Duchess relaxed. He admired her. She was a woman sufficiently proud never to ask for mercy. Nor would she need it, if she were clever.

"What have you done with him?" she asked at last. She spoke of the child as though it were a bundle, and he wondered if she had hated Piccolomini enough to hate the child, too, or if she was feigning indifference for his benefit.

He folded his hands and looked at her. He saw now that she could never be managed. She would have to be trapped. And that was a pity.

"In some measure Ferdinand and I are your guardians," he said softly.

"What?" She began to pace the rug from one end to the other.

"Well, we have made ourselves so, and there is no one to stop us." He leaned forward. "You should be grateful to me. If Ferdinand had the boy, he would dash it against the wall, as quickly as he did that dwarf downstairs."

The Duchess stopped her pacing. "Is he dead?" she asked simply.

"No, he is not dead."

"Then where is he?"

He paused. "I am the lesser of two evils. You may just as well make the best of me." He stood up. "Come, the child means nothing to you, except as a child. He means nothing to me, except as an heir." He came swaying towards his sister, with his arms outstretched, as though to bless her.

"What do you mean to do?"

"Nothing. Except to keep him from Ferdinand. Alive, he will one day rule. Dead, he could not do that. And Ferdinand loves property. So do I."

"What do you want of me?"

"Alive, one heir is quite enough. Let us leave it at that."

She gazed at him, and then fled from the room. The Cardinal did not follow, but stood there for quite some time, the only sound the hiss of the candle in its sconce, as it beat before a tricky gust of wind from the sea.

He felt sorry for her. He had only acted out of necessity.

24

By the next day she had regained her composure, whereas he had spent a sleepless night. He marvelled, looking at her, at the several abilities of women.

They had carried Piccolomini to the family tombhouse, which was attached to the cathedral, but could be entered only from the outside, through narrow lanes.

The tombhouse made the Cardinal thoughtful. He kept the Duchess and Ferdinand well in view. The *lazzarone* was nowhere in sight, and the secretary had yet to report. He did not like that.

To all intents and purposes the Piccolomini was the last of his line, which had not lasted long. Eighty years before they had started much as the Sanducci did now. They had built their tombhouse in Castel del Mare, as though not trusting their ability to hold Amalfi. It was a circular building stemmed to the church like an oak-gall, with a small garden of herbal knots and a cypress or two in good repair.

Inside, baroque monuments reared up to the ceiling, which had an oval hole to admit light. There were ten niches but only five Piccolomini, including the latest one. The late Duke had taken himself seriously, and seen to his monument while he was still living. The sculptures were in place, and pulleys and weights propped the lid of the sarcophagus ajar. His Highness's marble graces and engraved accomplishments would be in place by the end of the week. It only remained now to lower his coffin into its container, and the job was done.

Why the Duchess should have wished to see this ceremony was beyond him. She stood now under the rays of light which fell from the open dome, with Cariola beside her. The coffin swayed up in the air and then slowly settled down towards the immense marble sarcophagus. Workmen eased it into place. There was a hush in the building, a workman cut the weight rope, and the marble lid came down with a bang. Dust settled around the monument. Before the echoes had finally died, the little party turned and left the tombhouse, the verger locking the bronze doors with an enormous key.

Then the small procession wound its way back to the

cathedral, mounted horses, and went towards the palace. From there the Duchess would return to Amalfi; he and Ferdinand to Rome. The Cardinal rode well to the rear, watching his brother speak to her.

It was necessary for him to hear what Ferdinand was saying. His brother had always nourished an ugly passion for his sister. Now Piccolomini was dead, the Cardinal proposed to allow that passion to grow.

A burden seemed to have lifted from the Duchess. But she should not have worn that dress of silver and grey, which if he remembered she had had before marriage. Mourning would have become her, and not to wear it was an act of defiance. She rode slowly, but with a briskness she had not shown in some time, and while she listened to Ferdinand, she smiled.

Ferdinand's manner was more that of a lover than of a brother. Even when she was a child the Duchess had been his favourite. But then, Ferdinand might only be posturing again. One could never be sure.

The party reached the palace. The crowds applauded, but then they would applaud anything. Perhaps they wished to express sympathy. The Cardinal bowed and blessed them amiably, while he spurred his horse gently on, his heels concealed by his robes. As he entered the courtyard he caught a glimpse of the yellow-booted *lazzarone*, over in the corner with Ferdinand's soldiers. He frowned, dismounted, and went up to his rooms, to his secretary.

"What did you find out?"

"His name is Niccolò Ferrante. He had an introduction to the steward."

"From whom?"

"A nun at San Severo."

"And what else?"

"I think he wants a position here."

"No doubt," said the Cardinal. He was not satisfied, and he made his voice deliberately dry.

The secretary wanted very much to please. "There is one other thing. The Duchess's waiting woman knows him. She did not speak to him, but she knew him."

"So," said the Cardinal. He wondered what nun at San

Severo, but of course this lout would not know that. He went to the window and stared down into the court.

Bosola was swaggering uneasily on the edge of a dice game. He looked up, and the sun caught his face. With a start, the Cardinal withdrew from the window.

"So he calls himself Niccolò Ferrante," he said.

"Yes, your Eminence."

"Enrol him in my guard, but keep him away from me," said the Cardinal. Then he went back to the window, and leaned out thoughtfully, his hands on the stone sill.

He remembered the man now. He was pleased. A prince is successful only when he knows when to do evil, said Machiavelli, and for this purpose the best tools to his purpose are desperate and dangerous men. No doubt ten years in the galleys had made Bosola desperate indeed. The Cardinal had gathered another piece to move about his board.

FOUR

The Cardinal's titular church in Rome was in the old section not far from the Capitol. His palace was near by, and that of Ferdinand in the same quarter.

It was a long time since Bosola had been to Rome. He had exchanged his *lazzarone* costume for the Cardinal's livery, but he had not put it away. It was useful for roistering anonymously in the streets, and since he had not the means for the security he craved, he took his pleasure where he could. He was sure by now that the Cardinal knew his identity, and was only waiting for a summons. He had waited for six months.

One florid evening in May he changed into his *lazzarone* costume, and went clomping through the streets with Marcantonio, Ferdinand's bravo, who haunted the Cardinal's guard on orders from his master. Together they roved the back alleys, to pick a fight or a pocket, or go wenching in the cheapest tavern they could find.

Marcantonio led the way to the Piazza Navona.

It was a scene of carnival. Booths had been set up around the fountains, where food was sold. The square itself was dominated by two wooden platforms. There were street musicians and the unavoidable commedia players, and already flares and torches beat against the green dusk. Somebody had lit a bonfire, and from rug-hung balconies the inhabitants of the households were looking down at the square.

Marcantonio had taken Bosola under his wing, for he was a sadist with an unvarying instinct for a natural victim. Now he shoved Bosola to the front of the crowd.

The crowd was waiting for an execution. In the centre of the square stood a tall T-shaped gallows. From this some black-faced devil had been hanging in the strappado since morning.

28

He hung about ten feet from the ground, circling idly, and his face was congested with blood. It was time to take him down.

It was not so much the torture, as the effect of that torture upon Bosola, that Marcantonio was eager to enjoy. His face was pleasantly flushed in the flicker of the torches. Bosola was restive. It seemed to him that cruelty, like intercourse, should always be a private pleasure. He wet his lips. The crowd made him shy.

The strappado attendants were a quartet of scrawny boys from the slums, toughs too poor to feel pity. Now they scrambled over the scaffold, and lowered the prisoner. He was suspended by a chain, not a rope. He did not move when they released him. His limbs were broken and numb. He lay on the ground like a plucked chicken waiting to be stuffed, and no one did anything to help him. Among his own caste he was disgraced and knew it.

A priest was waiting with the next victim, a man who had stolen a lute, and who was now condemned to hang until dawn. The spectacle of what he would become by dawn was no doubt supposed to edify him.

He was just such a man as Bosola had been when young. Marcantonio seemed to notice that. He stood with his arms on his hips and chuckled.

Torture is both a sexual parable and an aphrodisiac. That was no doubt why Marcantonio had such a taste for it. He rubbed his shoulders, ignored the lowered man, and avidly watched the man about to be strung up.

It seemed terrible to Bosola that the new victim said nothing. It was also terrible that the boy was beautiful and would not be beautiful much longer. His arms would never again be slung from his shoulders in that easy way.

The attendants took him to the platform and laid him on his stomach. The priest followed. They pulled the boy's arms and legs behind him, fastening them swiftly together with the leather cuffs, as though he might struggle. But he did not struggle. Now he too looked like a chicken. His hair fell over his eyes.

The priest tried to exhort him, but could not see his face.

29

Neither could he crouch down to do so. Instead, raising his crucifix as though it were a baton, he turned to orchestrate the crowd.

The attendants attached the chain to the manacles and began to wind the winch. The man rose into the air jerkily and by stages, as though pausing for breath on the landings of an invisible stair. His arms and legs tautened into a triangle over his arched back, and he began to pour with sweat.

Marcantonio turned his head more and more upward, gaping foolishly, his eyes glistening with excitement. He was still rubbing himself. Bosola braced himself against the excitement too.

The chain had reached the top of the gibbet. The prisoner swayed in the air, but still he made no sound. It was a slow death. The attendants were artists in suspense. They waited longer than the crowd, the priest, or the prisoner expected. A torch flared up, casting reflections on the chain.

"Do it," muttered Marcantonio. He was beside himself. "Do it. Do it. Why don't they do it?" He was almost in an agony of delight.

Bosola felt faint.

One of the attendants released the ratchet on the winch. The chain roared down like an anchor. There was a roar of gratification from the crowd. The priest turned away and put his hand piously to his eyes.

The prisoner reached the end of the chain, which jerked back convulsively. His body bent into an almost perfect circle, and as his bones cracked, he gave a single, guttural scream. He was a sturdy man. He would live until dawn, and even after that, if such was living. But his beauty was dead.

That was what the crowd had come for. They liked to see beauty die. There was a long sigh of gratification, and then they looked round for diversion.

Bosola watched them and shuddered. This could happen to anyone, and what revolted him most was how thoroughly he had enjoyed that man's broken scream, for like the crowd he, too, was ugly. How had he become so?

He turned and fled back to the palace. When he arrived he was in no mood to learn that Antonio Bologna, the Duchess's new steward, had arrived to take up his duties. He sensed the meshing of invisible gears, in an engine as infernal as the strappado in the square. There is a point at which ambition becomes a form of terror. Yet he did not take fright. Why should he take fright? He had no reason to.

II

In selecting the Duchess a steward, the Cardinal had chosen well, and with his usual double purpose. It was one of the follies of the Duchess to make the request at all. On the other hand, she may merely have wished to be certain of the identity of the spy in her household. But the Cardinal was wilier than she. He would not send his spy on invitation. He had chosen Antonio for quite a different use.

His sister was a secretive person, but the Cardinal thought he knew her well. He himself had had many mistresses, and from them he believed that he had learned a great deal about the nature of woman. Their brains no man could touch, for they did not think as men did, but at bottom they were animal, and an animal can be trapped. It was only necessary to provide the right lure. He had studied his sister for years. She was discreet, but discretion has secrets of its own. If he had divined accurately, then Antonio should unlock some of them.

Now that Antonio was in Rome, on his way to take up his duties at Amalfi, the Cardinal arranged a tourney and asked Ferdinand to preside over it. Ferdinand was vain of his abilities at a tourney, but lacked finesse. Antonio was reputed skilful, and Ferdinand could not bear to lose any contest in which he engaged. It was the Cardinal's desire that an enmity should spring up between the two of them as soon as possible, and a tourney might well accomplish that.

The street before the palace was closed off, and there the guests would ride at the Saracen, the ring, and the handkerchief, all three sports at which, so the Cardinal understood, Antonio Bologna was proficient. He was, after all, a gentleman, of good family, and perhaps a trifle spoiled.

Bosola and Marcantonio watched the sport from the ground; the Cardinal, from a balcony. The Cardinal watched Ferdin-

31

and; Marcantonio, the sport; and Bosola, with some alarm, Antonio.

For Antonio was an astonishing man.

It was his whiteness that struck Bosola, for it was not the whiteness of alabaster or pampered skin, but the whiteness of an ideal. In truth, his skin was not white, but brown, and his eyes were dark. Yet this extraordinary whiteness of his was phosphorescent. He left behind him something shining as he passed, that lingered in the mind far longer than did his features. He was that special sort of man who is born to be deeply loved, and who therefore has the attribute of being lovable. He was a human epitome, and to see an ideal walking around on two legs, unconscious of not being an ordinary man, was a startling spectacle.

For the rest, he was a slim-hipped and a handsome man. His body was set in his pelvis as a stalk rears up from between parted leaves, and had the resilience of bamboo, which shudders and yields, but never breaks.

From his balcony the Cardinal looked down on him and was very pleased. His eyes sought out first Ferdinand, then Bosola, and he pursed his lips.

Ferdinand was in a bad mood. He was scowling. Indeed, a scowl was his habitual expression, as though he must always be Gianlorenzo di Medici, in the one famous portrait. But if Gianlorenzo was a lesser man, Ferdinand was lesser still.

Earlier the guests had tilted at the Saracen. The Saracen was a late medieval amusement, but Ferdinand was fond of it. It stood on a swivel post in the centre of the street, a gaily painted wooden bust with a black face and a yellow turban, holding a wooden paddle.

If one did not strike it exactly right with a lance, it swirled around on its pivot and unseated the rider with its paddle. It was a game that never unseated Ferdinand, and he was clearly glad to see Antonio fall in the dust.

Physical grace being an attribute of good humour, Antonio had the art of falling. He flew through the air like a cat, but the shock of hitting the pavement knocked him down. He tumbled over and came to rest at Bosola's feet.

"That man will not last my sister long. He cannot keep his

32

seat," said Ferdinand, and said it too loudly. Antonio had beaten him once or twice, and he could not abide that.

Antonio paused as he heard the words, and then smiled at Bosola, rising and dusting himself off. Involuntarily Bosola smiled back. Antonio seemed puzzled. It was as though he had found someone in the wrong place.

"We shall see," said Antonio, and got back on his horse.

The ring was held by a wooden arm fastened to the wall of the house. Now they rode at it, trying to pick it up on the tip of their lances. Ferdinand drank too much and brooded too deeply. He had not the steadiness to succeed in plucking the ring, and he was, moreover, angry at being bested.

Bosola watched with something like panic. He knew that look Antonio had given him. It signified curiosity ready to turn to pity. It is the look all receive who are not quite gentlemen, and yet who are clearly gently born. He shrank from it.

Ferdinand drove at the ring with a vertical cavalier rage that had nothing to do with correct form for the sport. When he missed it, he whirled with a baffled curse and tried again. His fourth miss set off a concealed titter. And the titter, in turn, drove Ferdinand mad, for there was nothing he feared more often or so much. He tried again and again, with short feints, his face black with fury. There were no titters now. The crowd knew him in this mood.

Antonio did not know him. As Ferdinand dismounted, Antonio came over and said something polite to him.

Ferdinand smiled sardonically and struck Antonio in the face with his jewelled cap. In itself the gesture meant nothing. If a lugubrious greyhound had been skulking in his path, he would have kicked it instead. Before this crowd the gesture meant much.

Antonio flinched and made to draw his dagger. Then his eyes narrowed, as though he had thought of something better. He smiled, leaped on his horse, rode towards Bosola, snatched up Bosola's lance, and wheeling, snagged the ring on the tip of it, and, without dismounting, shook it off. The ring, which was of metal, rolled in a drunken arc and then lay throbbing on a cobble at Ferdinand's feet.

Antonio returned to Bosola and handed down the lance.

33

Looking amused, he leaned over from his saddle and spoke to Bosola eagerly and boyishly.

"You are one of the Cardinal's men," he said.

Bosola nodded.

"You had better attend me. I have no attendant here, and the Cardinal will allow it."

Bosola blinked.

"Come. I like you. You would have helped me up," said Antonio. He turned and rode away.

Bosola did not like it. Like all men conscious of their own wretchedness, it hurt him to be liked.

He looked up and caught the Cardinal staring down at him.

III

And so, at length, after six months, he had his interview with the Cardinal. It occurred that night.

When he was summoned, he was in the guard room near the main entrance, playing primero with Marcantonio. It is a game which teaches you how to cheat chance. Marcantonio did not like the summons, being jealous of anyone who obtained special favour.

Bosola followed the equerry through the damp corridors of the palace and up the main stairs. It was a peculiar kind of fear he felt. He felt as though he were about to have an interview with his luck, and was afraid to be sent away empty-handed.

The equerry pattered ahead of him to the massive guarded door which led to the Cardinal's suite. There he was taken over by a secretary and ushered into the presence.

The presence was standing in shadow behind a candle sconce, gazing out the window. For the Cardinal stage-managed himself very well. He had the art of making an entrance merely by turning his head; and the magnificence of his rooms was designed to make the visitor feel shabby.

Bosola did not feel shabby. He felt naked. It had been ten years, and what did a man's enemy look like after ten years? What would the Cardinal look like?

For much more than Ferdinand, the Cardinal had been his model. Beauty is not always beauty. Beauty is to fit one's own

34

nature completely. And the Cardinal's nature was to be wily and devious. It was that spider mind that Bosola had taken as his etiquette.

The silence lengthened out. It made Bosola uncomfortable, even while he admired the skill with which that discomfort was accomplished. He looked down at the marble coat of arms in the floor.

When he glanced up again, the Cardinal was staring at him. In the candle-light it was a singularly boyish face Bosola saw, for guile has its own innocence. It is always a little naïve about virtue, and that keeps it young.

The Cardinal had fingers that seemed to play with invisible cats. Bosola had hoped for recognition. What he found instead was a kind of suppressed glee that was somehow transmitted to the finger-tips.

"Are you content here?" asked the Cardinal dryly.

"Quite content."

There was a faint impatient stirring of robes. "The Duchess's steward, Antonio di Bologna, has asked if you might attend him." The Cardinal's voice rippled over some inner hilarity, like water over stones when someone throws out a slop pail. "He seems to have been curiously struck by you." The Cardinal looked at him with mock curiosity. "You are from Brescia, I believe."

Bosola was startled.

The Cardinal picked up a sheaf of papers from his desk. "Niccolò Ferrante was from Brescia," he said gently. Behind the sconce, his face flickered deceptively, but in that flickering mask the eyes did not flicker. His eyes were his authority. They never wavered. Yet they could have been squeezed out like grapes. Bosola stared at them and his fingers curled.

"Antonio di Bologna is an excellent gentleman," said the Cardinal. "He will be our sister's steward. A man must talk to someone, and if he should choose to talk to you, that would not be so surprising. For he seems to have a preference for you."

Bosola understood.

"My brother does not like this preferment." He looked at Bosola innocently. "But perhaps Antonio has made an excel-

35

lent choice in you. We shall see." He seemed to grow bored with the papers before him, yet he went on toying with the sheaf as before. Finally he tapped them. "Perhaps you have forgotten, but you had excellent reasons for leaving Brescia," he said. "And Mantua as well. But that is not important here. How often in life we choose the wrong identity." He nodded his dismissal.

No wonder the Cardinal had smiled. For something like that would amuse the Cardinal. Bosola had made a mistake. He had forgotten that to assume another man's identity was also to assume his sins.

IV

Bosola's duties with Antonio were not onerous. He had chiefly merely to attend him, and for this he had a new livery, for Antonio had an eye for such effects. He loved to live in a world of appearances, and indeed, what other kind of world is there? Bosola's new livery was to the German, Gothic taste, as the Baroque would have it. He wore skin-tight scarlet, with a white bow on the right arm and another on the left knee, and a large Maximilian hat with a white feather. It made him look like a fantasy. Bosola had never lived in a fantasy before.

As for Antonio, he seemed as simple and as doomed as a grasshopper. Yet grasshoppers know what they are. If they imitated the ants, they would live no longer, so why should they not chirp and be gay?

About Antonio there was precisely that atmosphere of the sacred victim. It was because he was so lovable. Being lovable was what made him so beautiful, and beauty is its own shroud.

Bosola served him for the two weeks of his visit, and nothing happened until the end of that time.

Then something happened that shook him badly. It was Antonio's piety. Bosola came upon it unexpectedly, and it shook him. For from his sister, he knew very well what piety was. Piety was a career. It was terrible to learn that piety could also have the organic sadness of a flower.

Antonio travelled with a small portable shrine, and it stood on a chest in the embrasure of his window. It was a small statue of St. Nicolaus of Bari, a little wooden waltzing thing

36

set in a niche between two twisted columns, with a rack for three candles before it. The candles had to be replenished every day. Sometimes, in a Venetian glass ewer, a few flowers would stand there too.

One morning Bosola had to go in to replenish the candles. He was not thinking of anything in particular, except that his service to Antonio would soon be over. He entered the room without knocking, holding the white wax stubs of the new candles in his hand, and crossed to the embrasure.

Antonio was on his knees. His eyes were closed. And that was all. But it upset Bosola.

Sometimes we come upon people unexpectedly when they are in the midst of that special world where the self lives. We are abashed. We draw back. We catch a glimpse of each other across the landscape of silence. It is a look of mutual recognition from which we never recover.

Bosola set down the candles and Antonio rose. After a moment of insight, it is as though we had come suddenly into a darkened room. For a moment we lose our bearings. Our eyes still project the image of what we have just seen. And what Bosola had seen was goodness. It was unendurable. He turned and fled.

For the ambitious man should never be doomed to see the object he covets with the eyes of a man who does not covet it at all. Ambition must see everything from the front, or else die.

see p 130

That day the Cardinal was holding levee. Here were all the rich and great. And now they did not seem rich and great. Bosola passed them in the anterooms and shivered. He had wanted to rise by these people. Now it occurred to him that he would rather pull them down on top of him.

The one thing kept from the masses, is that the great ones of the world are freaks. They have been so pulled about by eminence that they no longer have any shape of their own. Greatness is like a cancer. It grows unseen until it is strong enough to gobble us up. Greatness is a disease.

Bosola with his eyes opened stood in the middle of a pest house, and it revolted him. For once in his life he saw the running sores of those who rode themselves too hard.

At the head of that procession pranced the Cardinal, with

37

his curiously asexual charm. For the man who is only one sex is not only rare. He is also a monster. Like the deaf mute, he is cut off from communication with far more than half the world. Yet the Cardinal was not effeminate. He was only clever, and as lacking in sexual differentiation as is the sexual act itself.

It was more than Bosola could bear. He had not the courage of his predilections.

So when at evening Antonio came upon him, he burst into a tirade as children burst into tears at a kind word from their mothers.

Antonio listened silently.

"Perhaps you do not belong here," he said. His eyes seemed to search Bosola's face for something that was not there.

"What?" The idea took Bosola aback. It had never occurred to him that he belonged anywhere else, for his nature had been bent on one purpose, as a tree is bent one way by the prevailing wind. Besides, though he might hate, hatred is the mulch of ambition. It burns the fingers, but it feeds the will.

"Why not?" asked Antonio. "I am going to Amalfi to-morrow. Something could be found for you to do."

"I cannot leave here."

"You do not belong here," said Antonio. "You are a good man."

Bosola shook his head. Goodness was a weakness, and he would not be weak. Goodness made him feel less than he was. Indeed, if someone tells us we are good, we feel a sort of helpless silliness steal over our faces, our knees wobble, and our testicles draw up, as they do when we are afraid. The worst tempters, after all, are not the devils, but the saints. Besides, he had his own reasons for not wanting to go to Amalfi.

Antonio left him and moved down the stairs to the hall. Bosola wandered restlessly through the palace, he did not know why, as it gradually fell asleep, for he clung to ambition as a blind man clings to his cane, or a leper to his bell. He could not give it up.

Far ahead of him, down in the main hall, towards midnight, he seemed to hear the angry rise and fall of voices. Only one sconce burned down there. Bosola crept to the balustrade of the loggia and peered down.

38

It was the Cardinal and Ferdinand, pacing back and forth in the litter of the hall, for the servants would not sweep it out until just before dawn. Ferdinand was manifestly in a temper. The Cardinal seemed alternately to be fanning him up and soothing him down. They talked in furious whispers. Bosola craned forward.

"He shall not go," snapped Ferdinand. "He shall not go to that strumpet."

"He is harmless."

"I know my sister. I know what she will do."

The Cardinal looked at his brother warily, waved a jewelled hand, and smiled.

"If she will do it now, then she has done it before."

"She is not to remarry. I will not have that man go there." Ferdinand was trembling like a wet dog. He seized his brother by the shoulders. "What are you plotting? What are you doing to me?"

The Cardinal shook him off. "I do not plot. I watch," he said quietly.

"You want Amalfi for yourself."

The Cardinal did not answer directly. "She is your sister," he said. "I hope you do not know why you are so angry, for that is a sin."

Ferdinand stopped in the middle of the hall and burst out laughing. "What would you know of sin?" he demanded. "Sin is a passion."

The Cardinal was very still. Then he moved towards the stairs, and his robes swished over the marble as he ascended, as though he moved upward on a raft of snakes. Below Bosola, Ferdinand looked up, and when he did, his eyes were white with fury.

Bosola withdrew.

Early next morning Antonio and his little retinue set out on the Naples road.

Bosola felt sad. When the company had vanished down the street, he stripped off his scarlet livery and returned to the guard. Nothing had happened, and yet life was no longer the same.

A month later the Cardinal sent for him once more.

By then Bosola had lapsed back into a scowling indifference. He had almost forgotten Antonio. He had spent the month roistering with Marcantonio. There was nothing more voluptuous than violence, nothing more satisfying to the soul while it was going on, nothing sadder when it was done. Indeed, the sadness was so unbearable, that it only led to more violence, like a drug, which enlivens the senses only the more permanently to impair them. It was the age of Caravaggio. Slitting the noses of a few gallants out late at night in the back alleys was a kind of joy. If he could be nothing, then it was something that they would never be the same again. The sides of their noses flapped and streamed with blood. We would take the whole world down with us, if we were able.

The Cardinal had no such ambitions. Bosola found him poring over a map of Amalfi and its dependencies, which had been flung out across the desk.

It was a beautiful map, blue and black on parchment, with miniature winds in the corners.

The Cardinal grunted but did not look up. "This is ridiculous," he said. "How long have you been here?"

"Eight months."

"We may as well drop the pretence," said the Cardinal. "If there is any hue and cry after you, it has fallen off by now. Still, you may as well be Ferrante for a while." The Cardinal glanced at him sharply. "Do you think I have used you harshly? Still, I do not think you are altogether happy here." Abruptly his manner changed. "I cannot keep you here," he said. "You are restless and I must be discreet. Besides, I have no use for you."

Bosola became motionless, like a stalked bird.

The Cardinal looked at him for a very long time, and something elusively like pity seemed to flood through the contempt at the bottom of his eyes. He gave a grunt and scribbled silently on a sheet of parchment, poured sand on it, blew the sand off, folded the letter, sealed it, and all this time said nothing more to Bosola.

Every year the Cardinal's insolence grew more kindly, more indulgent, and more smoothly adapted to its purpose, for some men are born adapted only to eminence, and what would be vices in a lesser station, become virtues in them. Bosola admired him, even while inwardly raging against him. The Cardinal now had that ultimate cunning that does not have to hide itself in order to work its effect.

His Eminence wet his ring with spittle, impressed his seal, and returned the ring to his finger.

"Antonio offered you asylum," he said.

"He wanted me to go with him."

"Just so." The Cardinal paced up and down the room impatiently, peering now and then at Bosola. "Why do you think I sent him there?"

"I do not know."

"My sister has a lively nature, so I am told." He stopped his pacing. "I am told," he said. "My brother is not. Do you understand me?"

"Yes, your Eminence."

"It is good the man has taken a fancy to you." The Cardinal held out the letter. "You need not mention this interview. I am sending you to my brother Ferdinand. He has a mission for you. If you are wise, you will accept it. If you are sensible, you will report everything he says and does to me. He will see you tonight. Then return here." He glanced down at the map before him. "I shall know if you lie to me. And there are spies everywhere, so I am told, even at Amalfi." He nodded, and then ignored Bosola completely.

It was perhaps one of his few mistakes, for no man likes to be taken up only to be ignored. To be bullied, blackmailed, tortured, that Bosola was willing to expect. But to be ignored fed his inner insecurity, and therefore made him rage the more. Yet even while he raged, he knew he would obey, for he sought advantage as a man trapped in a tunnel seeks even the smallest chink of light.

VI

Ferdinand was a man who could not sleep. It was not that he feared nightmares. His nightmares all took place during his

41

waking life. It was that he feared to dream, for his dreams had a forbidden sweetness more terrible than Eden.

He was the ruin of a passionate boy, burly, handsome, scowling, and muscular. He was also impotent.

His palace was ill-run and disorderly. All night long doors opened and shut down its corridors, and the least said about it the better. Bosola made his way undetected up the stairs, and then saw a dwarf peering down at him from the shadows. The dwarf disappeared as he reached the landing and turned towards the suite of rooms occupied by Ferdinand.

It was not difficult for him to find his way. The palaces in this section of Rome had been run up by a builder thirty years before, on speculation, and were almost identical. They were grandiose, but small.

There was nobody to announce him, not so much because he was unexpected, as because nobody was expected. He slipped into a long gallery and found Ferdinand pacing up and down the length of it, while torches fixed on the walls gave a flickering, uncertain light that turned the marble floor into a swamp of shadows.

"Who's there?" called Ferdinand, and his voice reverberated against the walls. He came swiftly down the room and peered at Bosola.

Bosola handed him the letter and explained his errand.

Ferdinand looked at the seal, slit it open, and then grabbed one of the torches from its socket and held it above Bosola. He began to chuckle.

"Yes, you'll do," laughed Ferdinand. "By God, you'll do." Instead of putting the torch back in its socket, he flung it on the floor, so that the sparks danced like a cloud of midges.

Bosola relaxed. He had not been recognized, for, like an animal, Ferdinand had little memory. He had only desires. The man was shaking with some sort of passion Bosola did not understand, and his voice was husky with rage.

"My sister would disgrace us all. She would disgrace me," he said. "She is a widow. She is a girl. Find out who she sees, and what she does. I would not have her marry anyone. Women are venal, lubricious, cunning without wit, and spiteful

42

as foxes. Let her do what she will, but marry she shall not."
Ferdinand rubbed his face with his hands. "Let her do nothing.
Why should she lie under some boatman or stable-boy? My
brother is foolish. He throws temptation in her way. Insinuate
yourself with that white-faced fool. Do you think I do not
know why she wants him there, or why my brother has sent
him there?"

He stood stock still in the middle of the gallery, in the one
dark patch the torches did not light, and it was as though he
stood at the bottom of a well.

"She shall not," he said tautly. "She shall not, shall not. Do
you think I have no thoughts? Men think I have no thoughts.
My brother thinks I have no thoughts. Why otherwise would I
walk here all night long? I do not sleep."

Out of Ferdinand's face there again peered that young,
adolescent face that had never gotten its own way, so that,
even though he was dangerous, there was something vulnerable and touching about him too.

"Go, tell my brother everything I say. She shall not drag me
through that filth. She shall not marry." Ferdinand threw a
bag at Bosola. "Go, and destroy her. For that is what you are
paid to do. And that is what I pay you to do, for that is what
life is."

Bosola stooped to pick the money up.

"Take it," cried Ferdinand. "Don't you think I know as well
as he, that the truth has to be doubly paid for?" Abruptly he
strode to the far end of the gallery and stood there, facing the
room, his face hidden in shadows, and the hall was quiet.

Bosola hesitated. The bag lay at his feet, with a long shadow
behind it, cast by the torch on the wall.

"Go!" shouted Ferdinand, and he sounded frightened.
"Go!"

Bosola retrieved the bag and went.

It was late, and he was very sleepy, but apparently the
Cardinal never slept. There was a couch in the little room he
used as an oratory, where he took naps, and that was all the
attention he had the time to pay to sleep. Bosola told him
what had happened.

The Cardinal listened as would a doctor to the symptoms of a patient he has no time to attend.

"In particular you will attach yourself to Antonio," he said. He picked up a letter from his desk. "You will leave now. That will get you to Naples by tomorrow dusk. There you will deliver this letter for me." He paused. "It is to your sister." Bosola started and the Cardinal smiled. "Are you fond of your sister?"

"She is an admirable woman."

The Cardinal shrugged. "No doubt. But since she did not tell me she had a brother, I presume she did not wish the fact known. But, as you see, I know it."

He held out the letter, and Bosola knew that it contained nothing. It was merely a pretext.

"That is all," said the Cardinal sharply.

So Bosola departed.

Late the next afternoon he reached Naples, and for once even Naples was overcast and dull. At dusk he went to the convent. Hate her he might, but he did not want to see his sister trapped. One of them, at least, should be set free.

VII

Sor Juana was the greatest female poet of her age. But in all her life she wrote only one poem because she could not help it. Like everything else she did, that poem was bland, twisted, sombre, brilliant, and yet deceptively easy. It was also knowledgeable, for knowledge was her passion, not poetry, not people, not God.

It was on the night Bosola came to visit her that she began that poem. She wrote it to dazzle. Instead it began to dazzle her. It was called *The Dream*. And because it did dazzle her, it lit up corners of her Self she had not wished to see: for it is true: the dream of reason produces monsters: and monsters are only what we cannot be, but others can.

As all such things do, the poem came quietly into her head, sat down, and then clamoured to be let out.

On an impulse she could not explain, but one that had sadness in it, she had gone to the nursery to see the child which the

44

Cardinal had left in her care. Though by now she knew perfectly well who that child was, she refused to admit that she knew.

> *On a dark night, the trees, the pointed towers*
> *like lichenous darkness, in Egyptian sleep*
> *I sat and wept beside the obelisk*
> *on a pebbled path whose stones were cruciform.*
> *Shadows and shapes would soothe me if they could.*
> *But another voice called from the heavy tree. . . .*

She found the child sleeping in its cradle, under a muslin canopy, and looking around her to see that she was not observed, she parted the flimsy cloth and then looked down.

She knew nothing about children except that, once, she could not remember what it had been like, she had been one. The more profoundly we experience the world, the more we are shut off from the general experience of it. Always, when we think we have mastered it utterly, we find that the mind has a false bottom, which suddenly gives way like a trap-door and drops us down into the basement of the soul. And very strange things are stored there. It is the lumber room of faith. It contains, among other things, the earlier models of the gods upstairs.

She had never wanted, and she would never have, a child. But she regretted any incapacity, and this child was doomed. Like a puppy wagging the tail that is soon to be docked, it had the pathos of confidence, and how gently it lay sleeping, and how beautiful it was.

> *. . . I sit alone,*
> *fearing this weeping that is not my own,*
> *since only the good can feel the sense of shame.*
> *Knowledge is only to know we cannot know.*
> *Dark creatures nestle in the wings of sense,*
> *and like an owl. . . .*

What owl?

It was in the nursery that Bosola found her, for he had the talents of a good spy: he knew his way into closed rooms. He knew how to find out what had not happened yet.

45

He caught a peculiar look on her face. It seemed quite genuine. As she bent over the cradle, the immense medal of St. Michel she wore by a chain round her neck dangled down and caught the light. He could see from the glance she gave him that she was furious to be caught in such a mood.

"I have brought you a letter," he said.

He handed it to her, and when she saw the seal, her long jointed fingers ran over it like a crab, reaching for its weakest spot and tearing it open.

"But it says nothing," she said, with a frown.

"What did you expect it to say?"

She looked down at the child in its cradle, pink and defenceless. She did not answer. She folded her hands.

"Then the Cardinal knows who you are." She sighed. "You should never have gone back there."

"Is that the child the Cardinal sent you?"

Her eyes widened.

"And do you know what will happen to him?"

"Nothing will happen to him."

A sort of helpless fury came over him. Every time he came to her, she sent him away empty-handed. She had nothing to give anyone. Knowledge she might have, but understanding she had not. "The Cardinal has sent me off to be a common spy," he told her.

"What else are you?"

He flinched. "The child is Raimondo Piccolomini," he said.

She looked swiftly round the room. "Hush," she said, and with that one word, he saw she was as venal as all of them.

He grabbed her arm. "Come," he said.

She tried to shake him off.

"No," he said. "Come." He dragged her out of the nursery and into the corridor. He hurried along swiftly, sure of where he was going, and pulling her after him, her long robes sweeping across the floor like surf. The corridor was lit only by moonlight coming through the unglazed arcades. He made for a bolted door at the far end, and threw back its bolts.

"No, you cannot go in there," she said. "No one goes in there." She shrank back.

"We live there every day," he told her, and pushed her

46

through the door so roughly that she stumbled. They were in a dark stone room, damp and unwholesome. Beyond that, down two stairs, lay a larger room, lit by moonlight.

What light there was came from windows set high in the wall in the groins of the arches. The stench was unbearable. There was no sound but snoring and the moaning of a man chained to the wall, with a crown of feathers on his head.

The others there lay sleeping, piled against each other for warmth. Many were naked, their flesh slippery with sweat. Most were men. A few were women. One or two were children. And though some had returned to the egg, and had lain curled up for so long that no physical strength could uncurl them, others clutched stray objects, one a wooden stick held like a sceptre, another with a medal on his chest that slipped and slid in lousy hair, but came from Compostella or Loreto. Bosola strode to the middle of the room and stamped on the floor heavily in his boots.

"Wake up," he shouted. "Wake up all of you." He seized the sceptre and beat the rump of the man who had clutched it. "Wake up!" Again he stamped, his heels rattling rapidly, like the warning of a snake unwillingly driven to violence by danger.

They woke. But they did not wake as ordinary people do. They woke slowly, and as they waked, began to repeat the only thing they any longer wanted to do, one standing on one leg like a chicken, the one with the medal gravely parading up and down, like a Prelate; and the man chained to the wall took off his crown and then, raising his arms, again placed it reverently on his own head. But most made the sounds of men chewing oatmeal, and these were the syphilitics.

It was the madhouse attached to the convent.

"There," shouted Bosola. "That is what your world is. That is what your goodness is. That is what the goodness of your Cardinal is. This is the court you shone at. This is the court where you want to shine. This is your Vatican, your convent, your kindness, and your faith."

He grabbed Sor Juana by the arms. "This is what you want to be. And this is the world where you want to be it. This is the secret you want to keep. Do you really think that because you change your shift once a day, you are sane?"

It seemed to him that in these faces he saw Ferdinand, Antonio, the Cardinal, himself.

"Do you think that because you are saved, you can damn me, or that boy, or anyone? You are not saved. Only the damned are saved. Only the damned know what salvation is."

"Why do you stare?" he demanded. "Why do you not write your silly poems here?"

But he had misjudged her. She was not proud of her own sanity. She was only proud of not going mad.

"Perhaps I shall," she said.

She felt sorry for him. For events are inexorable. They take place whether we participate in them or not, and that her brother had yet to learn. An hour later and he was on the Amalfi road.

FIVE

I

Of all the separate small countries of Italy, Amalfi was one of the smallest and most distinct. Had it anything to defend, it would have been impregnable.

There was no denying that it was a peculiar place. It had the furtive defiance of one of those pirate towns built in Tripoli or the islands of the Caribbean. And now that its maritime power was lost, Amalfi was stranded, as though the tide had washed it up against its own cliffs.

The night there was peculiar, too, for it did not have the insect stillness of ordinary night. It was a night haunted by cloth. At sunset the clouds piled up on the horizon in bolts of shot silk, that rippled away like lizards, bruised and turning purple or green as they fled down into the crannies of the dark. Amalfi had no ease.

Yet for once the Duchess did not see it that way. She was as excited as a girl, for now her husband was dead, she was learning how to laugh. That was very sweet. It was almost like having a friend.

The Duchess was not clever, but she did have a good memory, which often serves us just as well. She knew what her brothers were like and she knew what they were capable of doing. She had come back to Amalfi as a woman comes back to an empty house. She did not even have her son to stand between her and the people. So she shrank into herself and avoided everyone, keeping only Cariola by her.

Piccolomini had been in his dotage. For the last two years it was she who had ruled behind him. Now he was gone, she stepped forward and ruled for herself. It was an unusual occupation for a pretty woman, but it was the only occupation she had. If she could not be loved, she could at least be just.

Very often, at dawn, even before Cariola had risen, she

49

would sit in a loggia at the top of the palace and gaze out over the sea and the green sky. That was the half-hour during the day when it was safe for her to dream, so she dreamt, though she did not quite know of what. Her brothers had her child in custody. She thought the Amalfitani would loathe her for that. She loathed herself for it. So she hid. The townspeople saw her only when she climbed the steep, broad stairs of the cathedral. Her honeyed little court, which she did not trust for a moment, saw her as little as she could make possible.

But then something unexpected happened. A deputation of guilds waited upon her, hats in hand, and asked her to shoot the Popinjay.

She was deeply touched. It was the first honest gesture of respect she had had from the Amalfitani. Her face lit up at once. She thought it was a tribute to her justice. It seemed spontaneous, and spontaneous gestures are rare.

She dismissed the deputation and fled off to tell Cariola. After all, Cariola was her only confidante.

Cariola thought it might be some kind of trap.

The Duchess spoke to her sharply. "Nonsense. Haven't we had enough of traps? What shall I wear?"

This was a subject closer to Cariola's heart. They discussed avidly what she should wear, and decided on a tight hunting dress of green velvet.

"Your stomach is so smooth. One would never guess you had had a child," said Cariola.

When the deputation came to escort her to the gaming area, she met them with radiant smiles. It would be a long and fatiguing day, but she did not mind. She felt at last the world was opening up, and so she opened up to it.

And what was this Popinjay? All understood it, but few could say what it meant. It was a mystery, degraded to the status of a toy. But toys are mysteries to the children who use them. It is only their adults who have forgotten what they mean. So it does not matter what this popinjay was. The ceremony was as old as the death of winter and the birth of spring. If the year was to be full of life, then the popinjay must die. The meaning of it was as simple as that.

There was no level ground at Amalfi, except along the sea.

50

There, there was a broad esplanade, which might almost pass for a plaza.

The guildsmen conducted her forward through crowds lining each side of the way, and she was cheered. Thus they would have cheered the virgin come to trap the unicorn.

The Popinjay was set up on a tall pole on the south side of the embarcadero. It was a roughly carved wooden bird, perhaps two feet across, with outspread wings, which seemed to soar on the apex of the pole. It was a blue parrot. Ceremoniously the Duchess was handed the bow. Archery she had practised as a child, with Ferdinand, until she began to best him. She felt confident.

The crowd was suddenly hushed. One of the syndics had the honour to present her with an arrow, on a small pillow made of plush. She smiled at him, for he seemed a little worried, fitted the arrow into its notch, and drew back the bow. There was no wind and the sun stood high.

It was a moment of supreme joy. She did not want to let the arrow go. She wanted to prolong the moment. But the crowd was waiting, and the weight of the drawn bow grew uncomfortable. With a sigh, she released it.

The arrow flew unerringly up to the top of the pole. As it did so, other arrows entered the air. She tried to follow her own, shielding her eyes from the sun. Her own had a golden vane. The vane glittered, and the popinjay exploded, its loose wings turning and pivoting, brilliant against the sky. The crowd sighed and then shouted with approval. Only then did she realize that she alone of that company had known she would hit the target. Now they all knew it. It was a genuine triumph. She looked up at the fragments tumbling through the sky and shook out her hair. In that moment they were truly her own people, and she was their Duchess.

All was safe now. The year was born. Behind her she felt the presence of Antonio, her household steward. She turned, and was startled by the immediacy of his face. She had received him when he had come to take up his duties, but her heart had not been open then. It was open now, and she saw him for the first time. And Antonio saw her. Something turned over in him that should have been sleeping. He turned and walked away.

51

Antonio took his duties seriously. As the fourth son of a noble family far from rich, he had had to use his wits. He had used them here. It had taken him a month to assure that the Duchess would be chosen to shoot the popinjay. It was he, too, who had arranged the Triumph that was to follow.

The occasion was the annual feast day of the local saint, but the purpose was to enhance the power of Amalfi. It was a piece of propaganda, much used in Florence and the north, but not so well exploited in the south. There would be a procession to the Cathedral. So now great cars were hidden in side alleys and, to tell the truth, the clergy were somewhat pushed aside, for in this sort of procession religion came last. If that was symbolic, no one noticed it, least of all the clergy. The parade would wind slowly in and out of the streets, to arrive at last at the Cathedral. It was there, facing a little uphill square from the top of the church stairs, that the Duchess and the Bishop took their station to watch the festivities.

The Duchess had never seen a Triumph before. She waited impatiently, while the Bishop talked. She was somewhat on edge. She knew for whom this ostentation was designed, and she had more reason to fear her brothers' wrath than their timidity. But the day was a clear one and she was happy. She leaned forward at the first sound of music down the street, and the creaking of the triumphal cars excited her.

It was a diverse spectacle. It had an excitement the world has lost. For in those days people were not passive in their amusements. They did not watch a parade. They paraded themselves. And even those who watched it had sung and paraded once.

First came the lesser guildsmen, each led by a master, carrying banners and flags. They walked in silence. They were the overture. Next came the senior guilds, with drums, fifes, and even an angel to play the nun's fiddle on an allegorical cart. And with these came the first floats, each representing the patron saint of its guild. The floats were high and wide, and moved with rheumatic dignity through the narrow streets. A St. Christopher eight feet tall, clad in yellow satin, held an Infant Jesus above the crowd. An allegorical car presented the

Temptation of St. Anthony, but all the pretty demons were so tickled by the vibration of the car that they could scarcely help but giggle. St. George pranced by on a white horse. Behind him a blonde peasant girl led the dragon by a silver string. It was a delightful dragon, puffing real fumes. There were many more. St. Michael in silver armour led the Devil in chains. He was a green and scaly devil, like something from the sea.

There was an interval, and next came a cavalcade of all the previous Dukes of Amalfi, including her late husband, and before them, the Doges of the Republic, smartly dressed, and surrounded by a flurry of standards, as though they were being hustled back into history.

The centre of the procession had been organized by the Jesuits, who alone had discovered how to make the Passion entertaining. In love, in our daily chores, in the mere act of peeling a peach, we re-enact a passion every day. The Jesuits made faith visible. They also made it fun.

Drawn by camels, came the cart of the Nativity. On the roof of its stable angels gloriously sang, as on the next car they fiddled the flight into Egypt through the streets. The order of the carts had become mixed. Here was the Annunciation, a scene of great splendour, and what was the Queen of Heaven if she was not earthly too?

The angel might have been a page in her employ. He was clearly of good family. And over her prayers floated a white dove with outstretched wings, joggling up and down on a silver wire.

Round these carts capered some players, tricked out as devils, with big faces painted on their behinds, so skilfully contrived that the eyes blinked on their buttocks, and their hairy tongues slid in and out.

Next came the floats dedicated to the triumph of the Duchess. These she watched like a child, but her life was not like this. She grew tense again. She had thought she was merely watching a procession. But this was not true. She realized now she had been waiting for one special car, and was glad that there was no one but the Bishop to see her face. She was a little scared.

For the last of the carts devoted to her own apotheosis had

been designed by Antonio. It was the cart of King Psapho. King Psapho was a legendary king so eager for fame that he taught parrots how to repeat his name, and then released them to the world. The legend had perhaps become a bit scrambled at the hands of the Court Poet who had suggested it; but the intention and the compliment were clear. The Duchess felt very pale and very weak.

The cart was square, surrounded on three sides by a simple balustrade. At the four corners stood slim youths dressed in Roman armour made out of feathers, with scarlet feather cloaks, each holding a forked religious banner, and with beaks for helmets and buskins of gold. In the centre of the cart stood an immense cage, surmounted by the popinjay. In the cage a bird man taught some parrots how to speak, and mimics made them seem to shout: Aemilia, Aemilia, as the cart passed by the Duchess.

At the rear of the cart was a throne, over which a negro held a scarlet parasol. On the throne sat Antonio, dressed as King Psapho. He wore a twirled silk turban surmounted by a crown, a thin ruff, a surplice coat embroidered with stars, and red stockings tight over his elegant calves. In one hand he held a baton of gold. The other rested on the arm of his throne. He was perspiring heavily, and his face was flushed, but he bowed and smiled to the crowd. His white face was full of joy, and as he passed the Duchess he raised his arm and saluted her.

She did not see the salute. She saw his eyes. And indeed the eyes of someone lovable are terrible. They are bottomless and beseeching, and full of the terror of not being loved. But their true terror is that they recognize a lover.

The cart moved on. Crowding behind it came a derisive forest of those megalocephalic giants which today survive in Valencia. Their shadows flowed over the passing figure of Antonio, and their empty eyes were knowing. The Duchess's hand went to her throat and she moved uneasily. She wanted to flee. She thought she could do so, for we meet the inevitable person so seldom, that she still believed that love can be a matter of choice, as, indeed, for a little love, it can. But she was not precisely in love yet. She was only stunned by the sight of the future walking towards her.

Last came the religious procession, which peeled off from the rest and began to mount the Cathedral stairs. She looked down, and saw being borne up towards her the Byzantine reliquary of the local saint. It was a silver bust the colour of pewter, studded with yellow diamonds and amethysts. The head was harshly modelled. The eyes were of moonstone, as though clouded by a cataract. They stared sightlessly.

As the bearers negotiated the stairs, that face turned and glared down at her. She could have screamed. She fell instinctively on her knees. It was like a summons. Then the bust swept on into the sanctity of the church, and the crowd began to shout.

Her obeisance had pleased the Amalfitani very much. They could not know why she had kneeled down. She wanted to rush into the Cathedral and beseech that hideous and inexorable thing. She wanted to say, no, you are wrong. It will not end like that. You have no right to judge.

Unfortunately, we do not really make up our minds about anything. Our minds make us up. By the time we are aware of the necessity for decision, the decision has already been made. We can only follow willy-nilly. But in the meantime we are restless. We are ill at ease. We want to escape from something, we do not precisely know what. The Duchess felt that way, while Cariola was dressing her.

"Leave me. I want to pray," said the Duchess.

Cariola was disturbed. "Madam should not kneel in that dress. She will ruin it. And she looks so beautiful."

The Duchess looked in her mirror, but saw only the face of a young and wilful girl. She could not see herself at all, and something inside her truly turned to pray. "No, I am horrible. I am terrible," she said. With a heavy rustle of jewelled taffeta, she went to her prie-dieu, and indeed the dress was so massive that it sucked her down on to her knees; and so unwieldy that Cariola lingered in the shadows, fussing at the dressing table, until the time should come to raise her up.

Then, with Cariola behind, she left her apartments and was escorted down the stairs to the great hall. There had been no such festivities there since her marriage, and now the court was young again she would have to dance.

Antonio came from the north, from Bologna, which was ancient, settled, rich, and ostentatious. His duties there had been dull and well defined. He had wanted to get away. A seemingly chance acquaintance with the Cardinal, and some influence with the Bolognese Papal Legate, had brought him south. He found that strange mixture of splendour and squalor which the Spanish had installed in Calabria new to him. He found that he was expected to do everything, and do it, too, with very little to do it with.

Any other gentleman at Amalfi would have found the position demeaning. Antonio did not. He had a great many little skills which, since he was a gentleman, were dignified into accomplishments, and they came in handy when it came to contriving a pageant, the seating of a banquet, or the entertainment that was to follow afterwards.

The Duchess, like most gentlewomen and all children, thought the world came ready-made. She wandered through the world a little like Eve through Paradise before the Fall, and because everything was there, it never occurred to her to ask where it had come from. Courtiers were as matter of fact to her as trees.

But Antonio had worked hard to prepare this evening for her, and moreover he had enjoyed the work, for even as a child he had had a passion for the dance.

As a child, his enthusiasm had seemed amusing. But as he grew up, his skill merely became something unbecoming to a gentleman, so he put it away, like any other toy. But we never put away our toys for good. The dance was something that helped him to transcend himself. Once, on the deserted, wind-swept beach below Livorno, he had come across some gypsies huddled round a camp-fire, and they had let him dance with them. They had even cheered him on. It was the highest and most impersonal pleasure he had ever known. Yet he preferred that this passion of his remain unknown, and if it showed at all, it showed in the tight, smoothly defined precision of his calves.

But now, preparing for the Duchess's entertainment, he

threw himself wholeheartedly into the ballet which was to crown the evening. It was a *Silvae*, with court ladies for nymphs, courtiers for satyrs, the Duchess, Daphne, and Antonio, Apollo. He made certain that her steps would be easy, so she need not rehearse; but he did not know why he chose the part of Apollo for himself.

The dance was to be held in the great hall. He held not the customary one rehearsal, but five, and those serious ones; and he was still rehearsing as servants carried in trees in tubs to turn the room into a mock forest. The courtiers were taken aback, but then amused. After all, their lives were dull enough. For them a little exertion was a novelty. Antonio despaired of ever forcing them to dance at all. Indeed, they were so heavily dressed that if they could just keep to their positions and figures he would be satisfied.

He threw himself into his own role until sweat poured down his face, which was scarcely seemly. In the eyes of the others he was demeaning himself to the rank of a professional, a street player or a gypsy. He did not notice. He was too flushed.

Just before the performance he checked the hall for the last time. Trees stood about among the statuary, the tall fluffy oranges of Calabria, and a bush of laurel at the far end of the room, behind which the musicians had taken up their stations. It seemed to him that he had never looked better. He was wrong. For at whatever we do best, it is in that we give ourselves away. They were always a surprise to him. He did not know his own feelings until he had danced them out.

The Duchess reached the foot of the main stair, escorted by courtiers, and moved towards the dais at which she and they were to sit. The musicians struck up. It was a prelude designed to represent the end of winter and the coming of spring, on the recorder, lute, viol, and cembalo. Snow dripped. Ice cracked. The first water ran through the cembalo, and buds popped within the lute.

There came then a gracious aria, a chiming verse by the Court Poet, full of death, *morbidezza*, winter, and spring. As the chorus took it up the court ladies, disguised as the nine muses, issued forward in a ragged clump. Their only virtue was that they were young girls. Muses emphatically they were not.

57

Antonio sprang into view, striking a pasteboard lute, and drew them to and fro like a swarm of bees. He forgot how ungainly they were. The music apostrophized each of them, and then, with a stroke of his lute, he made them severally disappear.

The Court Poet's placidly plodding lyric took voice again, and spoke of Antonio's search for Daphne. Should he find her here, or here, or here? Each here was a variation which Antonio had worked out during the night, moving himself on the black and white floor of the hall, as though he had been a chessman.

Then, to a long descending scale on the cembalo, followed by a reedy tweak on the lute stop, he discovered Daphne where the Court Poet had intended her to be all along, and footed forward towards the Duchess, with those exaggerated but perfectly genuine mock gestures of pleasure and surprise that the period demanded.

Despite herself the Duchess was startled. She rose, looking down at his flushed, absorbed face, and it was like looking at St. Veronica's shroud. There was the same intense blindness in his eyes. Then she allowed him to lead her forward, down from the dais, and knowing that something was happening, she moved through her steps in a daze, retiring each time as he expressed desire, respect, bafflement, sorrow, enchantment, and despair. She had no time to think, for then came the chase. She had only to run upon her toes and flutter her hands at her bosom and in the air. Yet as she gravely fled before him, her flight became real to her. When she reached the clump of laurel, she vanished into its safety with gratitude.

She did not know what agitated her so. From the leaves she peered out at him, as his hands beseeched her not to be metamorphosed. Beside her the machinery of a clever transparency lit up and showed the actual change. His hands fluttered all around her hiding-place, like birds set free in a storm. And then came the same rapid rippling of his fingers down his loins that showed extinguished desire. The transparency faded. He did a dance of sorrow round the bush, and she saw his legs, his feet, his calves, his torso swaying like bamboo, and the long line of his body, sinuous and truthful, was something she

58

would never be able to forget. For it spoke directly. It told her it loved her. She wondered if he knew, and knew that so far he did not. That selfless *étude* of his, that graceful, hopeless movement of his leg, which tapered into nothingness, was an entire impassioned speech something inside her answered instantly. She clapped her hand over her mouth, so as not to speak, but it was too late. Without realizing it, she had fallen in love with a soul, and of all the forms of love, that is the only seemingly irrevocable.

The muses came back to lead him sauntering away. It was such an artificial sorrow. The laurels were hot and dusty. She must put on her public face, and step forward for the courtiers' applause. But she was shaken. She knew that this must never be.

And so, seeing her face like a glimpse of the moon through branches, suddenly did he. And that was why his dancing grieved so much. It was his body again. It had told him a truth it were better not to know.

IV

More than the Cardinal planned, his plot was in advance.

She made pretexts. After all, he was her household steward. It was natural she should see him every day. She thought that if she reminded herself of his inferior role, she would forget him. But though his role might be inferior, he was not. She could not forget him. If she sent for him, and he was away on some errand at Ravello or Salerno, her whole day was suddenly dulled. Yet she flattered herself that she showed nothing. There was nothing to show.

Then she began to feel that he was deliberately avoiding her. She was lonely. That thought made her lonelier. She had only Cariola to talk to, and these days she did not like the way Cariola looked at her. Cariola was fond of her, but she was a walking microscope to the smallest intrigue. She was so well trained to sniff it out, that she could scent it even when it was not there. She trusted Cariola completely. But she did not trust her with this.

Yet it was Cariola, after all, who offered a harmless solution.

The world of Amalfi was a small world, and a narrow one in

the physical sense. High on the left cliff stood the monastery of the Cappuccini; but apart from that the town huddled along the shore. Everyone knew everyone else by sight. There was no privacy there, and the Duchess was in need of diversion.

But above the yellow cliffs lay the mountain uplands, almost uninhabited, and little explored. There were vestigial forests there, small pools and brooks, and open fields which seemed to rock, in that intense light, high above the waveless sea. There was small game among those trees, and the privacy of the open countryside.

"Why not", said Cariola, "go hawking."

"I know nothing of hawking."

"You know how to ride. Leave the hawking to the hawk."

The Duchess would never have thought of it. Her heart sprang up. If she went hawking, it would be natural that she should take Antonio in her company. Now she might meaninglessly see him every day, for though there were other men at court who knew something of falconry, they were too old to wish to ride; and besides, intrigue kept them on a short leash. They could not bear to be away from their little plots for long. And such as would come would soon be left panting plumply behind. She thought all that and did not think of it at all. But she smiled. The idea appealed to her.

"I could not do that," she told Cariola. "What would people say?"

"You are pale indoors," said Cariola. "The air would do you good."

The Duchess shrank from the idea. She knew she was watched. She must do nothing unusual, or there would be trouble in it. She shook her head and said no.

The art of falconry had fallen into disfavour. It was no longer either the fashionable nor the customary thing to do. But this was the country for it. There was even a falconry attached to the palace. A week later she went down there.

It was a low, dank room attached to the stables, dusty, with a straw floor, and one narrow window high up, through which the light slid down the air. She went there on impulse, leaving the door open behind her. Most of the perches were empty, but there were three or four birds there, moving restively on their

60

perches, their hoods giving them the heads of enlarged blue-bottles. The alley between the benches on which the perches stood was narrow. There was scarcely room for her dress. The hooded heads looked testicular. The beaks protruded beneath ravenously, like those old Germanic pictures of hell, in which the devils have rending beaks instead of pudenda. One of the hoods had only to come loose, and they would attack her. They were furious with confinement, that taut, motionless fury that is the sure promise of violence. Her skirt caught on a leather jess, and its bells tinkled. The birds jumped up and down, and she moved away.

A shadow darkened the doorway. As soon as she saw the silhouette she knew instantly who it was. She drew a little back.

"I've done my best for them, but they need exercise," said Antonio. He was laughing. It was the first time he had ever spoken to her informally. His voice had a velvet burr, and his words flooded out over his emotions, like water over stones, tossing them about. She found his voice beautiful.

"I've never been here," she said.

"These were excellent birds once. But too old. You can get better at Salerno."

"So you know about hawking, too."

"Not very much," he said. But his voice was full of affection and pleasure. He seemed awkward for a moment, and then put one of the birds on his wrist, stroking it. She watched the movement of his hand. In the dim light it was a white blur. She was glad they could not see each other very well, and sorry there was but one way out of the shed. She wanted to flee. Instead she said:

"Order them. From Salerno. We will go hawking."

She felt rather than saw him smile, and realized that she had pleased him quite by accident. It was a long time since she had pleased anyone that way. It was even longer since she had met anyone who could be pleased that way. She felt oddly touched. But when they left the shed, she looked around to see if anyone was watching, and for some reason did not look at him. For some reason she did not want to see his face just then.

A week later they rode out of a clump of cedars, from which they could look down over a sloping meadow, to Amalfi

61

tucked away in the shadow of its cliffs, and some kind of oppression lifted from her breast. Perhaps it was the thinner air. Perhaps it was freedom. As spring survives the later, the higher we climb, so perhaps does youth.

From a bush far off she heard the solo of a bird. She looked at Antonio with quite honest pleasure, the first time she had ever directly looked at him openly, and they both smiled, and somehow, together, their horses cantered over the parched and yellow grass. It was impossible not to bring with them a little company, but the little company was easily left behind.

She was happy.

Of the next few weeks she remembered only certain things, but those so clearly that they filled up every empty chasm of her memory. She had had nothing worth remembering so far, and now she had so much. She saw everything for the first time, the way a child, a mystic, or a blind man suddenly cured, would see. A hawk does not dive directly through the air. That plummet seems to pause briefly at every floor of space, on the way to the basement and its prey. When a man rides easily in the saddle, with his feet in the *tapadas*, the creases of his breeches fall away from the kneecap like a gesticulating hand. When you lie on the grass, and look upward, the long slim green blades are like a forest of scythes, and through them the clumps of wildflowers stand up like pine-trees along a ridge. It is possible to play a fascinating game with small pebbles. You fling them into the waters of some shallow stream, and try to guess what precious stones they will resemble as soon as they become wet.

Rabbits really do scream when talons sink into their flanks. And somehow the patterns they make as they shuttle back and forth in terror across a field remain in the mind when they are gone. The patterns are like cradles made of string.

And why is it that the gesture of the nape of a man's neck, when he leans forward, is one of the most poignant and touching things in the world?

She did not know. But now when she laughed, she did it unconsciously, and did not hear herself do so, as usually she did. For she had discovered an intoxicating freedom. At first she did not believe it, and yet it was true. It was simply that

Antonio did not know. She had never known a naïve man before. For that matter she had never known a naïve woman, either. She found out suddenly that he had not one grain of self-interest. She had been taught that that was a form of folly. Now on the uplands she discovered that it could also be the source of a sense of well-being and of ease attainable in no other way. She relaxed. So long as she never met his eye, she might say and do anything she pleased. So long as she did not touch him, life could be innocent. For though he was older than she, he was still a boy. He was not yet awake.

Or so she thought, but she was quite wrong. He was boyish, but no boy. It was true he had no guile and very little wit, and that he laughed all the time, with that rapturous giggle that sits properly only upon Latin men. But he was a gentleman, and so he knew that the difference in their rank made it impossible for him to have her. And so he was very merry. He knew she saw nothing in him but a pleasant companion, and so it was safe for him to have at least this much, and to rejoice in having even that.

Yet sometimes, when we are holding an amiable conversation, suddenly that screen of words parts, and we know we are only talking against what we really want to do together. Then we become conscious of what we are saying, and hurry on, and cover the moment up, but the effort is useless. In that one little pause between words something has become evident, and we can neither take advantage of it nor even have the same ease with each other back again. That was the moment he inwardly dreaded, and he avoided it in every way he could. The trouble is that moment occurs at random and unexpectedly. We cannot prepare against it. So under the merriment he was very sad. He knew that they could not be innocent for long.

One day, coming over a rise, they came unexpectedly upon one of those saplings to which the farmers attach dead birds and voles, to frighten away the living from the fields, and perhaps as a warning to the curious. The bodies had mummified, and swayed in a stiff breeze, like frost-bitten pomegranates on a leafless tree. The Duchess pulled her reins and turned away. For some reason she was shocked. They came to a small stream, and dismounted while the horses drank.

Little by little, as the weeks had gone by, it had become established that the company with them should make camp under the cedars and wait for them. At first a page had been brought along for the sake of seemliness. But today he was ill. For the first time they were completely alone. It made them both uneasy, and the vole tree had upset them both, not so much because it was horrible, as because it had been unexpected. They had each been under greater pressure than they knew. They had said everything to each other already, without ever having uttered a word. And now, with the page absent, they found themselves where they had not meant to be. Each had guarded against making any beginning. But now, alone, they found it had already been made.

Nothing happened. The horses' heads were at the stream, and the hair of their manes parted smoothly and silkily. Antonio looked up, and saw the Duchess staring at him. A cloud scurried across the sun, it was true, but that had little to do with it. Antonio took an involuntary step forward, the Duchess's eyes widened, and then he pretended to be fussing with the saddle. That was all. But it frightened them both badly, and the trouble was now that each knew the other was scared. It had happened in the wrong place. They were within sight of the cedar trees. Both looked automatically that way.

But as they remounted and rode back to the camp, they talked as people do who have just had a serious quarrel, and are trying to overlook the fact, plodding through their words to the nearest exit.

It is by noticing such subtle changes that a court informer earns his keep. But there was no court informer there as yet, which was lucky for both of them. But Cariola was there, and though Cariola said nothing that night, when she helped the Duchess undress, her lips were tight.

"Madame should be more cautious."

"What do you mean by that?"

"You know very well what I mean."

"I don't! I don't! I don't!" said the Duchess, and smashed the glass vial she was holding. She was so young.

Cariola sniffed. "You had better send him away."

"No. I will go away myself."

64

"He will still be here when you come back. Madam, send him away. You do not know who watches you here."

Cariola was right. Nothing had happened, but she was right. But she did not send him away. It was too late for that. Instead she dismissed Cariola for the night.

The Duchess's bedroom was lofty and square, its arcaded windows giving on a large terrace. The enormous bed stood in the centre of the room, on a dais with three steps. The Duchess lay there restlessly until she fell asleep at dawn. If she had her eyes open, she thought about him. If she closed her eyes, she could see him, and that was even worse. No one had the right to have such eyes. No one had the right to be unique. His eyes seared her night. She would not take a lover. She could not marry. Her brothers would permit no course but chastity.

The next few days she did not see Antonio. She saw her courtiers instead. It did not do. To her everyone was unique. You could find one trait here, another there, but never could you find the same person. You may love a body, and there are a thousand bodies, all charming. There is only one soul. Love that in anyone, and lose it, and you have lost yourself for good.

Antonio had not waited to be dismissed. He had gone on a tour of her establishments. She admired him for that. He had more tact than she. But what was he thinking? What was he doing? Where was he? Every day she turned to speak to him, and he was not there.

There remained her little court. She was an heiress. She was young. She passed for beautiful. She had powerful brothers. The Spanish would be back in power some day, and it was not impossible the Cardinal might one day be Pope. She did not lack for suitors. They were all diplomats.

No doubt they were worthy men. They were not Antonio. And the pages, flunkies, and attendants? She might have taken any one of them. It would have been diverting for an hour or two. One or two might have lasted a week. This one was saintly, that was reputed animal in bed, was proud of it, and showed it, and wanted only a little favour in return, a parcel of land, a farm, a percentage on the fishing tax, a suit of clothes. That one was lubricious and wanted nothing. He was perhaps the better one. But we are not siege machines and she was not a town wall. She had no talent for the moment. What she wanted she wanted every day.

Yet every day she must be pert, well-favoured, fortunate, polite, tactful, and the ruler of the state. Every day people watched to see if she was this or that. It was their duty to amuse her, so she must pretend to be amused. Antonio was still on tour. He would be back soon. The burden was intolerable. She fled.

V

She went to Ravello. The town was very old, and was already falling into decay, but it was high on the cliffs, a thousand feet above and to the south of Amalfi. It had been built by the Normans, centuries ago. Now its noble houses were empty, and many of its churches were boarded up. The palace was at the end of the town. Its gardens stretched to the precipice. She took only Cariola and some domestics with her. The precipice fell sheer several thousand feet to the sea, and was backed by a *pineta*. One could look down and out to the small rock islets in the lonely sea, and Amalfi was hidden somewhere to the right. At the edge of the cliff there was a small gazebo, built by one of the dead Piccolomini. It was where she went when she wished to be alone, for it suited her thoughts. Here, with the gates closed, she could be safe.

She walked often by herself, over the hills, restlessly and thoughtfully, from one church to the next, from one empty house to the next, with only the peasants to speak to her.

The town was divided into two halves by a ravine. One evening at dusk she found herself on the far hill. There was an enormous church there, of unadorned brick, long boarded up. The evening was full of yellow light, as though it had been dusted with sulphur. Every time she turned a corner she expected to meet a stranger.

Instead she found herself in the piazza before the church, looking up at its twisted, eyeless façade. Attached to the church on one side was another structure. She thought she heard a horse somewhere, and, not wanting to be disturbed, tried the church door.

The interior was vast, shadowy, and naked of all ornament. The chairs were overturned, as no doubt they had been left long ago. There was no Host, and the altar had been stripped bare. The dust made patterns underneath her shoes. She picked up her robes, so they should not become soiled, and moved aimlessly down the aisle.

She came to an arch on her left, one step up from the nave. The opening was closed by a rusty iron grille. She peered inside. It was the ancient tombhouse of the Piccolomini, who had been little lords here, before they gained Amalfi. On an impulse she pushed against the grille, the lock gave, and the gate swung open. She hesitated and then went inside.

It was a very different affair from their baroque mausoleum at Castello del Mare. The room was long and square, with circular lights let in near the ceiling of the high roof, and a tall open arcade that looked down across the valley towards the sea. It seemed that the Piccolomini had crowded down to death in some haste, following one another pell mell, for the floor was a maze of statuary. She threaded her way to and fro, and let her skirts trail where they would.

She was young enough to find monuments of this kind full of a curious thrill, a certain charm. Here a woman life-size knelt beside a table tomb, thinking of nothing in particular, while her husband reclined on the lid, tapping with his fingers on a marble skull. There some knight rested with his feet up on an intelligent stone porcupine.

Farther along stood a marble countess in a farthingale, one hand on her breast, and with a stubborn, but gracious expression on her face. She stood among her children, of which there were seven, together with an eighth that lay in the cradle of her left arm. They were shown shrouded, with only their heads peeping out of their ruffs, and looked like ears of corn, stripped to show the cob.

It made her meditative. She had no children of her own. She had only the Piccolomini heir, and even he had been taken away from her. She wondered for a moment how ordinary people felt about their children. They must like them even when they were small.

She turned to leave, and thought she heard footsteps. She

hurried towards the grille and felt herself pulled backward. For a moment it startled her. The hem of her robe had caught a cherub carved low to the floor on one of the tombs.

Beyond the grille she saw the glow of a candle, and someone was definitely standing there. She gasped with exasperation and tugged once more at her skirt. But it would not come free. The grille creaked and the figure stepped forward. She looked at it wide-eyed. It was Antonio.

"What are you doing here?" she asked. She felt an overwhelming relief.

"The building is in disrepair. Something might have happened to you."

"Have you been here all the time?"

"I came to check the tombhouse, and the grille was open."

"You knew I was here."

He hesitated and then nodded reluctantly. He came no closer to her. That annoyed her. She tugged again at her dress.

"I'm caught," she said. Her hands moved idly, as though they had a life of their own, and wanted to say something.

He came forward, set the thick candle on the top of the table-tomb, and bent to release her. He had to kneel to do so. The light flickered restlessly. She looked down and saw the small black hair curling round the nape of his neck, and remembered those early days when they had first gone hawking. The well-cherished gesture of that neck suddenly made visible was too much for her. She watched her hand reach down to touch him, as though it were not part of her. He shook it off, and then, kneeling as he was, put his arms around her legs, and buried his head in the thick, embroidered folds of her dress, with a little stifled moan, that seemed to run up through her. She felt her hands rest in his hair, and burst into floods of tears.

VI

Tears bring release. They sometimes spring from joy. They are like rain. They renew everything. Tears are a promise. Tears are enjoyable.

Together they sank towards the floor. They had offered up six weeks to self-control, and now the sacrifice was over. It

68

made them solemn. It is curious how much more you can see of the world when you cry. When two people cry together, kneeling on a stone floor, face to face, they see even more.

He put his head on her shoulder. His fingers began to toy with her hair, and ran over the locket that hung at her throat, clutching it convulsively.

"Oh no," she moaned.

He wrenched away from her, but still knelt there, his hands on his thighs, staring at her. "Why should I not?" he demanded, and his voice made him older. He was not the harmless boy she had imagined after all. "Why should I *not?*"

He put his head in her lap. She could feel various parts of herself waking up. Abruptly she gave in to him. What harm could it do? It need happen only once, and there was no one to see.

There was a soft patter all around them. She sat up and wiped her eyes. Now their tears extended into real rain, as though the world had taken their emotion up. She leaned back against the table-tomb. He lay with his head in her lap. Through the arcade they could see the veils of rain sweep across the valley and meet in the middle like curtains.

Above them the candle spluttered, its wax rippling down its flanks and over the fancy stonework of the tomb. Its dim echo caught the needles of the rain and shimmered along them in waves of magic light.

He lay there for a long time. They were waiting for the right moment, and then it came. He stood up.

"Wait here," he said. She closed her eyes, and when she opened them, he was gone. She turned and leaned upon the tomb, gazing earnestly at the candle burning brightly in its little sea of liquid wax. Her eyes snapped and she smiled.

He came back again, with something over his arm. "Come," he said. He held out his hand to her, and they moved among the tombs. Close to the arcade was an open place perhaps six feet on the side. He handed her the candle to hold and threw down the cloths he had over his arm. They were gorgeous albs and chasubles from the vestry, where they might have been locked in chests for forty years. The candle-light caught the green embroidery, the saints, paste jewels, seed pearls, and gold and silver threads. The open space became a metallic meadow. He took her in his arms and the candle went out as she sank down into darkness with him. The fall seemed infinite.

Why are people so different by night and by day? His body was like his dancing. It had the same urgent, coherent suavity. She had slept only with Piccolomini, that vain old man who had had to be helped even to produce an heir, and to whom erotics were merely a branch of genealogy.

She laughed. She had not known that the emotions could be so easy. She was utterly detached from her body, and watched it as a nurse would watch a happy child.

In the darkness we begin to see with the finger-tips, and then the body has no shape, but only a meaning. It becomes transubstantiated into the nature of the thing it otherwise expresses only by its appearance. The thighs become a coast, the chest a platform, the navel an eager opening. How it clutches at the fingers when we put a finger there. Yet it was not the act that excited her. It was Antonio. His body was the symbol of himself, and that is why she loved it. People had no right to be so rare. There was a pathos in the way he bent his head, and his hair was like the feathers of some plaintive bird. And all that time they said nothing. What was there to say?

Outside the double window the rain began to disperse. It had been sated, and fell now more fastidiously, so that clumps of fine rain hovered here and there about the hills, like silver trees. Then even they were gone. The world slowed down and settled into place. The stars appeared.

They lay there quietly for a while. She noticed now, what she had not noticed before, that the studs, stones and threads of the copes had embossed her flesh cruelly.

She stirred and pulled down her dress. He stood up, and when she looked around for him, he was over near one of the tombs, gravely doing a slow arabesque with his right foot. She watched, fascinated. He was utterly unaware of her. Slowly the rest of his body followed his foot, and he fluttered gravely against the shadows of the tomb behind him, like a wounded sparrow. It was spontaneous. It was beautiful. It was heart-rending. He did not even know he was doing it, and it was a little ode of joy. She could not bear it.

70

"Stop that," she said. She did not mean to be cruel.

All the motion faded out of his body, and his head jerked towards her self-consciously. She had diminished him.

"I mean I'm cold," she said. "Oh, I don't know what I mean." She put her face in her hands. She put him back in his box like a naughty doll, and she would have given anything not to have done that, but it was too late.

He found the candle and lit it again. She drew away, formally, and they stood together in the stone shadow of the tombs, surrounded by the quiet effigies. He was a trifle shorter than she was, and that, as she stroked the back of his head, gave her back her sense of place and some command over him, and therefore over herself.

"We had better go," she said.

"There is only Cariola with you."

"Only Cariola," she said, and felt a pang of fear. Cariola would only have to look at her to know. She picked up her skirts and moved uneasily towards the grille. She had thought of rank as only a barrier between them. Now she saw that rank was a system of self-control, an armour to protect us from ourselves. The difference between a gentleman and a Duchess is greater than that between a Duchess and a peasant. For his sake, then, let it remain so.

He scooped up the copes and returned them to the vestry. Then they went outside.

The broken silhouettes of the town were black against the paler black of the sky. The night was cold and crisp. She sat on the pillion of his horse, while he led it by the bridle.

They passed across the church square. At the top of the stairs leading up to it, the church's green bronze doors stood open like the doors of a rifled crypt. Both breathed easier once they had regained the narrow lanes.

The palace was cut off from the town by a wall built entirely across the cliff, a wall with a narrow gate of wrought iron. The horse halted and the Duchess slid down to the ground. She half-moved towards Antonio, thought better of it, opened the gate, and fled inside, shutting the grille on his anguished face.

The white gravel path was thick with shadows, and bordered

71

with clipped yew and absurd Grecian hermæ. Despite herself, she glanced back, and he was still standing motionless, his white face a blur, gazing forlornly after her.

The palace lay to her left, very small, very low, and without a window on the garden side. She had done right. She had sent him away. But she could not face Cariola yet.

Instead she pushed hurriedly between the diamond-speckled shrubs, as the rain water ricocheted off on her dress, and went right to the gazebo. Far below her the fishing boats were out, each leaning heavily towards the water, on the side to which its net was attached. There was now a ghost of a moon. A thin, turbulent mist lay over the sea. Each boat carried a flare to daze the fish, and the sea was dotted with them, shimmering delusively in the mist, like fox fire in an autumn bog. The wind stirred her dress. She looked down. But even so she saw his abandoned face staring solemnly back at her, superimposed on the sea. Love, say the poets, is the only felicity. But love in great ladies is as culpable as crime.

VII

Ravello made her restless. So did Cariola. She was only too aware that Cariola knew that something had happened. She was equally aware of the church and tomb-house standing empty across the valley. None the less she forced herself to remain in Ravello a week, for she told herself that by the end of that time Antonio would have forgotten the incident.

At the end of the week she rode down to Amalfi along the cliff road. Since there was no freedom for her anywhere, it did not seem to her to matter where she went. She saw that we merely move from a larger to a smaller, a smaller to a larger cell in the prison of the world, at the whim of our gaolers, and are lucky if once in ten years we hear someone from the next cell scratching on the wall. And though commoners may take some comfort from being flung into the same dungeon, nobles, as befits their station, are locked up by themselves.

Cariola, however, was glad to be back. No doubt she missed the gossip of the kitchens and the halls. The Duchess could not feel the same enthusiasm. A town can have a thousand inhabitants and still be empty for the absence of one.

Court life did not interest her. Unlike her brothers, she had not risen by petty intrigue, but had been raised by it. It did not have for her the charm it had for them. She was only a woman, wedged between the world she ruled and the world that sought to rule her. She only knew that she must never look directly into Antonio's eyes, and never grant him a private interview, both for his safety, and for hers.

She had to sit for what she thought was to be a medal to commemorate the shooting of the popinjay. It filled up the empty hours. Her nerves were badly frayed, and the painter annoyed her. Everything annoyed her. She saw Antonio in public, and it was worse than not seeing him at all. She longed for him. It was ridiculous. A tension built up within her and could find no way out.

She had told him to stay away, but there are times when it is not so pleasant to be obeyed. She began to feel that he was avoiding her, even that he had done with her. She was mortified. She did not dare to find out.

She took to catching glimpses of him. She told herself these glimpses were accidental. Every morning at nine he crossed the yard towards the household offices. She could watch him from the loggia that faced the court. She did so for a week. It was the event of her mornings. He never looked up. He did not seem to know that he was being watched. His figure was so trim and jaunty. She would have wished it sad. When she received him formally, on business, it seemed to her that his eyes were sad. But perhaps his eyes were always sad. It was impossible for her to say.

On Friday he crossed the yard as usual, and she watched as usual, standing in the shadow of a column. He was very small below her, and too far away. He disappeared into the doorway to the offices. With a sob of exasperation she turned back towards her rooms.

Cariola was standing in the middle of the loggia. She said nothing, but she dropped her eyes, though not before the Duchess had seen the eager, gratified, faintly malicious look in them. She lost her temper.

73

"Send for him," she ordered.

"For whom?" Cariola blandly folded her hands across her dress.

"You know perfectly well for whom. Either that or you are a worse spy than I thought you were."

"I was not spying." Cariola eyed her mistress anxiously. "I don't like to see you this way."

"You love to see me this way. Bring him to me at once. At once."

"That would be unwise."

The Duchess did not care whether it was wise or not. If she was going to lose everything anyway, it did not matter greatly how she lost it. "Bring him to me tonight. Smuggle him in. I must see him."

Cariola stirred restively. "It would be most dangerous."

"I don't care whether it is dangerous or not."

"And what about him? Do you want to see him dead?"

"What are you talking about?"

"Your brother has arrived. He is down in the harbour now." Cariola looked around her. "It is not good to talk here. We might be overheard."

It was true. Ferdinand had come. He had come because he could not stay away. He had to see what she was doing. The Cardinal knew nothing of this visit. It was not to his interest that brother and sister should meet, for it was Ferdinand's jealousy he planned to make use of, and jealousy flourishes on partings, not meetings.

Ferdinand sent no message and did not appear. No doubt he was spying out the land, for he had never been to Amalfi before. Besides, Ferdinand was like a dog. If he had a master, then he whiffled on the trail, but if the master was away, he was apt to follow any scent that caught his fancy. He had that capacity to find ordinary people interesting that completely disqualifies some people for any career of their own. He approached tradesmen, dancers, fishermen, soldiers, even dwarfs, as a child approaches a grown-up, humbly, and with a desire to know how the thing was done. He seemed superstitiously to believe that the poor had a secret knowledge of their own.

74

The Duchess waited for him until four, and then could stand the waiting no longer. She did not want Ferdinand to see Antonio, so she had had him sent on an errand to Salerno. But she had to know why Ferdinand had come. She decided to go in search of him herself.

She found him still at the harbour, and approached him over the hard-packed, clammy beach, her skirts trailing after her. The light was low, the shadows long. The fishing boats were drawn up on shore, their painted prow eyes staring blandly out to sea, and the sand around them was corded with nets spread out to dry.

Since the Popinjay the Amalfitani had accepted her. They fell back respectfully as she approached, and she found herself looking at Ferdinand with some eagerness. The Cardinal she was afraid of, for she did not understand him. Something saturnine in his character had always kept her at arm's length. But when she was a child, Ferdinand had been like a big shaggy dog which once petted becomes the best of friends. It was only his monstrous need of her affection that frightened her and drove her away from him. If he had allowed her merely to like him, she would have liked him very much.

He was smiling, but when he looked up and saw her, his smile instantly drained away into something more serious, and his eyes became suspicious, as they always did.

She looked at him helplessly. She would have liked nothing better than to sit down in the sand with him and eat calamari with the fishermen, by the light of their flares. But he made such young and instinctive things impossible. Paranoia had cut him off from everyone. He could be friendly only in an empty room.

No doubt he had come with the best of motives. She knew that much about him. He really did love her. He wished her well. But when he saw her, something happened to his friendliness. He clouded up. His voice became choked. He curled his fingers into his palm when he talked to her, even if what he said was a compliment. And sitting in shadow, with one finger to his cheek and his legs crossed below the knee, he would let his famished eyes glower out at her until everything she did was wrong. And why did he act so? She refused to know. It was something she felt she would be better off not to know.

"You're well liked here, sister," he said, standing and brushing sand off his legs. He waved away the fishermen, took her arm, and turned towards the stairs leading up from the beach. "I hope you never give them cause to think otherwise of you."

That was the sort of thing he always said. He saw beauty only in a swift look round Eden, while the apple was being bitten. He came on stage always at the wrong time.

"I shall not," she said.

"You are too pretty. They think you must have a lover." He paused. "Have you been into the Cathedral?"

The change of subject startled her. She must have showed it, for he laughed and said no more.

But he was ill at ease, and that made her ill at ease. He was so eager to see her give herself away that she had an hysterical impulse to do so. Only the thought of the lover she did not, in truth, have, restrained her. She had need of restraint. Ferdinand's conduct that evening was to say the least curious.

He sat beside her like Minos, in a cartoon of the Last Judgment. It was indeed the age of Caravaggio, who turned the devil into a young man playing cards, died of malaria, and believed in everything but God. Ferdinand was a devil playing cards. It was not for some time that she realized what he was doing. He was memorizing the faces of her courtiers one by one, as though comparing them with some image in his own mind. Instinctively she knew what that image was. She was thinking of Antonio so intensely that he must be able to pluck that image from her mind.

He was sullen, but he found a chance to speak to everyone, to the young ones most of all. And when he rose to retire, which he did early, she saw he had been tensing himself to ask her something.

"That steward my brother got you, he is not here," he said.

"No, he is at Salerno."

Ferdinand dragged one foot on the floor and abruptly looked up at her. "Is he thin?" he asked.

She blinked. Surely Ferdinand had met him at Rome. "He's young," she said blandly. "Most young men are thin."

Ferdinand grunted and then excused himself.

76

She was sure it was not to sleep.

And indeed as she lay awake that night she heard surreptitious noises along the corridor which were not the usual noises she listened for. It was the sound of Ferdinand pacing up and down the night. She dozed off, and woke up abruptly to realize that he was standing on the other side of her door, afraid to knock, and even more afraid to come in without knocking. He was not pleasant in these little ways. He snuffled like an abandoned dog. She waited, breathless, and the footsteps walked away.

In the morning she rose early. She had once more to pose for her medallion. It was to be the last pose. Cariola brought her breakfast and the news that Ferdinand had packed up and was ready to leave. As she said this, she looked at her mistress significantly.

It was very like him. He was going precisely because he wanted to stay; and he was in a temper precisely because he had found nothing to be angry about. She wondered which member of her household had been got at and paid off, to send information on her movements back to Rome. She might never know.

She arrived at the sitting half an hour late. She sat down on her field chair and wearily presented her profile to the light. The artist had been fetched from Naples, and was a dapper young man. She would have taken him for an apprentice, had he not seemed so professional. She held the pose until her neck began to ache, and could see no reason why a simple medallion should require so many sittings. Even while she tried to look benign, she felt worried. She hoped Ferdinand would leave without seeing her.

Instead she saw him stride into the room. She did not break her pose, but squinted at him by swivelling her right eye, until the muscles ached.

"Why do you make this pretence?" he demanded.

She flinched. "What pretence? I told you a medal was to be struck."

"Do you mean to tell me you believe that?"

"Of course I believe it. It's true." When he was like this he was uncontrollable.

77

Ferdinand strode across the room and shook the painter like a rattle. "Who commissioned this?" he roared.

"Stop that," said the Duchess. "The citizens commissioned it."

"So then you do know," he said. "Which one of them?"

"I don't know what you are talking about," she told him.

"Don't you?" He threw the painter aside, grabbed her hand, and hurried her from the room and through the courtyard into the streets. They went up the steps to the Cathedral, and turned left into the cloisters, and then into a room opening off them, which had been set up as a studio.

In the centre of the room, on a large easel, stood an altarpiece. It was not yet finished. It glistened because it was still wet.

"Have you no shame?" he demanded, "to set your filthy loves up even in the Church?"

She had not been posing for a medallion after all. It was an Adoration of the Virgin, in the new style, painted in blinding light and deep shadow, and yet all pink and blue. The Virgin, her clothes fluttering in a spiral, floated in the air, her eyes cast up, her hair falling free, one hand to her breast, the other holding a drooping nosegay, and her elegant foot on an elegant crescent moon. Cherubs held back the clouds like vast silk canopies. She rose above a landscape of the Amalfi uplands, lightly brushed in. The Virgin was herself.

Frankly bewildered, she turned to her brother. "I knew nothing of this," she said.

"Did you not?" He sounded ironic, but was watching her closely. She tried to make her face expressionless. "Then look again."

The foreground of the picture was a small field of meticulous flowers. On this coloured grass knelt a crowd of adorers, all men of the court. Only one figure was unfinished. It had been lightly sketched in, and the body already painted, but the head mercifully was still bare sizing covered with one or two charcoal lines. It was the most prominent and extravagant of the adorers. The figure knelt, with arms upraised.

She knew every movement of that body, whose gestures were more personal even than the missing face. It was Antonio. And

78

of course Ferdinand was right. It was not an altar-piece. It was an erotic *ex voto*. It was bold, audacious, and beautiful. But it was an act of courtship, not of faith or civic pride. It moved her deeply.

Ferdinand took her silence for confession.

"Who is he?" he demanded, poking a finger at the canvas. "Which in that court, is your paramour?"

"I have told you, I have no paramour."

"And you pretend you had nothing to do with this shameless thing."

"Nothing."

Something in her tone must have stopped him. He peered at her, and then stamped out of the room. When she followed, he was waiting for her in the cloister.

"Perhaps I misjudged you, sister," he said. "But I give you warning. If paramour there is, I will find him out. And when I find him, he will not live very long or die very comfortably."

"You have no power over me."

"Do you think you rule here? We could snuff you out in an instant!" He paced up and down the cloister. "I will not have you with anyone," he shouted at her. "With anyone, do you understand?"

"You married me off to Piccolomini."

"That was different."

"How different? I had his child."

Ferdinand blinked his eyes. "I will not have you with any young man," he told her. His voice was low and earnest now. "You are my sister. You will not disgrace me so."

"And you are my brother."

He flushed and made an impatient gesture. "Do not anger me," he said. "It is not safe to anger me. Not even for you. Not for anyone." He looked suddenly like a small child. But he was not a small child. He was a dangerous man. She had feared him for Antonio's sake. Now she feared him for her own.

"I shall know everything you do," he said. "Everything. And have that abomination burnt, lest others know it too." Suddenly tears appeared in his eyes, and he took her hand. "I am fond of you. It is wrong of you to disgrace me," he said.

Later, when she was sure he had gone, she went back to the studio and looked at the picture for a long time. The artist entered, and seemed disconcerted.

"I want to sit here," she said. "Do your work."

He seemed displeased, but after all he had no say in the matter. She sat in a chair in the corner, and watched him busy himself with his palette and his brushes.

She sat there all morning, watching him, as rapidly Antonio's face took form. It was not so much that the painter created it as that it lay latent, and he merely rubbed it up until it gleamed.

The face added nothing to the body. It was not a cunning or an intelligent face. But it was a face radiant with feeling, curiously dumb, but with those intimate yet distant eyes. It was those eyes that decided her. For his own sake she must give Antonio up.

But the picture should not be burnt. She should not have it destroyed, for it was the only love letter she had ever received. Instead she would have it concealed, in the sacristy, where it would not be seen. Ferdinand would never go there. His brother the Cardinal had left him with a horror of the wash-rooms and council chambers of the Church.

But she felt suddenly tired. How could the mere attitude of a painted body say so much?

VIII

Antonio returned from Salerno late that night. She sent Cariola to fetch him at once. The court was asleep and it seemed better to see him before Ferdinand's spy should be on guard.

Cariola would bring him up the servants' stair that wound through the masonry. The inconvenience of this was that he would enter her room directly. And she did not know how she could face him directly. Now that they were to meet, she wanted buffers and barriers between them. And Cariola was no barrier. Cariola would only urge them on.

The stairs were steep. Servants were not supposed to dawdle, so the risers were ten inches high. This old palace was a rabbit warren of circuitous ways. She heard a noise. A door in the

80

wall opened and Cariola stepped out, followed by Antonio.

His appearance shocked her. She had somehow expected him to look different, but he looked exactly as he always did. That made her feel that it was she who had changed.

She told Cariola to wait in the next room.

The moment was awkward. The Duchess found she half wanted him to rush forward and fling himself at her feet, cover her with kisses, and talk her out of what she was about to do. It would have been heaven to give in to him. But he did none of these things. The moment when he could properly do them passed, and both watched it pass. There were times, she thought, when rank was not altogether an advantage: otherwise he might have flown to her at once.

He seemed to quiver there before her, as though tethered to self-restraint, yet longing to tug free. His lips were moist. His face was beautiful. He had come to her eagerly. Yet except for that first glance in them, his eyes had already given up. Perhaps it was because he had never been in these rooms before. She watched his eyes dart round at everything that belonged to her.

He was still dressed for the road. He stood there awkwardly, yet even in awkwardness his movements had an overpowering grace. Could he find nothing to say to her? Was she such a formidable creature in his world that he dared approach her only in hidden places, such as the tomb-house? Or was he frightened of consequences?

The more they did not speak, the more they managed to say to each other things she was in no position to say, and that he had no right to. It was safer to tie down the interview with words. The silence between them was treacherously comfortable. It could not be allowed.

Perhaps her imagination was too vivid. She could not see him as he saw himself. Instead she saw him as Ferdinand would have liked to see him, hanged, torn apart, or disembowelled, his face slashed to pieces, and his testicles hanging in a tree. Such thoughts are not merely frightening, but erotic, too.

"My brother has been here," she said. "He saw the painting in the church."

"Oh," said Antonio. It was not the reaction she would have wished. He in his turn seemed to become dry and ironical. Let one doubt impinge upon a Latin's certainty, and he will throw the thing away. He turns to ice. She did not want to hurt him. She only wanted to drive him away, whether for his good or hers she no longer knew. But if he turned to ice, then hurt him she must. She could get at him no other way.

"It was scarcely judicious," she said, and hated herself for the tone of her own voice. Yet some imp made her sound cruel.

"Did you show it to him?" he asked, after a moment.

"Of course I didn't show it to him. He showed it to me." This piece of wounded vanity upset her even more. "After all, you would have hung it up for all the world to see. I did not think you would brag of so small a conquest."

He did not quite understand what she was talking about. He was a little hurt. And that hurt was what broke down his prudence. He felt himself rushing forward, and then he had her in his arms. The distance that keeps people apart is as thick-skinned as the surface tension of water, but once break through, and down we dive. He gave himself up to sensation. And he had been right. It had been the right thing to do. He could feel her yield. He could feel himself sinking into her. He forgot his pride and caution.

There is a point of acquiescence beyond which it is impossible to turn back. Dimly the Duchess passed it and seized at it. She had to save both himself and her.

"Stop it," she shouted at him. "How dare you. Stop it and get out."

He let go of her at once. It was as though something snapped in him.

She was appalled by the look in his eyes. "I didn't mean it," she said. "I didn't mean it."

She stood there helplessly. She had hurt his pride, and so he would never be easy or spontaneous with her again. Something would always be held back. And in the pain of that she completely forgot that she had sent for him only in order to send him away.

IX

It was the next day that Bosola arrived, and it was because of this interview that at first he found out nothing.

He, too, came to Amalfi by morning, by boat, for like his master before him, he also intended to spy out the land. But he saw Amalfi far differently than had Ferdinand. For one thing, he was not helped from the boat, but landed wet on the shingle. For another, there was no one to welcome him there. Where Ferdinand had seen a heap of impoverished dwellings to which he paid no attention, Bosola saw a dirty, powerful, and inimical town. He came alone, without anyone to back him, and on the worst of errands. He could not be blamed for shivering.

Rather than go directly to the palace, he put up at a decent inn, though no inn in those days was really decent, and sent a message to Antonio. When the answer came, it was to say that Antonio could not receive him until tomorrow.

Bosola sniffed. It was his nature to think that Antonio was now too important to see him at once. But that happened not to be true. At the moment Antonio could not bring himself to see anyone.

When love turns out not to have been love, you go through the day very quietly. You tell yourself you have been very brave. And only when you are alone, and haunted by that adored face that will never again look at you in quite the same way, do you realize what your real feelings are. They are nameless.

Yet you are gratified. You are deeply gratified. You agree to all her terms. You agree it was not love. It was affection, or fondness, or fellow feeling, or indeed anything, so long as you may not be utterly dismissed. And if affection or fondness is left, then your love pours itself into that, and takes its shape, and so you have not lost anything. Yet you have lost something. You have both lost something. That can be felt as soon as you embrace. For that lost something you cry together, and it brings you closer, and you grow drowsy in a mutual tenderness. It is like twilight. Perhaps you have never been so tender with each other before. The memory of what you have lost ties you together more closely than passion ever could. You are still together. And yet that is what heartbreak is. Heartbreak is not to lose someone. Heartbreak is never to be able to bear to lose someone with whom something has been lost. You could have had that lost something with no one else, and so you go on with them. You love them the more for being there. Heart-break is marriage after the honeymoon.

For Antonio it had been even worse than that. Yet he had the feeling that the Duchess had not truly dismissed him. Such feelings are beyond words. They are not beyond the power of love, for if passion understands nothing, love is passion with the blinkers off.

So he was almost happy, knowing that he would see her every day.

But for the moment he could not bear to see anyone. That was why he would not see Bosola until the next day.

For his own part, Bosola was in his blackest mood, the one at the bottom that he almost never reached. He passed a bad night.

That did not prevent him from being efficient. He went to the palace next day with more information than he had had before. First of all, and best for his own purposes, he had discovered that Antonio was not popular in Amalfi. He was an outsider, and he held a job which otherwise would have been given to an Amalfitan.

About the Duchess public feeling ran a little differently. The feeling was that she would not last long, and since she was harmless and pretty, her subjects felt sorry for her. But they would not raise a finger to help her, should she fall into any danger, for they had backed the wrong side too often, ever to be moved by motives of chivalry. Amalfi had been given back and forth over their heads so often since the fall of their Republic that they were indifferent to their own rulers. They were more concerned with the price of fish.

A spy has two abilities. The one is to find out secret informa-tion. The other is to see the hidden significance of information that is not secret at all. Bosola possessed both. As he entered the palace and crossed the courtyard towards the offices, his practised eye saw many things. They added up to the fact that he was in the presence of pomp without power and the great silliness of an impotent aristocracy. He began to feel more at his ease.

Antonio kept up no pomp at all and received him at once.

He felt so friendless that he was longing for someone to befriend.

So Bosola's case was won before he had even spoken for it. Like all men of guile, it never occurred to him that others might do what he wished for reasons of their own, of which he had no inkling. He looked at Antonio, and saw that the man was not to be envied after all. He was a fool and he had not prospered. At the moment he seemed under some kind of tension, and somewhat thinner than he had been in Rome. His face, too, was as tanned as the skins of white-skinned people ever get.

As for Antonio, he saw a man he had almost forgotten, and one he did not altogether like the look of. For he felt instinctively that there was a wiriness in Bosola that might snap at any moment, and more than anything else he felt sorry for the man, as one would feel sorry for a poor relation. And indeed that is how men like Bosola manage to hang on at great courts, even though they think the reason is something quite different. What they attribute to their own cleverness is only the ability to inspire the same faintly uneasy sense of obligation that a second cousin inspires, a sort of family shame that does not do much, but at least keeps them from starving.

So the matter was settled simply, and Bosola found himself a clerk attached to the Purse and Wardrobe, a sinecure that would keep him fed, lodged, and able to follow his own business, which in this case was not his own.

Antonio proposed to introduce him to the Duchess.

This was something Bosola was not prepared for, not because of the Duchess, but for another reason. But having dared to make a pretext to see her, Antonio was in a panic about giving the idea up, and so the matter was arranged. They went at once.

The Duchess was in the great hall. It would be difficult to say why. Outwardly she was merely walking with Cariola, before going to her rooms. But actually these days she could rest in no particular room, but wandered aimlessly through the palace, in so far as that could be done with decorum, not in order to speak to Antonio, or even to meet him, but only with the thought of seeing him in the distance.

Antonio introduced Bosola, who knelt to kiss her hand.

She found the kiss repugnant. His lips were chapped and coarse, but that was not the reason. This meeting was not necessary. She was cross with Antonio for forcing it, even while she took hope from the fact that he had.

She did not recognize Bosola, and yet he seemed familiar. If he was Antonio's creature, she would prefer him. It would give her pleasure to do that. But she felt mistrustful, even while she bade him welcome to her court and added whatever meaningless phrases occurred to her.

Because Antonio was there, even because she did not look at him, she prolonged the interview. Beside her Cariola gave a start. The Duchess looked round involuntarily. But Cariola said nothing. She merely looked troubled.

The Duchess thought it was because of Antonio. And because the new man seemed eager to go, as well as because Cariola had brought her to her senses, she dismissed Antonio sharply and regretfully. But she did not leave the hall. She stayed there, watching Antonio until he had gone.

Left to himself, Bosola leaned against a wall, and mopped his brow. He had almost forgotten about Cariola. Thinking he was unwell, Antonio showed him to the rooms that had been prepared for him.

X

Technically, in the etiquette of those days, Bosola ranked with Cariola, several notches below those among whom he mixed, but still a member of the gentry. And in those days that meant a good deal. On the one hand it meant a vast and perpetual embarrassment not suffered, for example, by the likes of Antonio. But on the other, particularly in small courts, it meant that once given a position, and he was assured at least of adequate housing and honourable meals, a place or two above the salt. It meant that the gentry itself always knew who you were, but that the servants were sometimes confused, which was where the rub came. In our day the situation would be reversed.

The rooms given Bosola were small and grudging, but there were two of them, they were neatly furnished, and the window of the bedroom looked across the courtyard towards the

86

Duchess's loggia, and the corridor outside gave on the corridor leading to her rooms. It was there he waited for Cariola, for he knew she would come.

He had to wait a long time.

Cariola was with her mistress, watching her with something very like dread. Once she had wished that the Duchess would confide in her. Now she heartily hoped that she would not.

For she loved the Duchess, exactly as a nurse loves a child. She wished harm to come to her, but not too much harm, and never for too long. She wanted no one to worm out of her anything secret the Duchess might say.

No one would have thought, to look at her, or even to know her, that Cariola was a passionate woman. But she was. She was that sort of person who loves only once, and whose passion is not blind to the faults of its object, but sees them even more clearly. The person she had loved was Bosola. He had tricked her badly, but she knew him well. As soon as she laid eyes on him, therefore, she sensed, rather than knew, why he was there. The only defence she could think of was to go and tell him so.

But she also knew that he had used her before, and might use her again. For this reason she hovered over the Duchess with a special anxiety, unwilling to leave her, and at the same time urging her to go to bed.

The Duchess did not want to go to bed.

She had reached that stage of frustrated desire when one can think of a thousand reasons why one cannot have what one wants, and blames oneself for everything that has gone wrong. She had met Antonio privately only twice. The scene in the tomb-house she remembered only when she was exhausted with self-reproach. But the scene when she had told him to get out ran through her head interminably, as though it were joined end to end, to form a St. Catherine's wheel, on which her conscience ceaselessly revolved.

She was in such a position that she who should have been wooed was forced to do the wooing. And again and again, moving through the routine of her day, she thought of every mistake she had made. It was too much for a girl of twenty to endure. It was not her fault. It was not a position that a woman could endure with dignity, and it had no precedent.

87

Why, when he had come up the stair, had she not rushed to him like a girl? Why had she not poured out everything she had to say? She had so much to say. And most of all, why had something wicked and impatient in her told him to get out? Was it because she had done none of those things, and because he could not woo her? She was wrong to blame him for that. The position was impossible. But they could not go back and begin again. She must put him out of her mind. But she could not put him out of her mind. Her mind swung up and down, like a teetertotter, and carried her with it, now exalted, now depressed. And all this time Cariola fidgeted, brushed her hair, and turned down the bed.

The Duchess regarded the bed with distaste. No bed had any right to be that empty.

Cariola listened for a moment from the next room, and then slipped out into the corridor.

Antonio had a sense of protocol, and Cariola was Mistress of the Household. He had therefore consulted her earlier about rooms to be set aside for someone he wished to introduce into the staff. If she had known it was to be Bosola, she would have made them much meaner. With a tight-lipped expression, she turned down the shadowy corridor until she came to the turn at the far end, and then paused for a moment outside his door. She was about to knock, when she thought better of it, and slipped inside instead.

Several lighted candles stood on a deal table. Bosola was sitting there, doing absolutely nothing. His dimly lit face made him look not like a devil, but one of the damned. It took her slightly aback. She leaned against the door she had closed, and stared at him.

"Why have you come here?" she demanded.

He did not seem the least surprised at this approach. Perhaps it was more or less what he had expected.

"The Steward offered me the position when he was in Rome."

"At the Cardinal's." She almost spat the words out.

Bosola was alarmed. He had forgotten how much she hated him. She hated him because she had once loved him, and she thought he had used her. Well, he had used her. Yet it was not true that he had meant to do so. In the beginning his affair

88

with her had been quite genuine. That was the part he remembered. She, being the abandoned one, had remembered the rest of it. She could do him great damage here.

"I know why you have come," she said. "You will get nothing out of me."

"I do not want anything from you."

She sniffed. "You'll not get around me." She sounded more as though she were talking to herself than to him.

His eyes narrowed. He had caught the double inflection, and it made him consider her more carefully. It was a long time since he had felt any physical warmth, and his body was far lonelier even than he, for though we get used to loneliness, our bodies never do.

"Sit down," he said, and nodded towards the flagon of wine on the table. He tried to make his voice agreeable, and was surprised to find he felt agreeable.

For a moment she almost believed him, for he almost believed himself. His voice was sincere. His eyes, however, caught by the candle-light, were not.

She was filled with an immense rage that anything so fine as her Duchess should run the risk of being clawed down by a man like this, and a rage equally great that she was still attracted to him, and so might, willy-nilly, be the lever he needed.

He smiled wryly. "You might be wrong. Perhaps I am an honest man."

She was nervous. She snapped. "You are not a man. You are only somebody's creature." Unaccountably she felt herself burst into tears.

Bosola was startled. Then he pushed the flagon of wine towards her slowly, realizing before she did the real reason why she had come. And even while he did so, he was filled not only with savage self-contempt, but also with a most peculiar and unusual gentleness, the gentleness of a man who drives himself, and yet unexpectedly finds a moment to sit down.

XI

Sometimes we do not fully realize our own motives. He had

thought that he had kept her with him because it was the only way to calm her down. But once she was there, he found that he also wanted her to stay. They passed a strange night.

She came to him from time to time after that, but always without warning, and always very late. He scarcely knew how he felt about it, but it was an immense physical relief for them both, and if we cannot rest, it is at least something if our bodies can.

For the rest, he could find out nothing. Had it not been for the strange uneasiness he sensed not only in Cariola, but also when watching the Duchess, he would have despaired of there being anything to find out. And after a while his suspicions passed from Antonio elsewhere. There was nothing between them, he was sure. The mischief, if it did exist, must exist with someone else. He was reduced to sending the Cardinal minute descriptions of petty court intrigue, the opinions of the Amalfitani, and the condition of the State. It made him tremble for his position.

But days and weeks, and then months, went by, and nothing happened. It became autumn. Frost ran up the orange trees and touched the oranges. The sea grew angry and the court wore warmer clothes. The mountains looked colder.

All summer Cariola had watched the Duchess try one diversion after another. She had seen her grave, gay, wise, coquettish, full of laughter, and a little sad, taking an interest in the proposed convent, talking with prelates at dinner, or riding alone in the mountains, with a hawk on her wrist. Yet no matter what the Duchess did, Cariola was not deceived. She still caught her mistress watching Antonio from time to time. Outwardly Antonio's deportment left nothing to be desired, but something had gone out of him. He did not dance any more, and the court had grown sedate. His calves were going down. His legs were now wanly slim.

Winter was early that year. The first snow fell early in October, powdering the ground only lightly, as though with sugar. The year was almost gone.

Cariola hurried into her Mistress's bedchamber, bringing heavy furs from the storage *cassone*, to find her mistress kneeling and in floods of tears. She dropped the furs to the floor and put her arms around the Duchess, kneeling beside her. She hated to see grief.

For the Duchess it was not precisely grief. It was strain. She had controlled herself too long, so at last she had given way. It was the first winter snow that had proved too much. She could not bear that this year in which she had met him should go away without her seeing him again.

And in her own mind she had settled something. She had watched Antonio covertly for months. She had blamed him with every base motive she could invent, and every infirmity of character she could think of. She had believed him cold. But sorrowing self-control had made her see at last that passion could have a passive as well as an active form. She was convinced now that he was suffering because of her, and tried to compensate herself for the gulf between them with that. But now it seemed that nothing could compensate her for that gulf. She clung to Cariola, and cried in her lap.

"I want him," she sobbed. "I must see him."

Cariola stiffened. "You should not say such things to me," she warned.

"Why not? I must speak to someone or go mad."

Cariola thought how skilfully Bosola talked with her at night, and felt a sudden pity. But also she was curious.

The Duchess had had no one to speak to for six months. Now she had to say everything. Fear of her brother and utter terror of her own loneliness had paralysed her for too long. Besides, she was wary. She did not want to be taken advantage of. She saw all the faults in Antonio. She even saw faults of her own invention. And yet he had no faults. Nor was she any longer afraid of Ferdinand, even when inwardly she was afraid of him. After all, she was the independent ruler of a state. Why should she not do as she pleased? And no one need ever know. No one need know anything. It was not right that Antonio should suffer so, or she either. She did not even think of the Cardinal.

"Madam could send him away."

"I have sent him everywhere. If he wanted to go, he would go. Why then should he choose to stay?"

Cariola had no answer. But she did not want to listen any more. She saw a danger in hearing too much.

"You must be more circumspect," she said. It was all she could say.

In the small, stubborn lines of her mistress's wilful mouth, Cariola saw that the Duchess had decided on something that might be fatal to both of them. For an instant she thought of those maids whom Cleopatra had compelled to enter the pyramid with her, and then quelled the thought. It was disloyal. Whatever happened, she would tell Bosola nothing.

"We are going away tomorrow, to Ravello," said the Duchess. "You will bring Antonio here tonight."

"Oh no," said Cariola. But she saw that the Duchess's face had the rapt expression of someone who is afraid no longer, the expression of someone afraid of life, who has at last found something worth living for. Protest was useless.

She went in the evening to fetch Antonio.

When she came back, the Duchess was at the windows, gazing down at the patterns of the snow against the barren courtyard and its rocks. She was a little drunk with what she had decided to do. She felt exhilarated and giddy with joy. It never even entered her mind that he might not wish to comply with her requests. She grew arch.

Looking at her, Antonio saw something of what was going on inside her, and breathed deeply. It was perhaps better so. Self-restraint can cripple us, and no man would be a cripple if he had the choice. It was better to go on.

Cold air swept in from the window. It stimulated the Duchess and excited her. She dismissed Cariola. Then they were alone.

The Duchess had suddenly turned into comedy. She decided, even while her eye caught the slim shadow of his legs, to tease him.

She began to talk of rents and her estates. He clearly looked bewildered. For it was not easy for them. They had been separated for so long they did not know how first to touch each other again. He doubted the rippling undercurrent in her voice, and thought she was making fun of him. His chagrin showed so clearly in his face that with a glance towards the door, which Cariola had shut, she came over to him, walked past him, and

92

looked out the window again. The courtyard was deserted. She was aware of his standing behind her, and of his bewilderment. He shifted uneasily.

Then abruptly she turned, and he was looking at her with wide, sad eyes, slightly veiled, as though ready to be hurt. She smiled at him and stretched out her arms. Since he could not first approach her, it gave her pleasure to approach him. "Oh come," she said. "Oh come!"

He hesitated.

She smiled more fully, extending her hands palms up, and wriggling her fingers, and then he was in front of her, kissing her hands. She could not raise him up. That would not have made them equals, as they should be. Instead, she sank down to the ground and they knelt on the floor, facing each other, with their arms about each other, while the cold air from the window blew around them.

For a long time, embracing, they did not say anything at all. She could feel his body tremble, and his face lit up with a curious, impish, boyish joy. They sat there, and each began to laugh, and then was solemn again, and a little abashed.

There were, after all, no explanations, and no words. It was natural between them, as though they had been together for a long, long while.

She lay extended, with her head in his lap. "Why could we not marry, as other people do?" she said. "In some countries, contract in a room, before a witness, is legal marriage. Why could we not marry like that?"

He stirred uneasily. Suddenly he looked frightened, like some saint surprised by the stigmata. She did not like that look. She did not care for that glimpse of reality. She pouted.

"Suppose we were ordinary people. Why should we not be equals and so marry? No one need ever know."

"Your brothers would not allow it. You are Duchess of Amalfi. You have an heir and lands."

The image of Ferdinand's contorted face flared up in her mind.

"Privately," she urged. "Privately, to satisfy ourselves, not the world. I do not want to be married to that hideous, rotten old man they married me to. I want to be married to you."

93

He sat still for a long time. A little of her would always be wary. She had to know what he was thinking. She grew aware of Cariola in the next room, perhaps listening.

"There is a little town called Arosa," he said at last. "Do you know it?"

She shook her head.

"It is back in the mountains, a few hours from Ravello. No one ever goes there. It is only a collection of huts, and a ruined house or two. We could go there."

She misunderstood him. She did not care that they should hide out squalidly. "I am going to Ravello in the morning, with Cariola. I thought if I pretended to send you to Salerno, you could join me there." She must meet him on her own ground, not his.

But that was not what he had meant. "There is a church there. The living is in the gift of the Piccolomini. Thirty years ago your husband gave it to the priest who is still there. He is dying. He would marry us, and no one would ever know. We could meet there, if you like."

She was touched. She went to a chest in the corner. From it she withdrew a box, and from the box, a ring, massive, a baroque pearl set with enamel and small yellow diamonds. He watched her anxiously. She smiled at him.

"You shall give me this there," she said. "We shall be married with this." She handed him the ring slowly, looking into his eyes for the finer person she knew was there. She fumbled in the box again. "And I shall give you this. And——" She drew out a chain, and looked uncertainly around the room. If they were truly to be married, then they must not begin illicitly. He must go back to his own rooms, until tomorrow.

But this time he did not rush down the stair. He went reluctantly, as reluctant as she was to have him go.

Next day, in his report to the Cardinal, Bosola wrote that the Duchess and Cariola had gone to Ravello, finding Amalfi too cold; that the Duchess had graciously shown interest in the Cardinal's proposal for a convent foundation, and had asked who Sor Juana was; that the revenues from the fish catch had fallen off; that the Count Carriocciolo had abandoned his suit to the Duchess, but was having an affair with a tavern girl; and

94

that Mestre Antonio had departed on a mission to Salerno, in which there was nothing unusual, since the Duchess sent him there from time to time, on business connected with her house.

XII

Altogether the fates gave them three weeks of happiness. Since it was the only happiness they were to know, that was both kind and merciful. Not that the fates are either, but the fates are very busy. They cannot watch us all the time, and if we watch eagerly for the moment, when their attention is diverted, then it is possible to snatch a little joy.

The Duchess had not dared to take Cariola with her to their meeting. She rode along a faded track at the bottom of a steep gully, alone. Her thoughts were serious, and yet her face was merry. The weather was cold and dusty. Occasionally she passed a patch of pock-marked snow, and once she saw a ptarmigan.

She came out above Arosa at high noon. It was nestled in the groin of the valley, as though it had tumbled down the hills from all directions, and then come to rest in the stream-bed. It was dominated by a single tree, and by a little chapel. On the opposite hill a figure picked its way on horseback towards the same goal. She saw with excitement that it must be Antonio. It seemed to her symbolic that they should converge upon this ultimate meeting place simultaneously. It also seemed to her a good omen. She urged her horse on.

No woman tells a man how she feels about her actual marriage, for it has a symbolic meaning for her that it does not have for him. And then it only happens to a part of her. The rest of her is merely watching it. And so it will be with everything she does with him, even though she might want the matter otherwise.

When her brothers married her to the Piccolomini, that was no marriage, but only a deed of sale. This was her marriage, and she watched it bright-eyed and eager, determined to find it romantic. Well, it was.

The priest was truly ill, and a little dazed at the prospect of having something to do. If he knew who the Duchess was, he said nothing. A small boy was busy in the interior with a broom. The priest refused to let them enter the church immediately, but went in alone, and then sent the boy out to them.

He had wanted to furbish up the church. The damp gloom was smelly with newly-lit candles, there was incense in the air, and from somewhere he had dug out his best altar cloth. It had been so long since the church had been used by anyone but himself. He stood at the altar, vague, and nodding his head happily, with the child to assist him to say a Mass. He was clearly enchanted by the candles and by the air of consequence. In a town as poor and remote as this, a donation of candles seemed a miracle. It occurred to the Duchess to send the altar-piece here. It seemed to belong here. And if we cannot please God, we can at least make easier the last moments of his ministers. She determined that that was what she would do. Antonio could bring it privately.

So they were married. It filled her with tenderness. She looked at Antonio kneeling beside her, and it seemed to her no accident that the only light entering the chapel fell full upon his face. The baroque pearl was already on her finger. The priest moved erratically through his Mass. The wall behind the altar was bare. The altar-piece would fit it almost exactly. She wished the priest well.

She wished the whole world well.

When it was time for them to leave, the priest said good-bye to them reluctantly. Because her life was so full, and she was so happy, the Duchess felt sorry for him, and wanted to do him a good turn. Besides, the Mass had so clearly tired him out. She bent down from her pillion and told him about the altar-piece. His face lit up happily, and she was content. All she had wanted was to see someone smile. She rode on.

But Antonio was disturbed.

"Did I do wrong?" she asked, delighted to be meek.

He shrugged. "No, but it is a pity that we have to hide every trace of ourselves away."

"I only did it to give him pleasure," she said. But of course that was not true, and he knew it. The painting was hidden away in the sacristy, but even so, it would have been better if

96

it had never been painted at all. Here it would be better hidden yet.

It was evening when they came down behind Ravello. Once safely behind those gates, and the world was well away. Of course Cariola would have to know, but that only meant that she would have to be kinder to Cariola and more generous. There were no other servants at the villa. The Duchess had made these retreats even when Piccolomini was alive, camping out in the middle of the dusty, half-forgotten palace like a solemn child, sitting cross-legged on the floor, or dangling her naked feet in a fountain, like some Portuguese Princess.

She was too young to be a woman. It was nice to throw off that burden for a while and be a girl again. But not quite a girl. She had been a woman too soon and for too long to be able to manage that. Yet the imitation of innocence also has its pleasures, for then, and only then, do we realize what innocence can be.

She wanted to be private, but what do private people do? She did not know.

When Cariola brought in candles, and announced that such supper as they were to have was ready, she found them dancing in the undercroft. She was not to know they were married, for that would have frightened her. She would have more sympathy for an illicit escapade. So that is what their dancing seemed to her to be, and she looked at them fondly.

A dance without music is something peculiar. It makes available the secrets of a silent world. It is like moving gravely under the sea. Not since the court ballet, had the Duchess danced with Antonio, and now at last she could follow him into his secret world. The palace was built on the edge of the cliff. The undercroft was a long hall of heavy columns, open on one side to the distance and to space. It was always deep and shadowy. There they flitted like birds.

Cariola did not want to disturb them at once. It was a long time since she had heard two people laugh spontaneously together. The Duchess leaned against a column, and watched his white-clad figure, spinning in and out of the shadows. Then he circled around a pillar, and stopping in an open place, bowed to her gravely and extended his right hand. She went forward to meet him. Cariola coughed and announced dinner. They hesitated, and then hand in hand ran down the length of the hall towards her.

It was late before they went up to bed. The Duchess was not afraid of these corridors. She was used to them. She showed Antonio the way by the light of a single candle. Plaster had fallen from the walls, and some of the Cosmedin work had come loose and was tricky underfoot. The bedroom she had chosen was at the far end of the building, with a loggia over the garden.

The Duchess thought that it was not like that first night with Piccolomini. The marriages of great princes are half stud farm and half dynastic brothel. She had felt that way waiting for Piccolomini to dodder over her. Now, as she mounted into the great state bed, she felt gay. She nestled there complacently, waiting to be found, and knowing that she would be. He blew the candle out.

Darkness has its own geography, its flora and its fauna, a coal-black world of immense rustling ferns and almost intangible hills. Enormous beasts pad through that underbrush, and twigs snap under them like creaking furniture. There we float in the vast waves of a dry sea, in a world without barriers, under the thought of stars. In the darkness our bodies disappear, the flesh exists only to excite the finger-tips, and we are what we are. In darkness we flow in and out of each other as effortlessly as seaweed in a tidal pool, and then suddenly the current grows stronger, and we are all swept one way. We pour out of ourselves. Far off, over the spray, we may dimly hear the universal sea pounding down against the barrier reefs of the self, but we are no longer there. We swim together down a safe lagoon, beach on the most delectable of shores and, amiably exhausted, sleep together in the warm summer sand. There is no need to think of waking. The sun will wake us at the proper time.

Abruptly her fingers came away sticky, as though from a spider web at dawn. She marvelled. "Why are you crying?" she whispered.

"Because I love you."

She hugged him closer and cried too. Then she vanished

98

down into the endless passages of sleep, turning and twisting as they fell in each other's arms through the green layers of a kindly sea. For a while there was silence.

Then it seemed to her that far off she heard the fretful *io moro* of a lute. She woke up.

Antonio was lying on his side, his hair spread out against the pillow like the tassel of a black flower. He was very slim and boyish there, and very vulnerable.

She was playing a little game. She wanted to hide, so that he would come to find her. She dressed rapidly and then went out into the gardens, leaving him to sleep. The gardens were in the Italian taste, with herbal knots, shrubs carved into grotesque shapes which, from neglect, sprouted fronds like hairs in the ear, and tall avenues of narrow yew. She went down the gravel paths until she came to the pergola overlooking the sea, at the edge of the cliff.

She waited for him there, wearing an old dress that had lain too long in a chest, and had the dusty, faintly puzzling smell of daffodils. It was part of her marriage trousseau. She hoped it pleased him.

It was there he found her, and everything was as she would have wished it. For those three weeks they were children, playing with the idea of marriage the way children play with toys. For that period the world was scaled down within their reach, like an expensive doll's house. They made plans. They rearranged the furniture. They acted like grown-ups. They played house. Not even Cariola had the heart to remind them of reality. She stood silently by, and something in her that had come half-awake with Bosola, came wide awake with them.

They saw no one but each other until the gipsies came.

She would have remained hidden in the safe confines of the villa, but Antonio had a passion for the gipsies. As he rode over the Duchy on the Duchess's errands, he had made friends with them wherever he found them. This was the private side of his life that he had never shown to anyone. Among them he was a magic prince, and they were his spiritual kingdom. Therefore he wanted to show this kingdom to the Duchess now. He wanted her to inhabit with him every secret corner of himself.

99

He spent the afternoon setting torches about the path and garden. He would not tell the Duchess what he was doing. That night he and Cariola went out to set them aflare. Then he rolled back the massive iron gates, and the gipsies poured into the grounds of the palace. Antonio shut the gates behind them.

It was a motley company. Startled and a little frightened, the Duchess watched it from a window of the palace, for Antonio had told her nothing of this invasion. Gipsies were feared in those days, not merely as a thieving people, but as a supernatural one, as dispossessed and fallen in the world as fairies, but older than Egypt, and full of malevolent power. The torchlight caught a noisy, smelly crowd bustling about the gardens. Donkey bells clamoured in the shadows. Old women weighed down with grumbling and too much work set up the camp.

They did not seem so terrible. The swagger young men on the edges of the crowd did. They were the dandies, and like all dandies they had a ruthless air, and a male vigour that was disturbing. Slim and swarthy, black-eyed, in the torchlight angular and tall, with ear-rings, floppy boots, sleek thighs that flowed out of agile hips, and great open silk shirts, something in the angry way they held their bodies made them like predacious cats complacently licking themselves clean after the kill. When man is a restless animal with brains, there is nothing for him to do but kill, but there is something gorgeous in that violence. Antonio was at home with these young men. Giggling and laughing ferociously, he might have been one of them, and clearly they treated him with respect. He glanced up towards her window mockingly and joyously, and then came to fetch her.

A dais had been set up for her under a sagging awning. She was to be mistress of the revels, and he master. He led her up to it grandly, and suddenly she understood. They could never share her court. Therefore he would have her share his, as though to prove they were equals after all. She sat down and spread out her skirt. She looked at the faces of this strange court, and the savage young men formed a guard behind her. It had never occurred to her that the world had portable kingdoms, whose members were fiercely loyal to each other and beyond the grasp of the sort of pomp and power she and her

100

brothers had. She had always thought of Antonio as a prince in disguise, but it startled her to find that among these people he virtually was one, for among these people she had no authority. It meant that he was not really her inferior. He was inferior only for her sake. For her he had abandoned a whole world, and it made her own world seem the less. She did not altogether like that.

He excused himself, and when he came back he was dressed as the dandies were. It bewildered her, but it suited him perfectly. She saw that inside this was what he was. He made her feel ridiculous in her heavy court dress. He wore skin-tight striped pants, tight Spanish boots, a heavy belt, a white blouse, and a short black embroidered jacket. His eyes darted at the Duchess happily. She clenched her hands, and the castanets went even faster.

They wanted her to dance. But she could not dance with them. She did not know how, and her dress was too heavy, so she let them pull Antonio into their midst instead.

Firelight leapt and snarled in the garden. It turned the shrubs into furry walls. They might have been at the bottom of a crypt. On the floor of this trench dug through the middle of the night, the torches glittered like glass jewels. There were some negroes in that company. Where they had come from, nobody could say, but of all the dandies, they were the flashiest and the most venomous.

Antonio seemed alien to her, dancing bare-chested out there, as though she did not matter to him at all. She did not like it, even while something inside her liked it very much indeed.

The dance was a *folia*, one of the Spanish-American dances the common people danced. It seemed to absorb Antonio completely, and its sickening, ravenous rhythm made her deaf. She wanted to join him, but could not. She closed her eyes.

Cariola appeared and took her back to the palace. She went unprotestingly. She lay in her bed alone, wishing he would come, as her head went round and round, but he did not come. He was too happy out there. She felt herself sucked down into sleep.

When she opened her eyes, he was sitting on the side of the bed, and the night was still. She stared at him, unable to hide

101

the hurt at the back of her eyes. He laughed and leaned over her, supporting himself with his outstretched hands. He was very excited. Despite herself she was roused by him, and laughed. He tumbled into the bed beside her, boots and all. He was covered with sweat and grime, and his body felt alien and strangely taut. She was frightened and subdued to find him so changed, and to find also that in this mood he had control over her, which had not happened between them before. But though she resented that, she also adored it. She held on to him eagerly, and drew him down.

That next afternoon Cariola found them playing tag in the gardens, laughing their heads off, and with a negro playing with them. It was a bright, sparkling day, with moisture high in the air; and Mestre Antonio looked like a pirate, and her mistress in a peasant's blouse and skirt like something worse. Cariola sniffed.

The gipsies camped in the yard, slept late, and went off daily on errands of their own. When they returned through the gates, the fights, the dances, and the swaggering began again. Cariola scarcely recognized the Duchess any more.

As for the rest, God forgive them in that terrible age, for they were happy for three weeks. It was not their fault. It was a passion. They were prince and princess of the gipsies, and had forgotten who they were. They were to be reminded soon enough, so why should they not laugh while they could?

XIII

In Naples Sor Juana was having a triumph of her own. Hers, though sumptuous, was perhaps a little heartless and tinny. This was no accident. She preferred life that way, and so, for that matter, did the age.

Wishing some monument to himself, and not trusting his posterity, the Cardinal had decided to embellish the Cathedral. The work had now been going forward for several months, and the time of its dedication was at hand. What he had done was to break through a transept wall facing a likely piazza, and build there an immense baroque entrance. It was so contrived as to rivet the attention of anyone who chanced on the square, and to tell the truth, virtually obliterated the church behind it.

For this dedication Sor Juana had written a diplomatic pageant. It was her *Fiori di Cuore*, a work much admired in its day for its intoxicating rhymes. An engraved volume was already prepared, fulsomely dedicated to the Cardinal, and by his dispensation she had left the convent to attend the performance.

She, the Cardinal, and other notables sat on a dais facing the immense drape of black baize which shrouded the door. She reigned there like a little sibyl. Her fame was great and few had seen her, even fewer had seen her with the Cardinal, rumour was unkind, and in this case inaccurate, about their association, and so the square was crowded. That pleased her. She suspected the Cardinal of little reading, and saw no reason why he should not see her merits acted out before him. She sat prim and amiable, but her black eyes darted about the sunlit outside world she these days seldom saw, and she relished all of it.

She had sat in her convent like Achilles sulking in his tent, but now, if all went well, she would move freely once again, and do great things. It was one of the happiest moments of her life. She had forgotten *The Dream*, the madhouse, and her brother Bosola, and forgotten them with relief. The dark side of the soul did not interest her. This pomp she had made was of far greater worldly worth, and this was religion as she understood it.

To Sor Juana, and indeed to the Cardinal, theology was a branch of intrigue. God was a Grand Seigneur, with a court consisting of those in favour and those out of it, the three of them supported by loyal drudges and underpaid priests who, so long as they did their work and did not rebel, were of no real interest. When God's back was turned, one scrabbled for favour catch as catch can, and then turned up blandly the next morning as Master of the Bedchamber. One had to be amusing, witty, and unctuous. Above all, one had to flatter. The Grand Seigneur was much too busy to attend to affairs of state, but statesmen must never on any account be too busy to amuse the Grand Seigneur. His amusements, it was well known, were voluptuous. And the best way to rise, was to gain favour with

103

his favourites. Sincerity, in this case, consisted of a talent for amiable rhetoric, in return for which one was allowed to live at court, and accumulated estates for one's posterity.

The attitude of that priest at Arosa would have been incomprehensible to either of them. For one does not serve God. There are underlings to do that. One's sole duty is to keep one's self amusing and Him amused. And if one is beautiful or clever, and so catches His eye, so much the better. Thus Saint Teresa. Thus Bossuet. Thus the Cardinal. And thus Sor Juana. One could never become Grand Seigneur oneself. That was a matter of Blood Royal. But with patience and skill, one could, if one were Cardinal, become Pope; or if one were Sor Juana, marry into the family, and so become a Saint, a Blessed, or, like Teresa, a woman of affairs.

So, just as Antonio contrived triumphs and court dances, Sor Juana had devised her *Fiori*. It represented a battle between Sacred and Profane Love. Sacred Love was in court dress. Profane Love in Roman armour, with cuirasses, buskins, good knees, and waving plumes. The choreography was military and square. Each side declaimed the appropriate verses, which were certainly long, but the music was splendid, and the costumes marvellous.

The merits of Profane Love were undeniable. However, it was agreed by the contestants that the flowers of earthly passion fade. Sacred Love, on the other hand, was somewhat wan, though invested with a fine rolling eye. These flowers did not fade, but neither did they grow on earthly bushes.

Sor Juana had been tempted to continue the discussion, for the verse had flowed freely from her pen. She was, however, a mistress of stage mechanics, and she had sensed that the day would be cold.

So, in a united chorus of some twenty-five lines, accompanied by the roll of drums and some music for the trumpet, Love both Sacred and Profane announced that though the battle between them was endless, still they united in praise of the most high merits of his Eminence, Roberto, Cardinal-Bishop Sanducci. At this point the baize curtain was released, it dropped clingingly from the arch, and by a simple dramatic device the attention of the crowd was riveted on the gleaming white marble profusion of the Cardinal's gift to the Cathedral. Twisted columns, putti, graces, warriors, saints, and archangels swirled upward in a tangle of clouds, garlands, and flowers, almost obliterating the door, to where, twenty feet above the ground, two muscular stone seraphs held the enormous escutcheon of the Sanducci arms, crowned with a cardinal's hat, and surmounted by a dove.

The performance concluded with one of those conceited sonnets she wrote so well, upon the Cardinal's hatchments and bearings.

She could tell instantly that the Cardinal was well pleased. He turned to her and beamed, rising with an ecclesiastical prance; she was allowed to kiss his ring; and as she rose he had time to tell her that his sister, the Duchess of Amalfi, had been graciously pleased to take an interest in the proposed new convent, and in Sor Juana, whose name had in some way become associated with the project.

Sor Juana was delighted. The Duchess was clearly not an intellectual woman; was, in fact, a flibberty-gibbet, but perhaps that made her all the easier to flatter. Perhaps she might send her a sonnet and a memorial.

The Cardinal said not yet, but he, too, seemed well pleased. "It would not do to hurry the matter on," he said. "We must have patience. Perhaps in eight or nine months. . . ." His voice dwindled away, and lowering it, he asked about the conduct of the boy, who must for the moment be kept in strict secrecy.

That being the case, Sor Juana saw no point in telling him that Bosola knew who he was.

Pink-faced, unwrinkled, and beaming, with a look of blood-curdling benevolence, the Cardinal moved forward to receive the compliments of the company, leaving both his architect and Sor Juana well to the rear.

Sor Juana did not mind. It takes time to bring great schemes to birth, and nine months, after all, was only the normal length of any pregnancy. She returned to the convent in the happy thought that it need not contain her long.

SIX

Suddenly events caught up with them, for it is impossible for an honest man to keep his footing in a world of intrigue. He is like a man blindfolded. No matter how clever he is, eventually he is bound to lose his way.

It is impossible to understand how they managed to conceal their relationship for so long. Yet, though they could not see each other as much as they would wish, and though the Duchess was forced to confide in Cariola, no one knew what was going on, or with whom. Gossip, after all, soon wearies. It has to be fed constantly. Give it nothing to feed on, and it thinks the ground barren and passes on to other fields. That was their margin of safety. They forgot that it is not gossip that betrays us, but the truth of it.

In public she treated Antonio with a fine affectionate indifference. They both enjoyed that, for it meant their marriage was still a game. As a game, they were equal to it. What would happen to them when it ceased to be a game was something neither of them had thought about.

The court noticed only that she smiled again, and was pleased to see her smile, though even Bosola could not discover the reason for that joy. Then again, having Cariola, perhaps even he relaxed. Thus matters went on for many months. Spring came, and summer was warm to the hand.

One morning the Duchess woke to find that she was ill. She could think of no reason for it, and said nothing about it, but it frightened her.

She went at once to her glass, without summoning Cariola, and holding it in her hands, stood at the window, examining herself intently. She could see no change. She had slept alone that night. To be without Antonio sometimes made her restless. Often in the morning she felt clogged and dull after such a

106

night. There was in that nothing unusual, and the effect soon passed. Yet they had been safe for so long that she had almost forgotten the one consuming terror of passionate women of that age. She did not look at her body, because she was afraid to look.

But the days passed, and nothing seemed to be wrong. She relaxed. Only towards the end of the month was she nervous. She would not see Antonio. She could scarcely bear even to see Cariola. A week later she was ill again, and then she knew. She told no one.

She did not dare. She waited a day or two. Then, unable to sleep, waking before dawn, and before Cariola was up, she got out of bed, stripped off all her clothes, and stood naked and shivering on the stone floor of the room, looking at what she could see of her flesh in the glass. Her breasts seemed as small and firm as ever. Her belly was taut. She turned this way and that, as the cold air from the unglazed window rippled the fine hairs on her body. There was a faint almost imperceptible growth, for when she had grown the Piccolomini heir, nothing had shown for seven months. She had a deep, wide pelvis.

She felt like running away to hide, but only the anonymous can hide. The well-known and the famous have nowhere to go. She wanted to rush down the private stair, go secretly to Antonio's quarters, take him by the shoulders, and shake him. There must be something he could do to help.

Apart from panic, she felt astonishment that fate could change what had been so delightful suddenly into something so horrible, without warning, and overnight. She knew what it felt like to be trapped. She stood in the cold light, shivering, the mirror still in her hand.

There was a creaking sound behind her. She whirled, dropping the mirror, which shattered in all directions on the floor. Her hands flew over her breasts.

It was Antonio. "I had to come," he said. "I had to know what was wrong." He looked at her and his eyes widened. Whatever he had been expecting to find, it was not this.

He wrapped her in a cloak and led her gently back to her bed. She let him do so. She wanted to be comforted, and lost control of herself. She began to shake. To her overwhelming

107

relief and surprise he held her tightly in his arms. She was not a Duchess then. She gave way and became a frightened woman.

The door opened and Cariola came in, ready to wake her mistress. Her lips tightened with disapproval. Over the Duchess's head Antonio motioned her away. Cariola did not like that, but she went.

"Are you sure you can trust her?"

The Duchess did not know whom she could trust. "I think so." She drew the robe more closely around her, feeling immensely frail. Soon the palace would begin to stir. There was danger in that. Yet she could not bear to send him away.

"What am I to do?" she whispered. "If my brothers find out, they will kill you." They might also kill her, but she could not bring herself to say that.

He paused. "We must keep them from finding out. How long has it been?"

"Almost three months."

He paced up and down the room. When he spoke he was almost brusque. "Take Cariola and go to Ravello. I'll send you a woman there." As though realizing how cruel his voice sounded, he smiled at her timidly.

Something inside her shrank. "No," she said.

He shook his head. He looked abruptly old. "What else is there to do?"

She was terrified at his annoyance. She sat on the edge of the immensely high bed, her bare feet not quite reaching the floor. The room was still very cold. She swallowed bitterly: he was right. She looked up at him half shyly.

"Will you come?"

"I can't do that. It wouldn't be safe, for either you or me."

"Safe!" She could not keep the bitterness out of her voice.

The distance between them seemed ungulfable. They might just as well have been strangers. No doubt he thought she had tricked him. She did not like the way he stood watching her. She knew this scene was the test of something. The process was almost visible in his face. She found herself watching it almost impersonally, the way an alchemist would watch his alembics, sure that this ultimate test for gold would also fail, and yet rooted there by a last cynical shred of hope.

It made their love seem foolish and delusive. She forced herself to retain some dignity.

Then, she did not know how, he had his arms around her, and was smoothing her hair, with his head buried on her shoulder. "It has to be this way," he said. She scarcely heard him. She was too overwhelmed to find that he was still there, and had not fled, even though she was sure he had wanted to. That he had wanted to somehow made his presence more real and more secure. Something had changed in both of them. She wondered what it was.

"Go tonight," he said hastily, and pressed her hand reassuringly. "Do not tell Cariola unless you have to. I must find the woman. The gipsies trust her. Try not to be too frightened. I'll come if I can."

She let him out the private stair, and when he had gone, all the gratitude and warmth drained out of her. For no man could help her. She was alone with it. There was no escape.

They were not children any more. Much more than the ordeal she had to face, that was the empty terror that made her want to cry out. They had aged so soon.

She dimly understood. Youth is a garden, where for a while we are allowed to play. But when a sudden storm forces us indoors and we stand on the threshold of maturity, we see for the first time those shadowy corridors that only lead one way. Even if we have someone with us, they only lead one way. The corridors are lined with identical doors on identical death. It does not matter which one we open, for each one opens on an ultimate empty room. We move among the furniture warily. We dare not face those rooms alone. But the doors are tall and narrow. We can go through them only singly, even if we do not lose our companion on the way. And we are careful not to lose that companion, for once out of sight, and he or she may be gone for good. Sor Juana no doubt would have put the matter more subtly, and felt it much less. But the Duchess was not intellectual. She was caught alone in the full blast of the truth.

Bosola was bored, and the reason why he was bored, he ironically realized, was because he was content. If he could be content with so little, then surely that must prove that he was not equal to his own ambitions, and that was a truth he would not face. He despised himself for being happy where he was, for Amalfi was insignificant. He could not understand why the Cardinal should want to bother himself with it.

His duties were not enough to keep him occupied. That is the way of small courts surrounded by too much pomp; and a court ruled by a woman is no court at all. For women cannot rule without some tincture of the masculine, and the Duchess had none of that. He thought her ornamental, and therefore useless, and so he raged against her, and never thought that it might be because he was attracted to her. He had lived in a hard world. He could not understand the tyranny of something soft, and had no patience with it. Women wear men away gently, as water does a stone, so that they do not notice their enfeeblement until it is too late.

Had he been born a hundred years before he would have been one of the *condottieri*, those great clanking nobodies who sacked whole countrysides, murdered princes, and were high and mighty men until an arrow pierced their corselets. What he longed for was a civilization of mad dogs. But that age was long gone. Now the world had separated out into a wilderness of masters, servants, and spies. That maddened him. He could not bear to be a menial. Yet even Antonio was a menial. Everyone was a menial but the great ones, and a cage of chirruping mouldy birds called sculptors, artists, painters, scientists. Their chirruping meant nothing, but it got them attention, and they liked their cage. Or there was his sister, that downy one, who rose imperceptibly, by a kind of sacerdotal seepage, from the bottom of an ecclesiastical well, smug in the assurance that one day her fame would overflow.

But he was none of those things.

He was only an attendant on Antonio. What hurt him was that Antonio had made a friend of him. If that had been done with some purpose, Bosola would have been able to forgive it.

But now honour and gratitude confused his mind, and he did not know how he was going to betray him, should the need arise. To betray most men gave him a thrill of superiority. That was why he was a spy. But he shrank from the knowledge that with Antonio he would betray himself.

He would never forgive Antonio for having made a friend of him. It is dreadful to know oneself wicked, and then to find oneself liked. It totters everything that one believed about the world, and knew to be true.

With Cariola he felt much the same.

In the beginning Cariola came to him disdainfully, and that had filled him with a savage joy. It had made it possible for him to be brutal with her, with an animal ferocity that freed him from his own miserable body. She had loved that. She moaned and twisted and shrieked like a mandrake, and was a very different person from the starched, proud, haughty lady-in-waiting she outwardly seemed to be. That gave him pleasure. It showed how venal and rotten was even the most staid world. When he enjoyed himself with her, he delighted in the idea that that porcelain figure, the Duchess, if one but knew the truth, was as corruptible as they. If the good and beautiful were only an appearance and a sham, then the good and the beautiful were bearable after all, and even Antonio, who seemed so prim, no doubt had pleasures just as wild. In the midst of a sweaty night, hurting Cariola until her skin turned blue, he could avenge himself on the whole world, and rise superior to it. After all, human dignity is not much. Strip it of money, and crack it on the rack or wheel, and it soon shows it is as filthy as the rest of us.

But then even Cariola began to change. Their appointments became more regular, and she even condescended to be seen with him by day. She began to mother him. He resented that. Yet it was pleasant to be provided with better wine, or have someone stitch up his shirts. She became timid about it, and then placid. She would sit in his room and sew.

They might just as well have been married. She made little jokes at him, but they had lost their edge. And the more familiar she became, the harder it was to turn savage by night. Familiarity made brutality seem silly, and he became self-

111

conscious. He would suddenly collapse and lie in the warm bed next to her, and then she would treat him like a baby.

She came now usually on Tuesdays and Thursdays. He found himself thinking of her in a different way. It was as though energy and resentment had flowed out of him into a puddle, and left him someone else, the way we feel someone other than ourselves after a fever has left us, and we are still weak. Their life became matter of course, and silted up with small private events. It is impossible to become violent when life is matter of course. There is no channel down which our energies can rush. Instead the flood sinks harmlessly away.

On Tuesday she did not come. As soon as he missed her he knew how trapped he was. He was sinking into the mediocrity of other men. It was a warning. Yet here it was Thursday, and he sat alone in his room, well past the hour at which she generally came, and could not sleep. He had become as foppish as Antonio, and as useless and as foolish. After all, he was forty. It was no age at which to dawdle with women. No doubt the whole court knew their affair, and laughed behind his back.

Cariola never knocked. It was one of the things that annoyed him, as though she took it for granted that he would be alone and waiting for her. Now she slipped into the room, bearing in her arms a white bundle.

Cariola had also changed. She seemed happier and more assured. Her face now had a rested look, and her skin was healthier than it had been for years. Her voice had a kindlier authority, a tone that otherwise only the Duchess heard.

He was cross with her for being late, even while he felt relief at seeing her. He made no move towards her.

"I only came to say I cannot stay," she said. "I'm sorry. The Duchess is going to Ravello."

He was acutely disappointed, and refused to show it. "At this hour?"

"She has her whims." Cariola came no closer. They were both too old not to feel physically ill at ease with each other. But if he had bothered to look, he would have seen that she, too, was disappointed. She wanted so much to be motherly.

She held out her arms. "I brought your new doublet," she

112

said. "I've been working on it all week." She smiled at him uncertainly, put it on the table, and turned to go. He could still be difficult at times, but she liked him none the less for that. It was like having a child, and that is what a woman generally likes a man to be.

Against his will he said: "Can't you stay for a minute?" She smiled at him uncertainly, wishing he could be outwardly more affectionate, and then slipped out of the room.

Half an hour after she had gone, he got up and put on the doublet. It was white with gold trim, and with it was a pair of white fleshings, to be worn with half-boots, a fancy riding costume for the countryside. He did not quite know why he did so, unless it was because she had made them for him, and to put them on made him feel less lonely. He heard the horses jingle away, and then went for a walk alone. So much had six months done for him that it never even occurred to him to be curious as to why the Duchess should suddenly depart for Ravello in the middle of the night.

As he wandered about the deserted palace, his leather heels echoed against the cold, lonely stone. He saw from a light across the court that Antonio was still up, but felt too wretched to disturb him.

III

The night ride to Ravello took three hours. Cariola wished her mistress was not so capricious. She did not like this journey. It had something to do with the scene she had interrupted that morning, of that she was sure, and though she refused to give the thought a name, she sensed obscurely what was wrong. But it was not her place to say anything, and there were many things it would be better for her not to know. She reassured herself with the thought that the Duchess was often like this.

Cariola did not like Ravello, and liked it far less after having been privy to what happened there. She knew how ruthless those could be who wished to get at great persons through their attendants. She neither wanted to betray her mistress nor to be tortured into doing so. Nor did she like the gipsies. It was her opinion that Ravello was a diseased and haunted place, from

113

which no good could ever come. Worse, this was bandit country. It was both unsafe and unseemly for two women to wander about in it alone.

The Duchess did not like this journey either, but this she had not the courage to confide in anyone.

It seemed to her she was fleeing Amalfi. Something was happening to her she was impotent to stop. It was like standing in the surf of events, and being sucked out to sea, even though one did not move. The night was dark. The stars were like moth-holes in the fabric of a dusty black wool tent. The trail was narrow, and the horses oddly frisky. As they rose above the countryside they could not see a light anywhere, except for the fishing boats offshore. Whatever happened, the fishermen would always be out there with their flares and nets, totally oblivious of their betters. It was a lonely thought.

At last they came out on the plateau. The higher hills loomed in the distance. In the darkness Ravello glowered vacantly upon its flanks. It was totally friendless. They rode on to the palace, where Cariola unlocked the gate. It creaked open unwillingly, and the darkness of the garden swallowed them up. In this light it was not a real garden any more. It looked as though it were built of steel and semi-precious stones, like that garden Pluto made for the solace of Persephone, where everything glittered with life, yet had none. The Duchess went into the palace alone, filled with an unbearable sadness. Not even an insect chirped, and yet once she and Antonio had been happy here. It was strange to realize that was less than six months ago. It was not only strange, it was unbearable.

She would not even let Cariola show her to her room. "There will be a woman here in the morning," she said wearily. "Show her in. Good night."

She trailed forlornly off down the dusty corridor, while Cariola looked after her open-mouthed. She did not even raise her dress, as she walked, to keep it clean, and the wax from the taper she held ran over her hand unnoticed. In a few hours Cariola would know everything. How would they face each other then?

She was awakened by a great jangling clamour, and lay huddled in the bed. It was only just after dawn. She should get up, but she had not the strength to rise. She had perhaps fifteen minutes left to herself, and the sound of the bell twisted in her ear. She felt too apathetic to care. It was as though her body did not belong to her any more.

She was a devout Catholic, without ever having given the matter any thought, but what was about to be done to her was wicked in a way that had nothing to do with God.

Cariola knocked on the door and then entered. Her face was a mask. "The woman is here," she said.

The Duchess did not stir in the bed. "Show her in and then go," she said.

Cariola seemed to hesitate. "I think she wants hot water brought."

"Then bring it."

Cariola went out. The Duchess did not turn her head. She heard someone come in and move towards the bed. She sat up. The old woman was indescribably filthy, and carried something done up in a neckcloth. She looked down at the Duchess, her black eyes snapping in her wrinkled face, her horny, lizard-like hands folded across her waist, and burst into a flood of sibilant gibberish. No doubt it was meant to be comforting, but she spoke only Romany. The Duchess gazed at her blankly.

The old woman shrugged, patted her with a hot, crackly hand, and moved over to the window, where there was a low table. The Duchess sat up in bed to watch her, but the old woman's back was turned. She was unwrapping her bundle and muttering again. Whether it was a complaint or an incantation would be hard to say, but certainly there seemed to be devils in the room.

The Duchess did not move. The old woman's eyebrows went up, as though she found the gentry very foolish. She cast down some small instruments on the bed. One was a long hooked wire of the sort one plunges down drains, and the others were even more curious. They were made of iron, but though she had washed them, she had not been able to wash the rust off. They clanked against each other dully as they fell upon the bed.

The Duchess clutched the covers to her neck. Her head began to shake from side to side. The old woman grinned cheerfully

115

and patted her shoulder. Then, with a sudden deft movement she ripped down the coverlets.

The Duchess huddled against the headboard and screamed for Cariola. The old woman frowned. Cariola burst into the room.

"She shall not put those things in me," sobbed the Duchess. "She shall not."

Cariola took in the situation at a glance. She stepped rapidly to the head of the bed, and put her arms around the Duchess.

The old woman stood passively at the foot of the bed, her taut little eyes looking from one to the other of them.

"My poor lamb," said Cariola. "My poor lamb." The Duchess began to shudder less. She watched the old woman at the foot of the bed out of the corners of her eye.

"There must be another way," she said. "There must."

"Where did you get this woman?"

"Antonio."

At mention of Antonio the old woman beamed, and nodded her head significantly. Her attitude seemed to say that some people were overly nice, but it was not her place to ask questions.

Cariola gathered up the instruments, handed them to her, and made some sort of dumb show with her fingers. The old woman went off into a torrent of explanations. Neither of them could understand her. She looked disappointed, brightened, and began to act something out. She pounded something in an invisible mortar, put it on a stove, poured it into what seemed to be a syringe, and pumped away with her fingers. The sun would set three times, or the Duchess would take it three times, it was difficult to tell which.

"Tell her no," said the Duchess. She was more sober now, but she still clung to Cariola.

"What else can you do, my poor lady?" Now that she had grasped the situation, Cariola was practical.

It was true, there was nothing else for her to do. "I want Antonio."

Cariola was stern. "He could not come. He has done the best he could. Perhaps the old woman knows her business after all."

116

The old woman was undoing her bundle again, and brought it to the bedside. She held up various dried leaves and bits of twig, talking and gesturing. The Duchess recognized male fern, rue, and ergot of rye. Then Cariola took her off to the kitchens downstairs.

The Duchess had never felt unclean before. She lay there alone, plucking at the coverlet. One of the leaves had fallen there. It was blue-grey, and twisted into the shape of a screw. She had ridden over the bracken and gorse of this country often, and found them sinister, but had not thought much about them. Now she realized that the landscape was full of poisons. They must lurk in every leaf and twig, and there were those who knew how to use them. The whole fair world was poisoned, and plants had a venom as powerful as snakes. They would dissolve the life in her the way quicklime dissolved the bodies of the poor, cast into a common pit.

She clenched her teeth, and only hoped Cariola and the old woman would come back, and have the matter done. She listened for their footsteps down the corridor. She was determined not to cry out. But when the rough pewter syringe was inserted in her flesh it hurt her cruelly, and the liquid flooded her like burning pitch. It made her feel silly and weak. Not daring to cry out, she giggled and could not stop, until Cariola slapped her.

Towards evening she fell into a fever. She felt suffocated, as though the room were full of burning wool.

Ferdinand stood glowering in all the dark corners of the room. When she burned with thirst, he had his fingers round her throat, and what she saw in his distended eyes was not passion, but animal lust.

The treatment lasted three days. The old woman came and went, and the syringe became a great scaly snake. The lake of pitch seemed to eat her whole body away. She could eat only fruit, without knowing what kind of fruit it was, and drink only water, which did not slake her thirst, and tasted dusty. She thought she heard her brother the Cardinal's robes swishing in the corridor. He often smiled. The swish turned into an immense wave, crashing down on her, on whose crest lay the dead white body of Antonio, like Leander, wearing one white

117

sock and nothing else. He struggled to live, but Ferdinand, writhing with brown kelp, pulled him down and squeezed his eyeballs out. They exploded like the balls of seaweed on a childhood beach.

She slept and woke and slept again. She felt she was hovering outside her body, and could not raise it up enough to enter it. Indeed she did not want to. It disgusted her. Then she was trapped inside it again. The wave crashed down, and Antonio's head lolled limply in the foam of it.

She opened her eyes and he stood before her.

Cariola looked down at her, shook her head, and left the room. The Duchess shrank away.

"It didn't work," she said.

He made an indefinite gesture. "There are other ways."

She shook her head. "No, I'm glad. I want to have it."

"So do I. But the matter cannot be hidden long."

"I do not want it hidden."

"We have no choice." He was grave, and his voice soothed her. But she was irritated and rebellious, too. He could not know what she had been through. He could not force her to go through the same again, or worse.

"I am ruler here," she said. "Why did I marry that senile old man, if he had no power?"

He sat down on the edge of the bed. "We have no army. We cannot defend ourselves. Your brother the Cardinal covets your estate, and your brother Ferdinand is mad."

"Why should we not have a son?"

"You know why." He hesitated. "You have an heir. He could never inherit. So this child would be snuffed out and murdered."

"I have not forgotten the boy," she said. "They took him from me."

"Then what would they not do to this child? Even if they did not use you in the same manner."

"None the less. I am glad to have it, and I mean to have it. Why should we not live as other people do? We can conceal it somehow. I can transfer you funds and estates, and they can be settled on him. You can acknowledge a bastard. I cannot."

118

"As soon as you show me favour, the world will know. Only the poor can live anonymously and do as they wish."

"It can be done secretly," she screamed. She was pushed to the limits of endurance.

He looked down at her poor frail body under the coverlet, and had not the courage to tell her that nothing could be done secretly. And besides, it was true, it was his child and hers. Why should it not live? The Cardinal might fall from power. Many things might happen. And Cariola had said that she had almost died. "Very well," he said. "We will manage the matter somehow. The old woman is discreet. She will help us at the proper time."

But he was apprehensive, more for her even than for himself, and as he entered the courtyard of the palace at Amalfi late that night, tired and dusty and depressed, it seemed to him that someone loitered in the shadows. He was deeply disturbed, and cried out to the man to step forward, but it was only Bosola. Try as he would, he could not quite conceal his relief, and took the man to have a drink with him.

IV

On their side they had nothing but prudence, the loyalty of Cariola, which seemed secure, and the heavy dresses of the period. Great ladies are expected to have their whims, and if there were no fashion, women would have nothing to do. The court dressmakers therefore saw nothing strange in greater yards of stuff to a skirt and a plumper stomacher. These stomachers Cariola privately thinned down herself. The ladies of the court at first grumbled, but were delighted to have the excuse to purchase something new, and since difference is a kind of distinction, it was no great trouble to put the whole palace into camouflage. Indeed it was agreed that if one were young enough, the new matronly look was flattering.

Cariola had taken a great fright, all the same, and so Bosola was more than ever a comfort to her. There comes an age when we are even more grateful for the imitation of love, than for the real thing, for at forty passion would merely be a nuisance. Women who have reached that age must take care of their

119

appearance, and have no time for a lover every day. Their only danger is not to have one at all.

Yet Bosola bothered her. She had nothing to complain of, but she was afraid of losing him. She was that sort of woman who longs to be a mother. It may be an admirable quality in a wife, but is no way to win a fiancé. She had to find some other way to fit into life, so through the years she made a parody of herself, the way nurses do. She was good-humoured, so she did not mind doing that, but buried inside her somewhere was the little girl who had always wanted to be able to love somebody, and the little girl starved. She took it out in mothering her mistress and tyrannizing the household maids.

Then she had seen Bosola again. Few of us get a second chance at what we want, and she had always liked him, even when he deserted her years ago. Now, her heart had gone out to him against her will, for remembering what he had been, she could see the ruins of what he was. Where once he had been gentle, now he was importunate. Where once he had been sarcastic, now he was sour. Instinctively she knew what was wrong with him: he despised himself.

But though she had grown used to him again, she still did not trust him. And now that she had something beyond her own pride to conceal, she could not help it, her heart sank even when she realized how glad she was to see him.

She did the worst thing she could have done. She avoided him. It hurt her to do so, but she was afraid she might give the Duchess away. She did not realize that to leave a man like that neglected is as dangerous as to go away and leave an unwatched fire.

Meanwhile she sewed him shirts, for he scarcely had a shirt to his back, and she liked to sew, for alone in her own room she could be as domestic about him as she pleased. As the months went by, and nothing seemed to happen, she began to relax. She thought she could trust herself to see him again.

But if suspicion is smoothed away on one side, then it will fasten on another. Bosola had received no preferment, and therefore had sharp eyes for another man's rise. Besides, the Cardinal was beginning to press him, and if he could rise in one place, then certainly he did not dare to fall in another. The

Cardinal's prodding had made him alert. He began to notice things he had been a fool not to notice before.

First of all there was the difference in Antonio. He seemed worried and sombre. His light had vanished. He dressed like a married man, and went through his duties mechanically. And though it was true he saw more of the Duchess, there was now nothing in the attitude of either of them to suggest that they were lovers. The Duchess, too, was often unwell, and sometimes apprehensive. Bosola could only assume that there were other agents at court, undermining her in other ways.

The thought that he himself might be spied on frightened him. His reports to the Cardinal became more detailed, and he must have Cariola come to him more privately.

It was at this time that he was transferred from the Purse to the Household proper. Though it meant he saw less of Antonio, he was not displeased, for he had no head for figures. It was only with the arrival of the two bankers from Salerno that he began to wonder why the Duchess had ordered the change, and why no clerk had been appointed in his place.

There was nothing remarkable about these two men, but their appearance. They were Germans, and had all the tactless ostentation of that commercial race. Their clothes were trimmed with fur, and they moved with the hushed reverent self-respect of the recently rich. No doubt money was that regal in the north, but here they would have done better to begin with a title. They spoke to no one, and were often closeted with the Duchess. As Gentleman of the Household, Bosola could not help but notice the disappearance of certain jewels. It made him thoughtful.

Nor was he without sources of information of his own. Bribe a man's servants, and you know more about him than he knows himself. Titles and deeds had to be registered with the town council. Since favour does not always show itself publicly, Bosola had made friends with the custodian, on the pretence of interesting himself in confiscated property. The Duchess occasionally distributed lands to court favourites. It was in this way, accidentally, that he learned that the Fief of Arosa had been transferred to Antonio, with the right to fill the living of the church, and a gift to restore the manor-house there. Bosola was startled. The matter had not been mentioned publicly. Nor was it easy to believe that Arosa, in a small poverty-stricken district, was worth fourteen hundred crowns.

Bosola slipped away privately from the court, and took a ride in the hills. It was dusk when he came down over Arosa and drew rein on a ledge. Below him the reconstruction of a small house was going forward. The thin, spindly scaffolding of stripped poles stood around a half-decayed structure. Bosola turned back towards Amalfi. No orders for such work had come through the Household. He decided to become friendlier with Antonio. He rightly guessed that both the deed of gift and the construction were a blind.

Even then matters might have run smoothly, had not the Duchess unconsciously made a grave mistake, a thing so little she did not even notice it.

Because pregnancy is supposed to alter the complexion, she seldom appeared to the court now except by artificial light. At dusk it was her habit to walk in the cloisters between the palace and the cathedral, in a black dress, attended by the nobility and such of her household as she still dared to keep around her. She had grown accustomed to Bosola, but she still instinctively disliked him. Yet through Cariola, he had been able to join her intimate circle, and this meant much to him, for she was a beautiful and powerful woman, and he liked to be seen associating with such.

He almost began to bask in her favour, and if she had shown him favour, who knows, she might have gained a partisan. But whatever he might think he was, to her he was only a servant. The idea of favour never entered her head.

The Duchess had a small white and grey lapdog of the pattering kind, who ran back and forth like a spider. Usually it nestled in the crook of her arm, but now, at the end of the cloister, it squirmed, jumped down, and began its inane race among the courtiers' feet. Bosola had just gained the Duchess's attention, and to tell the truth he was showing off. Accidentally he stepped on the wretched thing and it screamed.

"Out of the way, you clumsy lout," snapped the Duchess. Her nerves were frayed. But the whole court was there, and heard her. It was the one sort of shame Bosola could not abide.

By the time Cariola came to him that night, he had brooded about the insult for hours. And something about the way the Duchess had started to bend over, and then thought better of it, lingered in his mind.

He launched into a tirade, but Cariola only laughed at him.

"She meant nothing by it. She was only irritable."

"She disgraced me before everyone."

"She meant nothing by it," said Cariola. "She was not feeling well."

"She is often ill these days," said Bosola. The look on Cariola's face stopped him. But it did not stop his thoughts.

He said nothing, but he turned over every glimpse he had had of the Duchess for months, and he knew that she had dismissed all of her attendants and would be waited upon only by Cariola. The rumour was that she feared poisoning. It occurred to him now that she might fear something else far more.

Cariola and the laziness of the court had lulled him into a false security. But now he learned that he was being spied upon as efficiently as he spied upon others. It would be useless to find out who the informer was. The mischief was done. The Cardinal forgot nothing. He wrote to complain of Bosola's reports. "You know the Duchess's serving woman," he said. "Now it is said you know her better. Use her."

The concealed threat made him mortally afraid. He would have used her, had not the letter arrived on the day that Cariola delivered her bundle of embroidered shirts. They stood now in a pile on his table, a crisp, freshly laundered testimony of her devotion. People gave him things so seldom that he knew the value of a gift. He had not the heart to use her, unless he had to. But there were other ways, and the shadow of the Cardinal drove him on. Besides, the Duchess had insulted him. He got his idea from the apricot trees which were now in fruit.

v

Antonio and the duchess had laid their plans with care, or so they thought. In ten days she would depart for Ravello with Cariola. From there she would go on alone to Arosa, where the

123

gipsies had installed a midwife and servants loyal to Antonio in the rebuilt house. Cariola would remain at Ravello. Should anyone come inquiring for her mistress, which was unlikely, she would say she was riding in the hills. As soon as possible the Duchess would return to Ravello, to be nursed by Cariola for a few days, and then reappear at court. The child would be handed over to a wet-nurse, and since the gipsies chosen spoke only Romany, there was little likelihood that gossip would reach those avid for it. Later, if all went well, they might reclaim the child. The money settled on Antonio would be paid for its keep, and for this, if for no other reason, the gipsies would treat it well. It could be brought to Ravello, from time to time, for the Duchess to see, in the gipsy caravan. At the very worst it would live: and privately Antonio was pleased to think that it might become a gipsy bravo.

It had been a strain on both of them. Now it was almost over. With the child born, perhaps they could be young and lovers again. That, at any rate, was the way the Duchess thought of it. She was almost gay, and she saw no reason why she should not see Antonio.

There was not much land at Amalfi, so the palace garden was at some distance from the palace, and was less a garden than a reconverted orchard, with herbal knots and shell paths underneath the trees, which were in late fruit, and a small fountain splashing against the orchard wall.

The Duchess was impatient. She could not understand why Antonio seemed to grieve. He might have been a mourner.

She wanted to have the child quickly. She wanted to have Antonio with her again, instead of standing forlornly in front of her like a petitioner. She hated to walk gravely and carefully, rolling along like a heavily burdened litter. She wanted to dance, for when Antonio danced, he was himself again, and everything she loved most in him became visible. She could have screamed at him sometimes, had she not longed to touch his cheek. She was weary of all this nervous gravity.

At dusk they walked in this arbour habitually, with Cariola as duenna. It had become understood that, as chief officer of her household, Antonio should wait upon her there. It was the one sad pleasure of her day.

That was where Bosola knew where he would find them, and he had come prepared for his experiment, so overwhelmed by the cleverness of it that he did not bother to think that it was also cruel. He had brought a gift for the Duchess. It would not harm her much. Nor would anyone think the proceeding extraordinary. It would be assumed that he was merely trying to seek favour again, after her rudeness to him in the cloister, about the dog.

It was Cariola who noticed him, pattering across the arbour in the dusk, and spoke to the Duchess. He had taken the precaution of telling her what he was about to do, and since she could see no harm in it, and knew about the scene in the cloister, she had agreed to pave a way. She spoke to her mistress, and the Duchess and Antonio instinctively drew apart.

The trees in the orchard were by now somewhat wan, and what fruit remained hung on the almost leafless branches like withered lanterns. The herbal knots were dry with too much summer, and even the fountain splashed dustily. The Duchess and Antonio stood there to receive him. To tell the truth they stood a little guiltily, like conspirators demonstrating that they did not know each other.

Bosola had taken some care to look amiable. He made a speech about his clumsiness with the dog. The Duchess was touched. She had regretted her sharp words to him. She would have been glad to show him favour, by way of making amends.

Even Cariola looked on approvingly. He held forth a wicker basket covered with a napkin. The Duchess smiled, took it, and laid back the cloth. When she saw what was inside she gave a little sound of pleasure.

Against the napkin nestled a dozen and a half plump apricots. They had been hard to find at this season, but the Duchess doted on fruits, and on apricots most of all. The fuzz on them was delicate, they were of a rich, coppery orange, and were as covered with freckles as a country girl. They glowed.

She reached for one instinctively.

Antonio made a motion forward. "You should not," he began, and then stopped.

The Duchess paused, and Cariola gave her a warning glance. Any hint of her condition would be dangerous, Bosola was

125

watching, and besides she felt fretful. She bit into the fruit. It was delicious. The apricots were of that stage of ripeness when the juice runs over the fingers. It is then they are most disrupting to the bowels, but she could not resist.

"Walk with us for a while," she said to Bosola. The fruit freshened her mouth. It was what she had been longing for. "These are very good. The gesture was kind." Apricots vanish rapidly. She took another.

She had a nature that took a greedy pleasure in very little things, and liked them better than anything ostentatious. Bosola watched anxiously. He did not altogether like what he had done, but it was done now. He had not counted on Cariola being there, and though the fruit was harmless, and the effect he hoped it would produce only natural, still he knew she would blame him. He shrank from that, but it could not be helped.

By the time they reached the end of the orchard, there were two apricots left in the basket. It was there, by the wall, that the Duchess turned pale and sat down on the rim of the fountain.

Bosola looked at her with a mixture of interest and clinical pity in which there was no compassion. She had been rude to him. She looked up at them like a fox trapped in a burrow. Bosola saw something milky in her eyes as they held his for an instant before they flickered on. The instant was enough. He knew, and she knew he knew.

He waited reluctantly to see how she would get out of it. He had forgotten that he could not very well leave at once, and indeed her appearance alarmed him. He had not meant to bring on labour pangs.

The basket fell from her lap into the fountain. The apricots separated out and bobbled near the jet. The napkin sank.

Cariola put her arms round the Duchess, and she and Antonio helped her rise. The Duchess could not withstand pain. Her head lolled sightlessly like that of a snake. Bosola made no attempt to follow them, and was jealous of how rapidly they had shut him out. He had found out what he wanted to know. That was enough.

At the gate in the wall, Cariola and Antonio whispered for a moment, and Antonio turned back.

It had grown dark very quickly, with the rapid night of the south. Bosola could not see clearly, but there was something ominous about Antonio's figure. His white face was stern, and his eyes burned out of the darkness. He passed Bosola and retrieved the apricots.

"If the Duchess *has* been poisoned, you'll answer for it," he said.

It was clearly a story they had made up between them, but something in his tone made Bosola panic. Suppose it was true? He had not inspected the apricots himself.

Antonio held one out contemptuously. "Eat it," he said.

Bosola did not dare.

Antonio threw the fruit against a tree, where it smashed into an ugly blur.

"Was it?" he asked.

Bosola half choked. "If it was, I knew nothing of it. I swear I did not."

"But you would not eat it."

"I was afraid," said Bosola simply.

Antonio eyed him angrily. "Where did you get them?"

"From a dealer in the square."

"Which dealer?"

"Piero Amici."

"One of the Cardinal's agents," snapped Antonio. His fingers clicked nervously, like crickets. He shifted from toe to toe.

Bosola broke into a sweat. He had not known about Amici, so poison was possible. He had been lax, and the Cardinal did not trust anyone. Perhaps he had plotted to remove him in this clever way, and the Duchess too. Or Amici himself might have thought of it, out of jealous rivalry.

Some of this must have shown in his face. Antonio watched him disdainfully. "Get out," he said. "Right or wrong, I do not care, but get out. You do not know what damage you have done."

Bosola could not think of anything to say. It would do no good to cringe. He turned and limped rapidly out of the garden, his only thought an agony to hide, he scarcely knew from what.

127

That night the palace was full of a peculiar bustle. Though you did not see it, it was everywhere. Domestic women came and went from the Duchess's apartments. Cariola let none of them enter. She stopped them at the door.

Bosola went to speak to her, but she would not even look at him. She merely gave him a glance, and shut the door in his face, but the glance was enough.

All had turned against him. Nor could he afford to change his plans, for the only ones who can afford to lose the world are those who have it in their keeping. Lesser men must keep what soil beneath their feet they can.

He had not known that he had an enemy down in the town. Proud of his position at court, he had treated Amici haughtily. One did not dare to treat anyone haughtily. Whether it was poison or not, and Bosola did not think even now that it was, Amici had not only the means but the will to destroy him. It was terrible for a weak man to have an enemy. The thought was unendurable. Amici might have written to Rome already to denounce him.

He paced up and down the silent corridors. Torches burned low in their sockets. He heard footsteps and drew back.

It was Antonio, pacing the yard below, with a nervous, help-less, tethered tread. Bosola could not help but watch. Antonio reached the end of the yard, stood against the rusticated wall, and looked up towards the Duchess's apartments. The moon-light fell full on his face. From those eyes, beseeching the moon, Bosola drew back.

Then he moved swiftly across the paving and into the palace by a door Bosola had not seen him use before, one that should have led him up to the loggia, but which did not. Nor, though Bosola waited, did any light go on in Antonio's rooms.

From down the corridor came a muffled scream, followed by tingling silence. Bosola hurried to his own rooms.

He hesitated before beginning his dispatch to the Cardinal, but he had to forestall Amici, and he was sure he was right. The pen drove across the paper, and he followed it willy-nilly. He had been foolish to feel secure, for the Cardinal's influence extended everywhere, and the spies he set upon his spies were multiple. Bosola wrote everything, dwelling much on his own cleverness, and promised to send further news at once. He wrote of the new house at Arosa, and of the church there, together with his own conclusions. He was even ready to name the Duchess's lover, though he was not absolutely certain as yet of that. Just why he held back he was not sure, unless it was to have one secret in reserve, as ransom for himself in case of need.

He sealed the letter, took it himself through the nocturnal streets to the messenger he kept always waiting, and then returned like a shadow to throw himself on his miserable bed. He saw now that Cariola had liked him only out of policy. That bed could not be too narrow for him now.

When he woke it was day. He sensed at once that something had changed. The messenger would be half-way to Rome, and there was still much for him to ferret out, if he was to defeat Amici. He dressed and went to the household offices, not daring to ask any questions openly, though knowing privately he must.

He was working there when a shadow darkened his desk. He looked up and saw Antonio.

The two men eyed each other warily. By now Bosola was sure he had fallen into some kind of trap, whether Amici's, the Cardinal's, or that of another made no difference. All morning he had been waiting to be denounced.

Now something in Antonio's manner caught his attention, and relieved his fears. Antonio seemed not only embarrassed, but still severely worried, and his stance was the brusque one of an honest man about to tell a lie.

Antonio walked around the room, avoiding Bosola's gaze. "I come from the Duchess," he said at last, awkwardly.

Bosola's eyes narrowed, as he considered the possibilities.

"I wronged you. She was not poisoned," said Antonio simply. With some effort he lifted his eyes to Bosola's. "It was merely the apricots. Her Grace's stomach is delicate." It was the wrong word, and provoked the wrong idea. Antonio frowned, and then smiled with that awful insincerity of the basically sincere trying to make a good impression. He shifted

129

hastily away from the subject. "The Duchess offers her apologies. So do I." He held out his hand.

Bosola took it, but inwardly he snarled. They were afraid of him and had come to bribe him, knowing he had seen too much and would have to be placated. Their words meant nothing.

But Antonio had more to say. "If you can watch the man Amici," he said, "we would be grateful." Bosola breathed easier. That meant he himself was not suspected of being the Cardinal's man. If it were not merely a clever deception. Apparently to Antonio the Cardinal could have only one man at a time. Also it meant that Cariola had not spoken out, even now.

It was difficult to believe that any man could be so innocent as Antonio appeared to be, yet Bosola was half willing to believe that he was. Antonio only saw the world from the front, and so, apparently, did the Duchess. It made them both vulnerable to anyone who moved backstage.

see
p 37

Her apologies he did not believe for an instant. For Antonio he felt compunction. But his letter was in Rome by now, and the comedy must be played out.

All the same he was glad that he did not have to look too long at Antonio. There was a pathos there that made him flinch.

VII

We do wrong to despise the ambitious and dispassionate as cold and bloodless. They suffer as we do, though not in the same way, for they have small finite emotions too delicate for us to measure. Great storms and rages are no part of true pride. True pride is worn away only by the small, steady trickle of regret.

The Cardinal had a mistress called Julia, a woman of good family and a little dull. He ignored her, gave her jewels, and saw her when he would. She was only a piece of voluble furniture, and she would last perhaps a year. Then there would be another. He slept with her seldom.

Yet what he needed in her was the echo of a voice he had never heard and the touch of a flesh he had never tasted, for

130

the intelligent, cut off from humanity, live by parallels. Long ago they learned that their true feelings would be derided if they showed them, and so they find an outlet in pretence.

All men live this way, but some have the hope that the pretence may become real. For a few it does. But the intelligent know better. For them it never does, for they can be easy only with others of the intelligent, who are in the same plight as themselves. But this does not mean they do not feel. It merely means that they have learned that saddest of all lessons, that they can survive only at the ruthless suppression of all feeling. A little practice and emotion is no more than a passing twinge. But the twinge is painful all the same.

And really it does not matter, for if one must learn to turn a deaf ear to oneself, then the pretence does just as well.

The Cardinal had just dismissed Julia, and the year had almost gone. At such times he almost gave way to panic, the way a man does who is locked in a corridor between two rooms with the doors jammed. He knows such feelings are irrational, but for a moment he cannot help it. Despite himself, the Cardinal remembered all the other times that he had had that feeling, and foresaw all the future times that he would feel it. For a moment he almost called her back, but that, he knew, would be unwise, for he did not really like her any more, and she had never really liked him. Insincerity, too, has its limitations. We can put up with it from someone only for so long, and then we must have it from somebody else.

It was at this time that Bosola's courier arrived. The letter was brought straight to His Eminence. And it was for these and other reasons that His Eminence found himself singularly reluctant to read it.

Finally, tapping it nervously on his desk, he shrugged and opened it. When he had read it he sat in the half darkness for a long, long time, until at last he became conscious of the coldness and the silence of the room.

For like most of the ambitious he had no real awareness of the bloody ruthlessness of his own plans, and so now he felt a sense of shock. He had no real grudge against his sister. As a child she had been a pretty, harmless thing, stubborn and wilful it was true, but he was rather fond of that.

131

He had plotted against her automatically. He had not intended, perhaps, that the matter should go this far. But since it had gone this far, he had no course but to go on with it, for if it was true that she was actually in this condition, then she would meet her fate whether he profited by it or not. It was for this reason he felt abruptly sad, for he realized that ambition does not plot against the foolishness of others. It is merely compelled to take advantage of the webs they weave around themselves, for it knows that if it does not, then others will, and that life has no other law. But still he hung back from showing the letter to Ferdinand. He could not bring himself to do so until next day, and that night he took a double sleeping draught.

Nor would he go to Ferdinand. He wanted some control over the situation, if that were possible, so instead he summoned Ferdinand to him.

He had not seen Ferdinand for months, and was encouraged by his brother's solemn manner. He misjudged it. Ferdinand was merely tired, sullen, and irritable after a joyless debauch.

But the Cardinal was pleased to see Ferdinand so seeming calm, for though he did not want to call him off, he did want to restrain him. He debated what to say, and then instead threw Ferdinand the letter, sitting back with interest to watch his brother's face.

To his surprise Ferdinand was tautly calm. "Why did my agent write to you?" was all he asked.

"Let us say we share him."

Ferdinand scarcely listened. The letter shook in his hand. "Is it true?" he demanded.

"If it is not, we shall soon know; if it is, we shall know even sooner."

"Who is the man?" demanded Ferdinand. He was angry now. He put his hands on the desk, and glowered down at the Cardinal.

"You will do nothing hastily," the Cardinal said curtly.

"Who is the man?"

"Lower your voice. I do not know who the man is. Neither apparently does the agent. He has a woman down there, and took some prodding."

"What woman?"

The Cardinal shrugged. "It's no concern of ours," he said.

"You know who he is."

The Cardinal had been prepared for Ferdinand's temper. He had not been prepared for a cyclone.

Ferdinand tapped the paper furiously. "No doubt this priest knows something."

"I do not know what, or from whom."

"I'll get it out of him."

"You will do nothing," snapped the Cardinal sharply. "He is a priest under oath to protect the privacy of the confessional, in my diocese, and under my protection."

It was the worst thing he could have said. That his brother had more power than he had, and secret information besides, drove Ferdinand furious, and always had.

"Very well," he said, and strode heavily from the room. The Cardinal watched him go with some compunction. But Ferdinand's rages soon drivelled away, unless carefully supported, and he had not the courage to make any move upon his own. The Cardinal knew that he could handle him until the proper time.

For once the Cardinal was wrong.

VIII

The priest of Arosa was dying and knew it. He did not greatly mind, for his life was now fulfilled. Months previously the Arosa altar-piece had been conveyed to Arosa secretly, and now, re-assembled, it glowed above the altar of the little church. To the priest it was a marvel, and tangible proof of the favours which had been granted him. Often, when he was well enough, he had himself conveyed into the church on a litter, and would lie on the stone floor, gazing up at it.

Then, at dusk, two boys would convey him out of the church. Today, at dawn, he had tottered through his last Mass, supported by both of them. In the painting he particularly loved the small, prankish flowers in the foreground. He glanced at them now, as the boys conveyed him from the church, locked the doors, and slipped the key into maculated hands too

133

weak to hold it. Then they carried the litter down the dirt road.

It was at this point that horsemen swept down from the hillside with a loud yip. There was no one to stop them, for the house intended for the Duchess was abandoned, and the gipsies had gone away long ago. There were three of the *banditti*, one stockier and more assured than the rest. They were dressed in bright velvet, and had a swagger to them that smacked more of Rome or Naples than of the *banditti* of the hills.

As they converged upon the roads, the boy bearers dropped the litter and ran for cover. The priest fell on the ground. The jolt shattered him. He heard the whinneying of horses. He shut his eyes tightly and whimpered, fumbling with his rosary. He had cataract. His eyes were taut and milky.

When he opened his eyes he saw dimly that he was lying at the bottom of a forest of knobbly black poles. Those would be the horses. Someone was bending over him, and roaring in his ear.

"Old man, we have come to ask you questions." The half-kneeling figure motioned the other two away.

The old man shook his head from side to side, muttering, no, no, no. It seemed to him that he had fallen among devils at last, and he wanted to get back home. Also he had lost the church key in falling. He reached for it and could not find it.

He was being asked something about a Duchess. He knew no Duchess. He did not understand. The terrible man in black must certainly be a demon. He wore a mask, and his bloodshot eyes were surely part of hell. The ground hurt his back. Surely it had something to do with St. Anthony.

"Answer." The black figure kicked him in the ribs. But that part of his body did not hurt any more. It was completely numb.

"I do not know. I do not know anybody," muttered the priest. "Only the two boys." He twisted his head, looking for them, and the forest of black poles jittered up and down.

The dark figure screamed at him and then stood up. "String him over that tree," it said. The old man understood perfectly. He was being martyred. It was a sign of God's favour. But that could not be true, for he was only a parish priest. The two others put a heavy rope under his arms, tied his legs, and dragged him across the rough ground. He began to scream. "Mercy," he cried. "Mercy for an old man."

"Answer then."

He would gladly have answered if he could, but answer what? He did not even know what they had asked.

Manning the rope, the two bravos threw one end of it over the projecting beam of a ruined house, and turning and twisting, he found himself hauled upward. A weight bit into his armpits, as though the rope were mouthing him. They raised him and then let him drop two or three times. His head began to wilt. His ears began to sing. Inside him something snapped and broke.

"Answer," screamed the third figure. The priest understood. It was the Inquisition. He would not answer. Besides, his mouth was full of dust and he could not speak.

He dangled a foot from the ground. They began to haul him up again, laughing loudly, and then quite spontaneously he screamed. The sound seemed impersonal to him but very loud.

"Answer," shouted the third figure, and began to kick him and belabour him with a short crop. The priest's body was so dry and light that each blow made it circle and dance at the end of the rope.

In ten minutes he was dead.

The bravos shrugged and let go the rope. The body toppled to the ground. But the third figure was beside itself. It gibbered and screamed and went on kicking the corpse. At last the figure stopped, while the others stood by uneasily.

"Strip him," said Ferdinand, "and take away the habit. When the buzzards have been after him, no one will know who he was." In a minute it was done. The three of them rode off the way they had come, up the valley, without even thinking of looking inside the church.

At Amalfi sunset sounded like a great gong. Gorgeous bolts of orange and vermilion silk fell tumbling through the sky, to reveal the first stars, like diamonds of a poor colour and inferior quality, and then the whole shabby splendour ripped apart and fell to dust before a sky putrescent green. High over the hills, without sound, the sleepless buzzards circled down.

It was on this night that the Duchess commenced her labour.

135

That afternoon a gipsy midwife had been smuggled in, but there was not much she could do. She and Cariola stood about the bed, looking down. Antonio came when he could, and found the sight terrible.

It had been four years since the Duchess had last been delivered of a child, and that had been the Piccolomini heir. This child meant more to her. Therefore she would not let them force her labour, and for this reason she refused the midwife's forceps and calipers.

Cariola was grateful that the walls were thick, the windows closed, and the doors to the ante-room well bolted.

The Duchess had become an animal. She sobbed and writhed and tore the sheets. It did not seem to help to hold her down. Her face was that of a desiccated albino fox, her hair was rimed with sweat, and her lips smiled with the horrible inhuman rictus of pain. She had given over all rational consciousness hours ago, for when pain takes us over, it nimbly flings open the hatches of the lower mind, which have their own systems of belief, and all the devils of doubt and self-betrayal come swarming up over us. There is no hope down there, begging softly to be let out. In the nocturnal devils we see the whole company.

So though they tried to quiet her, she cursed Antonio and everyone, for having got her in this plight. Sometimes he was there to hear her. Sometimes he was not. But Cariola heard everything. It seemed to the Duchess that she was a peristaltic grotto imprisoning a thrashing whale. And then the sheer spasmodic pain made her giggle. For ten hours she was not a woman at all.

Then the child was born, and the midwife cut the tangled cord and put the placenta in a basin. It was male and perfectly formed, but slap it and pummel it how they would, it was born dead. She was a woman again, but she had been an animal for nothing.

Together, the four of them could only stare.

However, even a dead child presents immediate problems. A live child may be concealed in another family. But bury a dead child, and who knows who may dig it up? Antonio set off promptly by the private stair.

136

Bosola had lately found out the existence of that stair, and he was concealed, watching it. He saw Antonio leave, muffled in a cloak and carrying a bundle. He waited a moment and then followed him. It was a long journey. Bosola had not dared to follow closely behind; and only the whinnying of Antonio's horse told him where they were. They were at Ravello. He concealed his own horse and walked to the deserted church.

There, in shadow, on tiptoe, by the grille to the tomb-house, he could hear the fall of a marble slab. Then Antonio brushed past him, shaking, with tears streaming down his face, and Bosola knew his relation to the Duchess for what it was.

It was high moonlight now. He waited until he heard the horse gallop off, and then slipped into the tomb-house himself. He had never been there before, and it bewildered him. There were so many tombs, all ominously alike, all glittering with shadows. Only the marks in the dust led him to the correct slab. He had not the strength to lift it, but he could push it aside far enough to peer within. He saw the dead child, wrapped in a rich shawl. It made him angry. It was for this futility they had walled themselves up in the consequences of their folly, and perhaps shut him in with them as well. He shoved the lid back and went as he had come.

On the way back he passed the walls of that building which might be Sor Juana's convent, if she had her way.

IX

As the first of her new dignities, perhaps as preparation for great affairs, perhaps for reasons somewhat more sinister and certainly very like him, the Cardinal had arranged for Sor Juana to be present at a somewhat unusual ceremony in the cellars of the convent of San Severo. He did not attend himself. It was not the sort of thing which he cared to see, for it was a side of religion not designed to please the fastidious.

There was a nun at the convent who was a great nuisance to the authorities. Her transgressions had been slight, but there were a great many of them, and she was the sort of woman who naturally attracts enmity. The Abbess, in particular, detested her. Her name was Sister Serafina. She was prone to prickly heat, and had no true vocation. Boredom and prickly heat had turned into a possession by the Devil, and possession by the Devil had made her difficult. She was a gossip, too; broke her vows, and saw more than it was wise for her to see. The ceremony was that of the *in pace*. The Cardinal had made it his express wish to the Abbess that Sor Juana should attend. He was a man who believed in teaching by example, and if Sor Juana had any fault, it was that of disobedience to her superiors. For her own sake, he thought the occasion well chosen.

At midnight Sor Serafina was conducted down into the cellars. She seemed docile. She may have been drugged, out of mercy, but that was unlikely. Sor Juana, the Abbess, and the bricklayers were already awaiting her.

She was led forward and made to stand on a small flag projecting from an embrasure in the wall. It was perhaps five inches wide, six long, and two thick, and about a foot above the ground. She was told to place her arms at her sides, and two nuns held them there, which made it difficult for the bricklayers to work among the skirts. The cellar was damp and smelly. A tray of mixed mortar lay on the ground and the bricks were conveniently stacked. It was their business to wall her up.

Sometimes nuns requested this penance voluntarily. More often, however, it was a punishment. Sor Juana watched and, despite herself, her eyes lost their twinkle, for it happened that Sor Juana suffered from claustrophobia, though she never mentioned it. So did Sister Serafina, and she had mentioned it often, for she had been put into the convent after a youthful escapade, by her embarrassed and eminent family. The bricks rose rapidly.

The embrasure was two feet deep. As the bricklayers worked, they had to push back Sister Serafina's habit, which became entangled with the mortar. Sister Serafina started convulsively, but the nuns held her firm, and once the bricks were up to the level of her chest, she could not stir anyway. The nuns moved away, and the bricklayers could therefore work faster. They reached the level of her chin.

She would stay there as long as the whim of the Abbess kept her there, in her own stench, fed once a day on bread and

138

water, in darkness unrelieved except by her gaoler's torch. It was a medieval practice, which had almost fallen into disuse. Thus it was that the Inquisition treated possessed nuns.

Something happened to Sister Serafina's eyes, and her mouth contorted, but no sound would come out. Yet that unheard scream somehow echoed round the cellars. She tried to move, to raise her arms, but she could not. The bricklayers, having finished their work, wiped off their trowels.

The others silently left the cellar, fastidiously lifting their skirts. Sor Juana understood perfectly. It was a parable. But for the first time in her life, inwardly she cursed, and was glad she need not face the Abbess for a day or two. It was a parable, however, which one might understand in several ways. That would not matter to the Cardinal, she knew, so long as it was understood at all. It was true: he was cleverer than she: but only because he had more power.

SEVEN

I

Ferdinand conceived what he thought to be a clever plot, and hurried to put it into execution. The adroitness of it pleased him so much that it almost put him in a good humour, but he made no mention of it to his brother the Cardinal, for his brother would only have delayed and temporized and cheated him of his revenge. The Cardinal understood only profit, and this was a matter of honour.

At Amalfi the Duchess was still listless. She needed to be amused. Antonio had gone to much effort to have put on an opera. The theatre was to be reopened with it tonight. The Duchess seemed almost eager, and the subject was well chosen.

After all it was over, and nothing had happened to them. They could scarcely believe that. There had been no furtive gossiping. Imperceptibly they had begun to relax. They so desperately wanted to be young and together again.

Now the child was lost, the Duchess seemed to feel that they no longer had anything to conceal, so she treated Antonio with too much public favour. That worried him. Yet he himself felt much the same. If safety was a delusion, at least it was a congenial one, and why should a Duchess not have her harmless favourites?

The theatre at Amalfi was one of the few happy thoughts of the late Duke Piccolomini. It was a large hall in the palace, fitted up after the Roman style, but in miniature. A semicircle of classic benches faced a marble scena with three arches, divided by pillars, and topped by elegant marble Gods, Goddesses, and Piccolomini, all white and all posturing. Through the arches architectural streets receded uphill. The hall was covered with an imitation sky across which pink horses galloped through clouds of Amoretti, and the walls were covered

140

with pinnacled stucco Roman masonry and more statues. In the middle of the semicircle state chairs stood for the court on a raised dais, like those for the vestals and senators at the Roman theatres. The Duchess entered and sat Antonio beside her, though on a lower chair.

The opera was Monteverdi's *Orféo*. The work was said to be affecting. The Duchess and Antonio found it so. They were watching their own lives.

There was a prologue. A muse appeared and sang of her powers to charm. She was a trifle breathless. Then Orféo came on stage. He had thin, vulnerable calves and a smudged face, but his voice and song were moving.

At least the Duchess found it moving. Sometimes love dies of impatience. Now it woke up again. She reached out quietly and took Antonio's hand.

The orchestra alternately swooned and leapt. Preparations were in hand for the wedding of Orféo and Euridice. The chorus prayed that no misfortune might befall the lovers. Orféo sang a voluptuous aria. But Euridice was bitten by an envious serpent, died, and the lovers were forced to go their separate ways, which in this life is quite death enough. It was what had happened to them. Euridice felt lost for good, and condemned to live in the underworld, at Pluto's court. But Orféo followed her. That was never to be expected, but it happened. The Duchess touched Antonio's fingers. She was deeply moved. So was the court. For everyone has lost someone, and no one ever expects the lover one has left to seek one out again. That only occurs in art.

"La tua dilétta spósa é mortà," the messenger had sung to Orféo. And it was true. Away from him she had died. She had withered away. But now Euridice would be allowed to return to earth with Orféo, on the condition that he should never look back. Not sure she was following, he did look back, and lost her for ever.

It was an affecting moment. The audience wept. And looking down, the Duchess saw that Antonio had crossed his slim and shapely legs. She turned quickly to the stage.

With Euridice lost, Orféo wandered heartbroken through the Thracian wilderness. He begged trees, rocks, and nature to

141

lament with him. For this Monteverdi had provided one of his most pathetic arias. The orchestra grieved.

The Duchess felt moved to tears. It would be agreeable to believe that when we die there actually is someone left behind to whom our death makes any difference. Monteverdi's plucked strings made grief real. Again she glanced at Antonio, catching only a glimpse of his tangled hair.

From the proscenium descended a rickety machine, a gilt pasteboard chariot drawn by white horses with ostrich plumes. Apollo stepped from his car in gorgeous armour, as Orféo, astonished, looked up on tiptoe from his grieving. Apollo sang the dénouement. Grief had made Orféo immortal. It had made Euridice immortal. It had made love immortal. He would rejoin her in the stars.

Stage fire glowed red, blue, and green. Out of the orchestra spiralled a hushed and fervent music, cool and audacious as a wet tongue against the flesh. It was the music of the spheres, that sound heard only in the outer air. The stars danced. The orchestra became delightful. It was the climax, in which the company danced a celestial morisco. Suddenly the Duchess wished to see Antonio dance, and herself to dance with him, now together, now separated, and now turning gravely to the whistling of the stars.

She got her wish. The opera was followed by a ball.

She was still under the enchantment of the performance. So was the court, for the effects of art seldom wear off before an hour or two. From one end of the great hall she watched Antonio prance towards her. Indeed, he was Orféo.

And she was Euridice. They were together, as they had been at first. For no one ever remembers all of a parable. He remembers only the part of it he likes best—which is unwise, for parables are inexorable, otherwise they would not be parables at all.

It was in the middle of a *courante* that she looked up and saw who stood on the pillared steps leading down into the hall. She lost the measure, and something in her tightened up. She whispered to Antonio, and while the music went on, lifted up her skirts, and with him slightly behind her, moved gravely towards the stairs. There she curtsied slightly.

142

Ferdinand looked at them both out of his little eyes. He seemed amiable, and only the Duchess knew that that was if anything his most dangerous mood.

"Sister, I have come to visit you," he said. He paused for a moment. "I have not come alone."

This was obvious. Two or three bravos hemmed him in. No matter who he had about him, Ferdinand's companions always looked like executioners.

There was nothing for the Duchess to do. She turned to Antonio, who bowed and withdrew to make arrangements for Ferdinand and his little host.

"Who is he?" demanded Ferdinand. "He has a familiar look."

"Antonio di Bologna, my household steward. No doubt you met him in Rome."

Ferdinand grunted. The music ground to a stop. The court was watching now. Standing beside Ferdinand was a burly, sullen-faced blond youth with tow hair and heavy inert complexion. He shifted uncomfortably from foot to foot. He was a young brainless tough, who no doubt meant well, and fawned on Ferdinand like a spaniel.

"Do you think it proper to dance with your household steward?"

"I think it proper."

Ferdinand clapped his hands loudly at the musicians. They started up uncertainly. "This is Ciampino, dance with him." He looked over her head at the hall, without making any effort to descend the few remaining steps. The Duchess watched him anxiously.

"Well," said Ferdinand.

She allowed Ciampino to lead her forward, and for the rest of the evening Ferdinand would let her dance with no one else, except, once, with himself. He seemed to have nothing to say to her. When he touched her, as sometimes the dance demanded, his grip was hot and too firm. He merely seemed intent upon enjoying himself.

The Duchess knew better. Ferdinand never enjoyed himself. And all evening long she was conscious of his eyes following her, as she moved back and forth across the hall.

143

That night she slept alone. And for the next few nights as well. Ferdinand said nothing about his purpose, but he was everywhere. His servants were also everywhere.

She could not stir without finding herself alone with Ciampino. He might almost have been called attentive. But though he plied her with stumbling compliments awkwardly delivered in a furry voice, he was one of those muscular young men who are at ease only when hawking or on top of a horse. It was comical to see the difference in him then. His awkwardness vanished. He was, in short, one of those truculent, successful young gallants with defensive eyes who understand everything but people, and expend their love on greyhounds, falcons, horses, and dumb animals. A total lack of imagination makes it possible for them to lead golden lives, and it is only when their muscles begin to grow flaccid that they become grumpy. The Duchess found him pathetic and a little dull. Having no brains of their own, such men do as they are told.

It was on the fifth day that Ferdinand came to the point. People like Ferdinand are enormously cunning about things that other people take as a matter of course. It had taken him that long to devise some method of intercepting her casually.

So, in the afternoon, when she went to the walled garden for her stroll, wanting to be alone, she found him sitting on the cope of the fountain, clearly waiting for her, and clearly pretending he was there by accident. She cast her eyes up to heaven, but she had to discover just how much he knew.

For a while he managed to talk of idle things. Then, looking at her curiously, he said: "Sister, it is not wise for you to rule here alone."

"Perhaps I prefer it."

That seemed to anger him. "The difference between a gentlewoman and a Venetian whore is only a husband," he told her. "I would have you marry."

She was angry. She was also chilled. Ferdinand, she knew, would never have her marry, unless it was to some hollow shell such as Piccolomini, and then only on the Cardinal's errands. So this must be his trap, and therefore he must know she was married already.

"I have scarcely been a widow a year," she said. Rumour

might have told him the truth, but there was no one else who could but Cariola. She must find out, too, if Antonio's identity were known.

Having set forward his plot for weeks, Ferdinand was not to be hurried. She saw for the first time that his eyelids were red-rimmed, and that he was hectic with lack of sleep. She would have to humour him. Unconsciously she began to walk faster, as though to shake him off.

This garden was a place of ill-omen. There was no life in it, but only clockwork. The gravel underfoot was little whitened skulls.

"What do you think of Ciampino?" he asked blandly, but his voice was not bland. It was angry and urgent.

"I think nothing of Ciampino."

"He is an excellent young man. I favour him."

"You cannot dispose of me now," she said. "I rule here. The people are loyal."

"Are they?"

"They are."

He lost control of himself. "Sister, I know what you are. I know what my brother is. I am not the fool you think me."

"I do not think you a fool."

"But you will have nothing to do with me."

"I am your sister," she said sharply.

His face was livid.

"Very well," he said. "You are deceitful. Your state rots, and you are like all women. I shall announce your engagement and force your marriage to Ciampino."

"To that lout," she said scornfully.

He glared at her. "Can you marry him?" he demanded. He was full of a suppressed fury that was close to rage. "Can you?" And then, half stooping, he scuttled towards the garden door.

For a moment she could not move. She looked up at the acid sky that seemed ready to burst over her, and turned away.

II

The rest of that day was unendurable. Ferdinand did not

145

appear, and that was ominous. It was like knowing a mad dog was in the building, but not to know where.

She could not force a smile for ever. She retired as early as she could decently manage without occasioning comment, and went directly to her room. There she was careful to bolt the doors. She had seen that maddened lust in Ferdinand before.

It was when Cariola was undoing her hair that she thought she heard a noise on the private stair. She sent Cariola away at once, and turned to face the wall. She was not even sure it would be Antonio. Others now might know the secret of that stair. In her hand she held a brush, and found herself clutching it like a sword. The door creaked open. She let out her breath and sank down on a bench.

It was Antonio. He stood in the centre of the room.

"There is some mischief going on," he said. "I came to tell you."

"Wherever my brother goes, there is mischief. He makes everything unsafe."

"This is in the town." He ran a hand through his hair. "Someone is stirring the people up."

"Against me?"

Antonio hesitated and then nodded.

"Who?"

"The Cardinal has an agent here. A man called Amici."

"We could have him dealt with," she said.

Antonio had not expected that tone. He looked at her closely. "It would make no difference."

The Duchess got up and paced the room. "If it came to a struggle, could we defend ourselves? Suppose there were a siege, or an invasion? What about the court?"

He shook his head. Her popularity with these people had only been a whim. There was not enough money in the treasury to make them loyal. And courts are the same anywhere. If she had nothing left that they could take away, they would shake her out like an empty money sack. She kicked her skirt aside, and glanced warily at the door.

"My brother came here to force my marriage," she said. "He knows I cannot marry. I am sure of it."

146

Antonio sat down, facing her, with his hands between his legs. "There is something you should know," he said, and told her what had happened to the priest of Arosa.

It was the sort of thing Ferdinand would delight to do. She shivered.

"There are no records. He was too ill to speak. The church was locked. He cannot be certain," said Antonio.

"But we cannot be sure."

He was silent for a moment. "No," he admitted slowly. "We cannot be sure."

They sat silent, facing each other. The room was shadowy. They made no attempt to touch each other, for there was no shelter for the two of them together. Now they would have to shelter separately, just when they had most hoped that the storm was over. Happiness had been only a lull, while intrigue gathered its powers. They had only to close their eyes to see that surf, and feel that grinding reef. It suddenly seemed there was no security anywhere.

"We have a few days," said the Duchess. "Ferdinand will not dare to act without the Cardinal. He is a coward. And this is not the Cardinal's hand. This man, Amici, are you sure we could not deal with him?"

"It would only set the town on fire."

"Do you think they know who you are?"

He hesitated, glancing instinctively towards the closed door, and shook his head. Neither one of them even thought of Bosola.

"I could go away," he said.

She shook her head. She could not bear that. Her brothers had no right to tear them apart, and she could not do without him. At the same time she saw him, mutilated, as Ferdinand would have him.

She thought again of Amici. "But how could he find out? There must be someone here."

Again Antonio looked towards the closed door, but she refused to accept that. Not, at any rate, until she had time to think of it, for surely someone in this world must be loyal, and Cariola had been with her always.

"You should not be here," she whispered, but she made no

move to force him to leave. And neither did he have the will to go. Yet there was no safety in this room. There seemed to be a ticking in the walls.

Most of the time Bosola lived in such an agony of frustration that he forgot his appearance, and thought that he must look the way he felt.

Because he often woke at night glistening with sweat, he thought his body must be sordid, but this was not so. It was as though it had been beaten out of purple pewter, and much use had only tempered it.

None of this had escaped Cariola. To her Bosola was not so much a man as a principle. And a woman who first finds a man at forty is not apt to abandon him simply because of his character, or because of loyalty to someone else. Cariola sulked.

The intrusion of the Cardinal's brother was something for which Bosola had not been prepared, and of which he could make no sense. He kept to his quarters.

But his quarters turned out not to be defence enough. Ferdinand had no reverence for doors.

At between twelve and one of that night, when Bosola lay on his bed, unable to sleep, cursing the music and revellers the Duchess had left behind in the hall below, his door was literally beaten in. Bosola leaped from his bed and lunged for his sword.

Two guards in the Duke's saffron livery stood before him, with fixed staves. One of them was Marcantonio. Marcantonio looked as astonished as Bosola did. Daggers twitched at their thighs, and on their heads were saucer helmets. Ferdinand turned to them. "Enough," he said. "Get out."

They slung their staves over their shoulders, and went out, banging the sprung door behind them. Bosola put down his sword. No doubt they were still loitering outside in the hall. A sword would be useless here.

Ferdinand strode up and down the room. It was easy to hear that under his doublet he wore a link corselet, and his massive boots swallowed up his legs, as though he were dressed for flight. It was so he always dressed when bent on violence, and violence was clearly what he was working himself up to.

"So you are the Cardinal's spy also?" he said.

Bosola wore only his shirt and pants, and a bully always goes heavily armed when there is bullying to do. He waited.

Finally Ferdinand stopped in front of him, hands on hips. "Who is this man?" he bawled. "Who is this man?"

Something kept Bosola from answering. Perhaps it was resentment. Resentment was stronger than fear, and he could not bear to be bullied.

"Answer!"

"I do not know." It occurred to him for certain that the Cardinal knew nothing of this visit. This was not the Cardinal's way. And from that thought he took security.

With a vicious swipe of his gloved hand, Ferdinand swept him aside against the table and lifted one enormous heel to kick him, not with the toe, but with the spur. Bosola scrambled hastily aside, and stood behind the table, panting.

Ferdinand laughed.

"What do you know?" he demanded, and began to advance around the table. In that state there was no way to deal with him. He stuck out a cruel leg, and tumbled Bosola down again. But he made no attempt to kick him. He only toed him repeatedly and hard. Ferdinand used his feet as another man would use hands.

"You have a woman. The Duchess's woman-in-waiting. You must know something. I have only to stamp your face in, and what would she make of you then?"

Bosola panted, clinging to Antonio's name as another man would have clung to decency. With the great one must always hold something back.

But there were other ways.

"There is a private stair to the Duchess's apartments," said Bosola. "I think it is used."

"By whom?" shouted Ferdinand.

"I do not know." Bosola was hurt and tired. Let Ferdinand find out for himself, and then the matter was over and no responsibility of his. He could be torn two ways no more.

Ferdinand kicked Bosola again: "Show it me," he bellowed. "Get up and show it me, or I'll have you carried there." He put his fingers to his mouth, and the guards sprang into the room.

With one look at Marcantonio Bosola got up and showed him the entrance to the stair. It was not really concealed but might easily pass for a closet door at the end of a corridor.

Ferdinand disappeared up the stair.

IV

Some second sense warned them, some different sound in the relaxing walls. They had only an instant, and there was nowhere to hide. The Duchess sprang up and pushed Antonio half-naked into Cariola's room. Whether they dared trust her or not, they had no other choice. Then she returned hastily to her bed.

The door in the wall opened and Ferdinand clattered into the room. He sniffed round the room greedily, but saw nothing. Then he headed for Cariola's door. The Duchess grew tense. But beyond the door she heard nothing but Cariola's indignant voice. Ferdinand came back and banged the door behind him.

"Where is he?" he demanded.

"There is no one here."

"Then why this stair?"

"It was built by my lord Piccolomini. These are his rooms. I understand he made use of it in his own way." She folded her hands before her, lay back on the pillows, and closed her eyes.

"Do not look at me like that," shouted Ferdinand. He had never been in her bedroom before.

"My eyes are closed."

He swaggered uncertainly, the fire gone out of him, and suddenly flung himself against the bed, tripping against the dais and falling face down upon the embroidered coverlet.

The bed was huge. In the old fashion, it stood in the centre of the room. Piccolomini had been such a little man that he had taken his ducal pretensions seriously. The bed was therefore a throne for sleeping. It was shadowy and vast, about seven by seven feet. Baroque columns supported the baldachin, where wooden angels soared and swooped after a ducal

150

coronet. The Duchess did not stir. She looked at Ferdinand at the foot of her bed, huddled up like a wounded child. He was very drunk.

"I sit in Rome and think about you," he said into the coverlet. He grasped the stuff in his fists, face down. "I wonder what you do, and why you will not see me. And my brother sits there and plots against me." He raised his head. "Do you think I do not know what I am? Do you think I have not always known? He laughs at me. He married you to that dirty old man. Did you think I liked the thought of that?"

The Duchess moved uncomfortably. She wondered if Antonio and Cariola were listening. There were some things even they should not know.

"I want you pure," he said. "You are my sister. I always watched you. You were the best one of us, the one my brother could not touch. You had no part in what we do."

"And what are you doing to me now?" she asked. The words slipped out of her bitterly.

"I?" He raised his head. "Nothing. You will not let me see you, so I came." He half sat up on the bed and looked at her. "I thought of you with that old man. I could see you both, and what you were doing. I saw it all the time. It was horrible."

"It was not very pleasant. We know what marriages are."

"Do we?" he shouted. He clamped his hands down on either side of her body, and stared down at her. "Do we? Then why did you marry again?"

"I did not marry again."

"You lie. You are like all of them, all women. You lie."

"There is no one." She could not quite keep her voice level. Their eyes were too close. He could read hers, and she could read his.

"No? But I warn you, if I find him, I will kill him. I will kill you. I will not have you do this to me."

"No one is doing anything to you."

"You are," he whispered. "You are."

She tried to slip from under him. But he would not let her, and she wanted to do nothing to rouse him.

Over his shoulder she could see the closed door behind which no doubt Cariola was listening to everything.

151

"I shall have to kill you," he muttered. His voice broke, and he half-fell, half-threw himself on her. Despite herself, she began to scream, beating him with her fists.

He stumbled, and then turned to her, furious and yet beseeching. The door behind him burst open, and Cariola and Antonio rushed into the room. Antonio had a dagger in his hand.

"No," she said. Her hand went instantly to her mouth. "Get back." She knew Ferdinand must not recognize him.

But Ferdinand whirled without even seeing them, and ran back down the stair.

Now he knew for certain there was someone. But at least he did not know who it was, and in that there was still some safety. She could think only of that.

"So that is the truth of it," said Antonio slowly, coming towards the bed, the dagger still in his hand.

The Duchess glanced warningly towards Cariola, and then gave up. "Yes," she said. She had not realized it before, but it was so. She could still feel Ferdinand's hot, dry hands on her body, and she shuddered. "Yes, that's the truth of it."

"He must be mad."

"It does not make him any the less dangerous," said the Duchess. She leaned back wearily. "You must go."

v

Ferdinand was so terrified of himself that the Duchess hoped that he would run away to hide. It was what he had always done after giving way to violence. But this time he did not. That complex creature was too much for her. She kept to her rooms, and would see no one. She wanted the private stair walled up. As she moved about uneasily, she was always aware of that door, and she kept Cariola by her.

Late in the afternoon Ferdinand sent up a messenger. He was leaving. Would she accompany him through the town to the harbour? She thought it best to comply. The situation had gotten beyond him, so he was fleeing to the Cardinal.

She went down the state stairs slowly, with Cariola beside her. She had worn a black silk dress. She wanted to look as unattractive as possible. She dreaded seeing her brother.

152

But Ferdinand was in the oddest of all his moods. It was one even she had never seen before. He stood in the middle of the hall, surrounded by his court of bravos, talking to Ciampino. There was no real malice in Ciampino. He was only a dog who had nothing to do, and whose master, at the moment, did not smell quite right. Her life would have been simpler with someone like that. For the first time the Duchess really looked at him, with a certain weary relief.

He was not like Antonio. There was no fire in him. But fire can burn, and then we need the salve of mediocrity, to take away the sting. He stood there sturdily before Ferdinand, his arms crossed, balancing self-consciously on one foot, with the physical ostentation of the healthy young, staring up at his master's face, confused. What Ferdinand was saying she could not tell. But men like that have no speech. They grunt at each other companionably, and that is enough.

She reached the foot of the stair and Ferdinand turned to her. He was up to something. When he spoke, she could not make out his manner. She was disturbed. His cleverness was childish, but it was also ruthless. And the behaviour of children, like that of birds, is unpredictable. Death and life are all one to them, and it is not until long afterwards, if at all, that they are sorry.

Their horses were waiting in the yard. Antonio held her palfrey. She thought she saw Ferdinand look at him thoughtfully. If so, she pretended to ignore it. Ciampino would have ridden beside her, but Ferdinand took that place. Cariola was forced to ride behind. With a jingle of silver bells on the harness, they left the palace and entered the town, pacing slowly. The streets were virtually deserted, but what people were out stared after her with closed faces.

"The people are sullen," said Ferdinand shortly. "Have you noticed?"

She shrugged, but wondered what he was up to.

"I do not think they will applaud you any more," he told her. He kneed his horse aside, towards an alley.

"This is not the way to the harbour."

"There are many ways to the harbour," he said. "This is the darkest. The day is hot. It suits me."

153

He had his company about him, and they rode in tight formation. There was nothing she could do but follow.

They came out into a small square, shadowed by tall rickety houses. Here a crowd surrounded the open door of a shop. Hearing the horses, they turned to watch. They said nothing. But their faces were sullen, and one of the men tightened his fists. They turned their heads to watch, as the horses crossed the square and entered a street, on the other side.

Ferdinand smiled. Just as the horses reached the far street the crowd began to boo. It was a deep guttural sound, full of anger and something like contempt. It was a sound the Duchess had never heard before.

Ferdinand grunted. "Would you like to know why?"

"Not particularly."

"A man called Amici was found murdered in his shop this morning."

"What has this to do with me?"

"They think you had it done." He shrugged. "You didn't, did you?"

"What is this game?"

"He was tortured first. He was very popular here. At any rate, he is popular now he is dead."

"And why did I murder him, if I did?"

"He was the Cardinal's spy. Naturally they believe that there are certain things you would rather not have found out. At any rate they believe it now."

"You saw to that?"

"I saw to that," said Ferdinand. They came out of the back alley, and on to the quay that faced the sea. There was no wharf. The company would have to ride through the surf to the boat. Ferdinand nudged his horse towards the water. At the surf he turned.

"You rule here by our whim," he told her. "Have you ever seen a mob storm a castle, drag out their ruler, string him up in the streets, and beat his body with their fists until someone sets fire to it? I have. They may come at any time, and who knows what sets them off?"

He looked down at her angrily and contemptuously, with that strained masculine giggle he reserved for his own clever-

154

ness when it had pushed him too far. "You have no place to hide, and I know where to find you. You will not trick me again, and you will not rule here long."

He forced his horse into the surf. Ciampino had looked puzzled at this exchange. Now he gave the Duchess one of his innocent smiles and made haste to follow his master. Cariola came up to the Duchess. The two women stood there, watching. The horses got in up to their bellies, and shied at the weak waves. They could hear Ferdinand laughing as he urged them on. The sound came over the water like the tolling of a bell.

The horses were hoisted up on to the boat, riders and all. The Duchess turned to face the town. In the bright sunlight it sparkled like a prison. Only the church rose over it, and even that was hauled half down from heaven by the heavy tiled roofs that closed it in.

She could not know that Ferdinand had been lying. She thought that now the Cardinal knew.

VI

First she had to protect Antonio.

She realized that as soon as she returned to the palace and had time to look over her meaningless little court. They were not much. All these little lords and gentlemen were loyal only to their own perquisites. Chivalry and honour had shrunk, for them, to the dimensions of a law-suit. To them she was not a woman. She was merely a source of favour. She would give them nothing more. They knew that. Dukes and duchesses meant much to them. The people who were dukes and duchesses over them meant nothing to them at all.

They were venal and uneasy. They were less loyal than her servants, for servants work for a fixed wage, but courtiers could only be bribed. They had no fixed price. And it was clear in their eyes and their deference, that just as mice know when it is raining, so they expected a change of reigns. Their unctuousness was so obviously a matter of filling in time, that it disgusted her. She would have none of them.

For these reasons she never thought of giving Antonio up, for he was the first real thing she had ever known. She had

155

quite a different plan, one that came to her mind so easily that it must have been there all along. She did not stop to think about it. She merely grasped at it with relief, and sent Cariola off to fetch Antonio.

Cariola did not want to go. The Duchess had had enough of opposition. She flared up angrily.

"What does it matter?" she snapped. "You will do as I say."

It was seldom she ordered Cariola to do anything. She had not meant to be so harsh. Cariola went. When she returned with Antonio, the Duchess could not help seeing how pale and hurt she looked. She had never seen quite that look on Cariola's face, and she did not like it. A little doubt flickered in her mind.

"You may go," she said. Cariola went reluctantly.

"What has happened?" he demanded.

She shook her head. "Nothing has happened. But there are some things we must do at once."

He glanced warningly towards the door.

"Cariola is all right," she said.

"Is she?" His voice was unexpectedly hard.

"I must trust someone."

"She is too frightened to be dependable. She listens to you, spies on you, and says nothing. Why should a loyal woman do that?"

The Duchess was impatient. She had not forgotten the look on Cariola's face. "All servants do that." It was the wrong word to have Cariola overhear. In her own mind Cariola was no servant.

"Suppose they tortured her," he urged. "She would not be very loyal then."

"Perhaps you are right," said the Duchess slowly. She had unconsciously been edging away from the door. Now she led the way out into the loggia and the hot, stifling night. There she spoke urgently to Antonio.

"The Cardinal knows," she whispered, and hated herself for feeling the need to whisper. She told him what Ferdinand had said and done about Amici. "You must flee. I will say that as my steward you cheated me. I shall discredit you utterly. They

156

will believe me. They believe everybody cheats. I shall say you have mismanaged my accounts. I shall be utterly disillusioned." She smiled at him sadly. She could see that he did not like the idea. "What else can we do? Any stratagem is better than none."

"Very well," he said slowly. "But I cannot leave you alone here."

"I shall not be alone long. There is safety in publicity. I plan a pilgrimage to Loreto, I shall go with a large company, very slowly and ostentatiously. I will think of some excuse, some pretext to please the Amalfitani. No one will dare to molest me, not even the Cardinal. You will go to Ancona. It is close to Loreto. I will manage to slip away. Then we will take ship from Ancona."

"And then?"

"Who knows then? But we will be out of their clutches." She smiled at him again. "The important thing is to escape. We could join your gipsies, perhaps."

He shook his head. It exasperated her. "Why not?" she demanded. "It is a poor plan, perhaps, but what else can we do?"

It was true. He could not think of anything else. But he would not consent to it until she granted him permission to join her in disguise, as she neared Loreto. She would need someone to protect her, he argued. And she had not the heart to deny him.

"We are slipping away like fugitives," he said.

She looked around the shadowy loggia, and shivered. "We are fugitives," she told him sadly.

They returned to her room. She went to summon Cariola. There was no answer. They opened the door to her chamber. Cariola was gone. They stood in the empty room, looking at each other soberly.

At four she sent him away, into the yellow dawn. He rode out of Amalfi on a horse well laden with saddlebags, for what each of them thought would be the last time, and headed for the hills. The tracks up there were known to him and unknown to others. It was gipsy and *banditti* country. No one would follow him. It was the safest way across the peninsula, for him.

Cariola had overheard everything. She had run away to hide. She had served the Duchess loyally, only to discover that loyalty counted for nothing. She was merely a servant. She had been supplanted and cast out. She wept for shame. She also wept for terror. The idea of torture was unendurable. Yet if she was cast out, where could she go? She said nothing.

Neither did the Duchess. There was so much for her to do.

That afternoon she summoned her court nobles to appear in the great hall. She delayed in going to meet them. Despite herself, she had a conscience. She hated what she was about to do. She had no will to denounce anyone, let alone Antonio.

Her emotional turmoil actually contributed to her plans, for it gave conviction to something that otherwise would have had none. It made the court believe that hers was the real anger of a woman who had been deceived, and not the guile of a woman bent upon deceiving. Only Bosola took the matter differently, but then it was his business to take all matters differently.

He stood in the throng, almost unnoticed, until he saw Cariola watching him, with a crestfallen expression that seemed friendlier than her manner had been for some time. He could do nothing about that, but he took note of it. He wondered what was coming next.

The Duchess slowly passed down the room and mounted the dais at the end of it. She was solemnly dressed, and mounted the dais as though it had been an executioner's block. When she turned to face them, Bosola was startled by her appearance. It was impressive. In some way she had aged. A real grief gave her presence dignity.

The court was uneasy. Ferdinand's presence had disrupted them, and they knew that there were disturbances in the town. They did not care about her. But should the mobs riot, it would be their property that would be damaged. It was to their interest to slick those troubled waters down, and that would cost money. They did not like that.

The Duchess cleared her throat. Her voice was unexpectedly firm. She began to speak.

158

Bosola listened with disbelief. It could be a clever trick: still, somehow he could not help but believe that it was true. Yet when he thought of Antonio, he knew that it was not true. A man who is born honest can change his own nature as little as a hunchback, a dwarf, or a cripple. It is a stigma he must bear for life.

A ripple ran through her audience. It was caused by self-justified delight. That impressed Bosola. When Antonio was in favour, the minor courtiers had circled round him like dogs wary for scraps. They had scarcely known how to gain his favour. But they knew very well how to denounce him.

The Duchess had something more to say. The tone of her voice had changed. She announced that it was a shame that this had happened on the eve of her projected pilgrimage to Loreto. At this Bosola pricked up his ears. So did the courtiers, though for different reasons. They were delighted at an excuse to leave Amalfi, until the mob was quiet again. And a pilgrimage might even serve to quiet the mob. They were a pious people. They admired it when the quality followed their example. A few more bones in the reliquaries of the cathedral made them feel that Amalfi was still an important place.

Bosola thought her shrewd. Moving at a leisurely pace and in public across the face of Italy, surrounded by such of her court as went with her, she would be invulnerable. But he was not taken in. He sensed that her whole purpose was to deceive. What her plans might be he could not guess. But he was sure that this sudden act of piety was the part of some plan.

Then she appointed him steward in Antonio's place. Despite himself he was gratified. He was wary, for he thought it was part of this new cleverness he had not expected from her, but he was enormously pleased. He was also enormously busy. He had not much time to spy. On the other hand she seemed entirely open about her prepararions for the cavalcade, and these went forward rapidly. She even seemed eager for his advice.

He was puzzled. He had not thought her guileful. He need not have been so puzzled. For though she could act with vigour, guile was beyond her. She had looked around for someone she could trust publicly, and caught sight of him.

She was revolted by her court, and he was the only outsider there.

Cariola was miserable. The hammering and scurrying back and forth necessitated by the departure for Loreto drove her to distraction. She saw herself cast aside. It seemed to her that the Duchess was no longer at ease with her. She did not understand her mistress's moods and tempers. She thought that Antonio had gotten rid of her. Inside she raged against him. She could not help herself. She began to believe that Bosola was right. Little people were crushed underfoot by these highnesses, who had no kindness in them. She had always resented Antonio. Now it seemed to her that the Duchess had been taken away from her. She had to talk to someone.

When she came to Bosola, she thought that it was only to complain. But the strain on her had been too great. She let him take her. It relieved both of them. And when people are together in bed, they talk. They seem to believe that things said in the darkness of a shared bed will never be repeated and are outside the moral system which controls our days. She told Bosola that Antonio was the Duchess's lover.

Even then that might not have turned him against her, but a quick vengefulness in her tone took him by surprise. He pretended that he had not known, but inside he instantly despised her. For she had waited until the hue and cry was up against Antonio. She would always go over to the winning side. To save her own pride, let alone her neck, she would betray anyone. He said nothing to her. But something inside him that she had once almost thawed turned hard again at once.

She herself was flustered. She was ashamed. But also she was secretly glad. Inside her something rejoiced in having given Antonio away. Those phrases she had overheard now hurt her less. But it was this secret gladness Bosola heard in her voice, and he would never feel the same way about her again, as a result. Disappointment in her turned him savage.

Of this betrayal the Duchess of course knew nothing. The night before her departure she summoned Bosola to her, and gave him a casket containing such jewels as she could not publicly take with her. These she bade him conceal in his saddlebags and luggage. She was rather grand about it. She said she trusted him. He was to accompany the caravan as far

160

as Naples, then slip away to Rome, sell them, and convey the money to a merchant at Ancona.

There was nothing to do but accept. Bosola was appalled. He bowed low and withdrew. Through her folly, he had been caught up into her web, and he did not know what to do. The jewels were useless to him. Alone, he could not dispose of them. Nor could he sell them in Rome. The Cardinal would hear of it at once. But if he did not sell them in Rome and proceed to Ancona, his position would be found out by the Duchess and Antonio, and then everything would collapse. Nor did he underestimate Antonio. The revenge of an honest man is even more determined than that of a scoundrel, once he is aroused, and he knew of Antonio's acquaintance among brigands and gipsies. A knife in the back can come from anywhere. He broke out into a sweat, and wrote to the Cardinal at once.

VIII

Bosola need not have been so worried.

When he learned what Ferdinand had been up to, the Cardinal was extremely angry, but then he smiled. Like doctors, who can keep six patients in six rooms, and treat them all without fumbling their prognosis, the Cardinal was most efficient when he had most plots in hand. Occasionally he overlooked something, and a patient died, but not often. He knew better than to compete with chance, but he believed in being there to snatch away its benefits for himself. Therefore he had merely to fit Ferdinand's fooleries into his own plans. The adjustment required was not great.

Bosola presented quite a different problem. He was too much of a gentleman to be a reliable villain. The Duchess seemed to trust him. He might therefore change sides. He wrote him at once, telling him what to do with the jewels, but also he wrote to Sor Juana. She had had her lesson, if he was not mistaken. That should be enough to keep her loyal, since she was ambitious for her convent, and she should be able to find out if her brother had any secret schemes. That done, he proceeded to Ferdinand, and considered his day profitably spent. Soon Amalfi would be his. It never occurred to him to wonder why

161

he wanted it. It was merely a course of action he had embarked upon, that unwound now whether he was there to take advantage of it or not. He bore no malice towards his sister, and was a little sorry that her folly should have made her course so short. But after all, he would not be there to see what happened, and he had much to do.

At Amalfi the caravan was ready to set forth. The show it made was in every way a splendid one. The Duchess had made it purposely so, and her nobles always welcomed display.

The company was given the episcopal blessing from the steps of the Cathedral, after a solemn Mass, whose incense still clogged the interior. The sonorous organ peeled out into the square through the open bronze doors of the entrance. The crowds were respectful, and respectfully fell back, as the company took its way down to the shore.

Sackbut and trumpet wafted them off and cleared their way. The court poet dependably produced an ode. It was almost as though they were setting forth on a little crusade. In the harbour the ships lay waiting. They would go by sea to Naples, and then set forth across country towards Loreto.

As they pulled out from the harbour, and the sails caught the wind, the Duchess, with Cariola, stood on deck and watched the shore recede. Now Amalfi was less a town than the ghostly shell of one. It was as though she had never been there. It was meaningless.

She felt a lump in her throat. Now she was a Duchess without lands, without estates, without an army or a populace. She had not even a home. She was in flight, but must pretend to be leisurely. She was not going to Loreto: she was going to Antonio. She knew she must hold to that thought, and never think of the future at all. But she could not help but think of it. Who would give them sanctuary? Where could they possibly seek refuge? Peasants might run away, and remain hid. But rumour had made her famous. Where could they go?

As the ships stood out to sea, the promontory of Ravello came into view. She said nothing. She did not even stir. But she watched it. As they drew away from the shore, Ravello turned black against the morning sky, as though it had been sacked and burned. She had been happy there.

EIGHT

Knowledge of this pilgrimage had preceded them. They were received in Naples with respect. The Duchess had chosen her pretext well. If one was upon a pious errand, and could not go to Rome, one went to Loreto. Like a journey to Mecca, a journey there was sacrosanct. Merely setting out for Loreto made one untouchable and therefore safe, providing one went with a large and public company.

The baroque taste for showy marvels made the shrine popular. Nor was the Duchess less devout for taking the matter lightly. We can believe and disbelieve in the same miracle at the same time with equal fervour. After all, if we prove a miracle false, then it only becomes the more miraculous, and the story of Loreto was well known. It was, after all, the house of the Virgin Mary, spirited from Palestine by a tempest.

But first there was Naples to be dealt with.

Perhaps because she had been born there, the Duchess was not afraid of Naples. As soon as the ships drew in to the mole, she felt more secure than she had ever felt at Amalfi. It was as though she had escaped from a prison. Farther down the coast was Castel del Mare, her husband's abandoned fief. But in Naples she felt self-assured. The day was halcyon, and in that light all colours sparkled. If only Antonio had been there, she would have been content, but even without him, her spirits rose.

For on a clear day, and there almost all days are clear, the Bay of Naples makes the heart soar. The heat haze seems to tremble with an invisible music. That dangerous magician, Virgil, has his medieval spell cast out like a fishing net, to drag the world in.

The purple bulk of Vesuvius casts its ostrich plume against the sky, and the world seems swathed in gorgeous silk. Care slithers away like a scarf flowing off a table. If Naples is evil and grotesque, it is evil and grotesque in a singularly cheerful way.

The Duchess decided to disarm her brother the Cardinal. He had some interest in that nun, Sor Juana. Very well, the Duchess would receive her. The more religion they had the better. Let her brothers think she had had a change of heart.

When she discovered Sor Juana could not leave the convent, she shrugged her shoulders, and said that she would go to her. Why should she not? It might be amusing. She had never been to a convent before.

Bosola did not like the idea. He had the feeling that they should not meet. Nor did he wish his sister to see him in that entourage. But there was nothing he could do. The Cardinal's web was drawn too tight. They were all in it now.

To the Duchess, however, it was merely amusing. She was interested now in everything.

The Duchess had no idea that she was going to visit the guardian of her own child. She had come to patronize and to be gracious. She could not know that to Sor Juana she was not a gracious lady, but an inconvenience. She picked up her skirts and moved sedately up the convent stairs, with Bosola at her heels, Cariola behind, and other members of the court trailing behind her round the landing.

The Duchess was neither literary nor pious. Therefore the usual preparations made to receive visitors did not impress her as they had been intended to do.

Since she had no ceremony of her own, Sor Juana made use of her monastic circumstances. It suited her very well to have the world come to her, and she made the most of it. Such state may have been ridiculous, but scholars and great nobles are not noted for their sense of humour.

The Duchess had come only to see the age's leading curiosity, as in Venice people might visit the zoo and the convent on the same afternoon, pausing to marvel first at the rhinoceros, and then to gossip with the nuns. She was prepared to be condescending.

The landing was deserted, except for a bevy of nuns hovering about some empty chairs set companionably to the cloister

164

windows. The Abbess came forward to receive the Duchess, bending commendably low. They were seated and served light refreshments.

Only after a dignified pause did Sor Juana see fit to put in her appearance. She hated to bow to anyone, and through the years had contrived to solve the problem in her own way. She would bustle forward busily, attended by her servant girls, as though just interrupted, drop a quick curtsy, and be seated as the girls fussed about her chair. Then, bright-eyed and amiable, she would turn to sparkle at the company. She swept in now.

The Duchess was startled by this procedure. She was accustomed to the manners of the Court Poet, who worked diligently in order that poetry should salute rank, as was only proper. It had never occurred to her that poetry had its own pomps. Besides, there were bits of steel in this woman that she did not care for. Sor Juana looked too prosperous. She should have been more afraid of the world.

She had expected a pretty and precocious nun, not a business woman whose hard eyes believed in nothing but herself, and whose skin was that of a court beauty beginning to lose her looks. By that time even Sor Juana realized how much her character had changed her face.

"But she must be formidable," the Duchess said. "She is a little nobody." She sat back, waiting to be dazzled.

But Sor Juana had decided not to dazzle. She was badly rattled. The presence of Bosola in that audience threw her off. She had not expected him. She did not want to see him smirk at her. And she felt cautious. If the Duchess did not know her son was here, why otherwise had she come?

The complications her mind invented were not pleasant. She would have quailed if the Duchess had been older or less bland, or had more power. Sor Juana had not lived at the viceregal court for nothing. She had early learned that pomp is meaningless without a standing army.

They discussed the theatre, the Cardinal, and the plans for a convent. On the subject of the convent the Duchess was vague. She said the matter was up to her brother, the Cardinal. In this she lost both Sor Juana's attention and her respect. She had been vigilant. She thought the Duchess had come to bargain. Now she relaxed, seeing she had not.

Watching his sister, Bosola hated her. For her attitude towards the Duchess diminished him. Sor Juana recited one of her keepsake sonnets, written for the occasion. The Duchess accepted a copy of it. Nobody listened to it. The company rose to leave. Bosola contrived to stay behind. A look in his sister's eye had convinced him that he should. He loitered in Sor Juana's cell, waiting for her to come to him.

Now she had the Cardinal's favour, he was quick to note, her manner was brusque. She was no saint. She was as bad as he was. She did the devil's work for nothing.

She came into the room rapidly, with a flurry of skirts, and dismissed her two maids. She wasted no words, but when she saw him dressed so properly, her lips tightened.

"What is happening?" she demanded.

"We are making a pilgrimage to Loreto." He bowed mockingly. "Perhaps we have turned devout."

That merely made her impatient. She was very certain of herself. "Rumour has the matter differently. What has happened there?"

Bosola shrugged. "Your convent will be quite safe."

"What do you mean by that?"

Her tone was sharp. Again that great weariness came over him which was always his reaction to her presence. A little gentleness would have done her no harm. She did wrong to show her hand so soon and so obviously.

"How strange", he said at last, "that we should both toady to the same man." He was not angry with her. Only tired of her. Therefore he could choose the words best suited to hurt her with efficiency.

"I toady to no one," she said. But there was a guilty expression in her eyes that showed him that in some way she had realized what the Cardinal could do to her, if he chose. "She is fleeing, isn't she?"

"I don't know what you are talking about."

Finally she came out with it. "She does not know the boy is here."

Bosola hesitated, but she did not give him the time to lie.

166

She seemed much relieved. The boy clearly meant much to her, the Duchess nothing. Perhaps no one any longer meant anything to her. Like him she hurtled through life impelled by the impetus of an ambition she had long since left behind.

He turned to leave.

"I am not afraid of you," she said. "You are only a great man now on the losing side. Enjoy it while you can."

He looked at her. Her face was cold as metal. So was her voice. So he knew that in some way he had shamed her, and that therefore she was now his implacable enemy. He had always wanted to pull her down. But he did not flatter himself that he had done so. The Cardinal had done so. He wondered how.

He could know nothing of that nun walled up down in the darkness below her. Yet he had the curious feeling that he was seeing her for the last time. He lingered. He did not want to be sent away like a stranger. There must be warmth in her somewhere. For some reason he felt sorry for her, even when she made him angry. He saluted her mockingly and strode down the stairs.

II

Next day the caravan set out from the Rome gate. Bosola would accompany it until it was time for him to turn off for Rome.

It was one of those crisp mornings when the world is full of music, and the air seems to tinkle against the trees. Flutes sound in all the gorges, and organs rumble like the wagons of the law. Birds chorused out of the grey cliffs and yellow hills of central Italy, and for a while they followed the coast of that magic Roman sea.

Since they made the leisurely public progress of those days, the company did not go more than fifteen miles a day. As they approached each hamlet or small town little boys and beggars ran out to meet them. The spectacle was a noble one. The landscape would be empty. Then, over the nearest rise, the first outriders would appear, peaceable and imperturbable, in the Piccolomini livery, with standards resting in a stirrup strap, and very vain of their sinuous legs. Plumes on their bonnets ruffled in the breeze.

By choice the Duchess rode next, side-saddle on a palfrey, surrounded by a small bodyguard, with Cariola respectfully half a length behind her, and others riding up to talk to her from time to time. Behind her, for a quarter of a mile, stretched out the heavy wagons and carriages which carried supplies, offerings, and household goods, both her own and those of the nobles who had come with her.

Progress was so slow that it was possible to go hawking in the hills, and still rejoin the company at its destination. Bells jangled. The horses snorted. The carts lumbered uncertainly up and down the rutted roads.

To the Duchess it was a new experience. She looked around her with delight. She had never travelled before, and she had a mind to take delight in new scenes, that special eagerness to see what is round the next bend which makes the traveller. She had sat in Castel del Mare and Amalfi all her life. Now she saw the world could be an endless series of next bends, with something round every one of them. And somewhere, far across these hills and valleys, was still another sea, the musky Adriatic, salt with shrimp, and a town called Ancona, which would make her free.

She began to make a favourite of Bosola, and found him more pleasing than she had found him before. During that five days she forgot her suspicions and began to depend upon him. Nor was she entirely misguided, for Bosola had changed. Had that trip been endless, he would in truth have been dependable.

For Bosola had relaxed. For five days he might do as he pleased, and enjoy favour. It was something he had never done before, to ride well dressed and respected at the head of a caravan, and have the confidence of a Duchess. She preferred him over her own nobles. That made the nobles both angry and uncomfortable.

Only he knew that the situation was not permanent. Therefore he took pleasure in it for what it was. He liked the spectacle of these gentlemen forcing themselves to toady to him for nothing.

Those five days were the happiest of his life. Only when he looked at Cariola, and remembered how easily she had betrayed Antonio to no purpose, did he become more solemn, and remember that this pageant was only a game. On the other hand, he saw no reason why he should not enjoy Cariola, too. When they paused at houses along the way, he did so. If she sensed something was wrong between them, that was her own affair. But she was subdued. She watched and said nothing. Only in bed did he feel how hysterical she was underneath. She lay in his arms like a rabbit straining to bolt.

The Duchess, he thought, was better at this game. She seemed thoroughly unconcerned.

Indeed, for a few days she was. Like him, but in a different way, she snatched at the pretended ease of a time between and managed to believe it real. It was a little like having a honeymoon alone.

When they reached the cross-roads for Rome, and Bosola turned off down it, on the sleekest horse he had ever owned in his life, she looked after him with a sense of dis-ease that soon turned to panic. She did not quite know why, except that the cares she had managed to suppress now flooded back on her. She missed his ironic tone.

She looked up into the sky and saw blackened hawks slowly circling over the only tree on the hill above her. As she rode along she kept glancing aside, until Bosola had disappeared.

He had diverted her. Now he was gone, she was alone with her retinue, and if she flinched even once she knew it would turn upon her mercilessly. She longed to urge the company on, but did not dare to do so. That would be too obvious. But rather than seeming closer, Ancona seemed impossibly far away.

The landscape now was not fresh, but dusty and dry. It was a landscape of rumour. It seemed to her that she moved like a dot across the face of one of those gold and azure political maps whose heraldic designs splashed the walls of the council rooms of palaces. There was nowhere for her to go but on, and therefore she had somehow to get there.

She had not forgotten Ferdinand. By now Ferdinand must know that she had fled. When she saw two sentries talking at dusk, or interrupted the gossip of courtiers, she thought that it was on his errands that they looked at her.

The countryside had changed. They were now in those ragged turbulent hills which stood between central Italy and the eastern coast. As they wound through dry *arroyos*, there was ample time for ambush here, and the region was poor. Brigands and *banditti* were everywhere. Ferdinand had used that disguise before. Or he might hire others to do the mischief. The rest of her company was wary here. They did not like it either. The pompous caravan tightened up, and seemed pathetic against the hills.

It was here Antonio was to meet her. There was no sign of him.

On the third week of the progress, they came out of a bastion of rocks, high up, and saw the Adriatic for the first time. The sunlight was mercilessly clear. So was the air. She drew rein and looked down.

The hills fell away on either side. Between the cliffs and the ocean stretched a level plain, dotted with quincunxes of trees. Here and there in the plain rose a massive butte. They could see peasants and labourers going about their business in the fields. Out to the Adriatic stood little ships, which scarcely seemed to move. Not a bird hovered in the sky. And in the far distance sparkled the white walls, turrets, and campanile of Ancona, turning the pale breasts of its cathedral domes up to the sky.

Loreto lay hidden in hills far to the right. She turned her horse in that direction, bitter to tears. Something, she knew, had gone wrong, and she had not the courage to go on. She ordered the caravan to halt, and went to rest in the tent soon pegged out for her.

She had to hide, for she was trembling. For a little while she wanted a respite from being so perpetually watched, and the one thing she must not betray publicly was anxiety. Even Cariola did not know the real purpose of this journey.

As she rested in her tent one of her guards came to announce that the company had fallen in with a troup of tumblers and strolling players. He thought that they might amuse her.

The Duchess smiled wanly. She was touched.

170

Cariola bustled into the tent. She was severely agitated, and stood behind the guard anxiously.

"Very well," said the Duchess. "Show them in."

"Oh Madam, don't," said Cariola.

The Duchess's eyes widened. "Why on earth shouldn't I?" Again she smiled at the soldier.

Cariola started to say something, and then thought better of it. Her face was pale and frightened. She left the tent.

The Duchess hesitated. "Send them to me," she ordered. The soldier smiled, saluted, and went out. The Duchess leaned back in a cushioned field chair, and prepared to be dutifully amused.

It was a commedia del' arte company. Rapid tumblers rushed into the tent, and there was even a dwarf, who played the viol. Then came Sganarelle, Bombard, and the others, all in grotesque masques and peaked caps. Despite herself the Duchess laughed. They were amusing. Their dialogue was very good. They had decided to mimic her company, as though they were themselves on a pilgrimage. Their vulgarity was soothing. She felt much better. She decided to send for the court. She could face her nobles again now.

Sganarelle pirouetted madly, stumbled, and fell against the rug on which her chair stood. He let fall his masque and laughed at her.

It was Antonio.

III

In Rome it was raining, with the quick, emphatic rain of ruptured summer. It turned the unfinished city into a sea of mud, in which cobblestones rocked down the rivulets of unpaved squares. The yellow poles of scaffolding stuck up like fractured bones. Water whipped capriciously round the interiors of unroofed naves, and poured over the waltzing statuary of a hundred false façades.

In those quick August cloud-bursts the heavens open like a sluice. The Forum was a swamp. Rain freshened the stench of incense, which hung in the city like the miasma of a plague. The Forum cats huddled in acrimonious groups of three or four, sleek as rats and utterly miserable, staring out of niches

171

and holes at the weather, their natural enemy. Even they were better off than the scuttling poor. The doors of the Pantheon stood open, quivering in a lashing gale. Rain poured down through the circular hole in its roof like a waterspout, and deluged the high altar with gusts of spray.

Huddled in a sodden cloak, Bosola on his horse picked his way towards the Cardinal's palace. The street before it was a river in spate, and there was no one in sight anywhere.

Water coursed down his horse's withers and his own legs. His shoes were pulp. His splendour was ruined, and he had not brought a change of clothes. He had every reason to be in a temper.

Nobody disturbed him. The courtyard was deserted. In the loggias the rain whipped against the inner walls. Bosola went directly to the Cardinal's apartments.

The Cardinal was waiting for him with his usual patient, slightly defensive smile. It is a mistake to think that that which does not move us is therefore not moving, and he eyed Bosola narrowly. The man was not honest, but he was sentimental. Indeed, sentimental people are never honest. He wondered how much Bosola was keeping back from him. On the other hand the man was dripping wet, and his clothes were ruined. He would have to be soothed. The best way to soothe him was to ask him for advice.

"Does my brother know they have fled?" he asked.

"I do not think so."

The Cardinal looked at the box in Bosola's hands. It had four lion legs, and was of wood with silver mounts. When the box was placed on the table, the Cardinal raised the lid. He had never seen the Piccolomini jewels. He looked inside with curiosity.

"Is that all?" he asked.

"She has much money with her. The rest she gave to . . ." Bosola stopped suddenly, "her paramour."

"You know his name, then. Have you known it long?" The Cardinal did not wait for an answer. He turned the box out on the desk, and looked at the little hoard, somewhat ruefully. "What a pity she should run such risk for so little." He held up a sapphire. "How is she?"

172

He seemed genuinely concerned. Bosola did not quite know what to say. The Cardinal looked up at him. "We do not always do as we wish," he said. "But what others do should play to our advantage." He was sly now. "Do you understand me?"

"No."

It was the first sign of rebellion Bosola had ever made. The Cardinal looked up thoughtfully. Then he sighed and put the sapphire down.

"You will sell these and take her the money. To Ancona, if she wishes that. It was Ancona, wasn't it? They are only trumpery things." He paused. "It is Antonio di Bologna, of course?"

Bosola did not answer.

Again the Cardinal sighed. "I see," he said. He smiled. "A man called Niccolò Ferrante once came to me. He was a fugitive from the galleys. I gave him preferment. Now I find he is wanted in Pavia. I have only to send him there."

"I am not Niccolò Ferrante."

"A dozen men will say you were. You said you were. They would behead you if I turned you over to them. And why should I not? You are nothing to me."

"It was Antonio de Bologna."

"Of course it was. I suppose they will meet at Ancona. The idea is romantic, but not paid for." Suddenly he stood up, rustled round the table, and glared down at Bosola.

"I am sending you to my brother." He was not angry. He was merely contemptuous. And it was the contempt that Bosola would always obey. They both knew that.

"You will do as he says. I suppose you think you have risen. Perhaps you could have once. But power is not the same thing as a new suit of clothes." The Cardinal began to pace up and down the room. "Yes, you will do as you are told. Do you think we cannot do what we please with you? You, and your sister, too." The Cardinal glared at him. "She at least is clever enough to get what she wants. But on our terms. You have not even the brains for that."

He tried to look amused. But his forehead was sweating. He sat down again and glanced up at Bosola with oddly candid

173

eyes. "My brother cannot be stopped. Treat her gently if you can. She is very young."

The room grew quiet. The Cardinal shoved the jewel box forward towards Bosola. "Do as he says. But tell me nothing until it is done. Now get out."

Bosola got out. He had seen more than he had wanted to see. It was as though they had been talking at the end of a dark alley, and someone had held up a lantern to both of them.

He did not mind what happened now. He was caught. He sought out Ferdinand. He would throw himself away, contemptuously; and it would be a pleasure to be whipped. If we can make ourselves grovel, then what others make us do so does not hurt nearly so much. It was useless to be Bosola. He had become Ferrante now.

IV

That news travels fast does not disturb us. What takes us aback is that it arrives so suddenly. One moment it is not there. The next it is.

The Duchess's party was encamped upon a hillside, half-way between Ancona and Loreto. It was morning and something had disturbed the birds. The air was thick with doves, who wove low webs across the air, and called and cooed their trouble as they flew. Only a hawk sometimes could make them dart that way. Or it may only have been their play. Who could tell?

The Duchess woke drowsily, roused by a flurried murmur round her tent. It was the doves. She glanced around the tent, expecting walls. The light was pearly grey, and therefore disturbing. She turned to Antonio for comfort, expecting to find him asleep. He was not asleep. He was lying passively on his side, watching her. She looked at him so seriously that he smiled, but she could see that he was serious too.

"It's early," he said.

"Yes." Something disturbed her. She did not quite know what it was. Something about their night had not been quite as things used to be.

She did not want to get up. She wanted to snuggle away

174

from the world with him, at the bottom of the bed, as though that were protection enough. For a while then they lay in each other's arms.

There was no real security in it. The inside of the tent was hung with frail white curtains, several layers deep, and looping about the bed as they cascaded from the ceiling. These now moved restlessly, and now fled abruptly up into the air, tugging at their rings, in invisible gusts of wind. The Duchess watched them. Outside the tent the birds sounded agitated too. Then, as the curtains were whipped in a particularly violent flurry, there came the tinkle of bells and the creaking of harness.

It was not easy to dress rapidly in those days. Cariola was nowhere about. The Duchess sent Antonio out to see what was happening. Shoving himself hastily into his clothes, he strode out of the tent, closing the flap behind him.

She was alone. She could not help lying there to listen. The sounds were louder now. They were anxious, worried, surreptitious sounds. Antonio was a long time in coming back. When he at last did so she could tell from his face that something was seriously wrong. He did not undress again, but stood above her, looking down at her.

"Some mischief is up," he said. "They are standing about, whispering to each other. You had better call Cariola and get dressed."

"What is it?"

"The Lord of Montferrato has turned back for Amalfi. I am afraid the others are going to follow."

"But they would not dare."

"They are frightened. Therefore they would dare anything. I'll find Cariola."

"Can I stop them?"

He hesitated, and shook his head slowly. Then he turned and went for Cariola.

When she at last came she looked awed and frightened.

"Is it true?" asked the Duchess.

"Yes," said Cariola. "Oh, what does it mean?" Her face showed that she knew what it meant.

"You may go, too, if you wish," said the Duchess.

"But where would I go?" The answer was anguished and

175

trapped. The Duchess straightened to look at her. "Poor Cariola," she said. "Then come with us."

"Where will you go?"

The Duchess started to explain, but something held her back. "Never mind," she said. Cariola's fingers were trembling more than her own. At last, dressed, she was ready to see for herself. At the flap of the tent she paused. Then, while Cariola thrust the flap aside, she stepped out through it, and blinked in the hard cruel light.

The encampment was on the crest of the hill. There had been perhaps thirty tents. Now there were at most fifteen. Below her she could catch glimpses of Montferrato's caravan weaving uncertainly down the bumpy road, surrounded by his company. They had no pinions flying. Clearly they were in furtive flight. The biggest coward, perhaps, went first.

She had only to look around to see what was happening. The servants were packing up. The nobles were nowhere to be seen. As she stood there, the rising wind toying with her skirt, she saw one of her precious following come out of one of the tents. He was in travelling costume. He saw her, hesitated, turned aside, and then came towards her. It was the Lord of Torcello, a very minor member of the company. There was something crestfallen and apologetic in his gait.

He, at least, had the decency to speak to her, though she had too much pride to listen to his excuses. He was a practical man. He had to go where the others followed. But even he was not concerned about her. He was concerned only to make his own conduct dignified. She could not bear to hear him. She dismissed him, to his obvious relief, and went back to her own tent. She sat there with Antonio and Cariola, listening to the sounds of departure, which were hushed and muted. Did they still think she had any power over them? If they had, they would not have dared to flee. They did dare to flee, therefore this furtiveness ill became them. But then few of us have the courage to run away in pomp.

Suddenly it was quiet. Even the birds were still. There was nothing left to agitate them.

She jumped up, with a glance at Antonio, and went outside.

"What does it mean?" she asked Antonio.

"I do not know." He went forward to investigate.

For the tents were still standing. They quivered in the off-sea gale.

Antonio came back to report that they were empty and abandoned. The company had left in some haste, Montferrato having drawn all of them rapidly after him.

"What did they know?" demanded the Duchess. "What can happen to us now, that is any worse than what has happened?"

Cariola looked anxiously at her mistress. The Duchess fell silent. Then she turned and climbed the hill, holding up her skirts. The others followed her. From the top of it they could see the several retinues of the various nobles, wending their way silently through the harsh landscape, inland, back to an Amalfi that was hers no longer and would always be theirs, no matter whom they had to sacrifice to keep it. She swallowed hard. There was no music now, no outriders, and no flags. What she looked down on was the flight of locusts. She turned to face the other way.

To her left lay Ancona. A ship was entering its harbour. It sparkled and glittered like a mirage of safety. To her right, down the coast, hidden by hills, lay Loreto. She looked at Antonio, who held her arm, to steady her.

"Which?" she asked. But she knew which she would choose. Her eyes went back to Ancona.

He shook his head. "Someone must have started this. The Cardinal must have agents here. If we went there, we would be intercepted at once. We could not defend ourselves. Better to pretend to make for Loreto, and then slip away by night. The players are still here. They will help us." He looked sternly at Cariola. But so long as she spoke to no one she was safe enough. Now there was no one for her to speak to. He shrugged.

"We *must* get there," she said.

He pressed her arm more firmly. "We shall."

An hour later, surrounded by the sparse company of musicians and drolls, who did not seem so merry either, they were headed away from safety, towards Loreto.

"But if the roads are watched, how shall we get back?" asked the Duchess.

177

"We will not use the roads." Antonio stood in the stirrups and gazed at the hills. "There are bandits here, and gipsies. We will trust to them." He called one of the players to him, murmured something and sent him off.

Both he and the Duchess watched the montebank post towards the hills. He was their messenger to hope.

Behind them, on the knoll, stood the abandoned encampment, its tents still unstruck, and flapping unattended in the wind. Later, the bandits would come down from the hills, to pillage what they could, Turkey carpets still on the earth floors, and serving vessels tumbled on the ground. The tents they would leave as too bulky. A wind might knock them over. Perhaps it might take the winter to destroy them, or the season's sun would rot their fabric away. Meanwhile they stood along the crest, like a row of architectural ghosts, and the wind flapping through them made eerie and minatory noises.

Ancona fell behind. Out of sight of it, and the Duchess drew closer to Antonio.

v

Antonio was right. There were agents in those hills. What he did not know, and what the agents themselves did not know, was that there were two sets of them. Like a farmer, the Cardinal was driving cattle down a narrow funnel towards the yard, and he counted his brother with the cattle. But the Cardinal moved only behind the scenes. Of this Ferdinand knew nothing.

Night and day he had posted across Italy, with Marcantonio, two more bravos, and Bosola. Now he drew rein on a rocky outcropping above the Ancona plain.

Bosola looked at him warily. He had never spent so much time with Ferdinand before. He realized Ferdinand was like Marcantonio. Even when his head was clear, the man was physically insane. And of all the forms of insanity, the physical is the hardest to control and the most intemperate. Like any other kind of insanity, it has its own logic, and its only means of self-expression is violence. And an insane body cannot be reasoned with. Violence is amenable only to violence, and Bosola had no strength.

178

Certainly Ferdinand's mad rush to Loreto had been peculiar. For one thing, he would not let Bosola leave him, which made Bosola uneasy, for though he might appear to be serving Ferdinand, he knew whom he was really serving, and he was supposed to go on to Ancona. He did not quite dare to do that. In his present mood Ferdinand might destroy anyone for any trifle. Nor was travelling with Marcantonio pleasant. The man had nasty little ways to enjoy himself when he was bored. Men like Marcantonio lived by choice in those torture chambers of the mind where Bosola lived only by necessity.

Or did he? He no longer knew.

Now they looked down on the deserted camp. They had already met the noble caravans returning to Amalfi. Ferdinand saw that was his brother's work. He spurred on, until his horse's blood dropped on the road. Figures came out of the tents, and looking up to the horsemen on the ridge, themselves mounted and fled. Ferdinand and his company came down on the deserted tents.

Ferdinand strode moodily through them, kicking aside here an ewer, there a rug the robbers had been in the act of rolling up.

"How did they know we were coming?" he stormed. "How?"

"Perhaps they did not."

Marcantonio had found some wine in an ewer. He sat down with it. Ferdinand looked at him contemptuously.

"Where have they gone? Loreto?" he demanded. "Why Loreto?"

Bosola had said nothing about Ancona. That was on the Cardinal's advice. He knew he must get there, but he did not know how to get away.

"We must not alarm my sister," said Ferdinand. "My brother would let them off. In other words, he would keep them for his own purposes. We must take them by surprise, and him." He grinned. He would let Marcantonio have Antonio. He had already promised him that. He was content to watch. Marcantonio knew so many things to do. He would have the Duchess watch also.

"So," he grunted. He turned to Bosola. "Ride after them.

179

We will follow through the hills." He grinned. "I know whose thing you are. We will keep a watch on you. We shall know what to do when you find them."

Bosola hesitated and glanced towards Ancona. Ferdinand followed the glance, but said nothing. "Go," he said. Marcantonio put down the ewer of wine and stood up, hands on his hips, and stared at Bosola.

"Well, go," he echoed his master.

There was nothing else for Bosola to do. He mounted his horse, and turned it aside on the Loreto road. It was a little after noon. The sun stood to one side of the meridian, and both he and the horse poured with sweat. All afternoon he passed through the landscape, and saw nothing. The Cardinal would have some message waiting for him at Ancona, so he must get there, but he knew better than to make a break for it until darkness fell. For though the landscape looked empty, Ferdinand and Marcantonio were grimly following him along the ridge. They were itching for violence. They trembled with desire for it. Any false move from him, and they would string him up behind his horse and send it galloping through the stony dust. The only thing he could do was to dawdle. That would make Ferdinand furious, but Ferdinand wished to remain concealed. His brother might also have agents here. He would not descend the hills to make Bosola go faster.

So Bosola's pursuit of the Duchess and Antonio became an agonized amble. At dusk he would make for the shore, on whose sands riding would be swift. But he dared do nothing until then. He was a prisoner in a landscape without walls.

Thus the curious triple pursuit went on all afternoon, each side dawdling so as not to reach its goal, and each side moving furtively in the bright, paranoic sun. Towards evening the shadows began to turn purple. They lengthened. The sparkle of the sea grew dull. The leaves of the olive trees rattled crisply in an off-shore breeze. Only an occasional church bell cracked the silence.

Fortunately there would be no twilight, for in those regions dusk did not descend. It plummeted over the unwary like a gladiator's net.

It came.

Bosola instantly spurred his horse down the first *arroyo* leading towards the sea.

VI

The Duchess and Antonio had not been able to dawdle slowly enough. They had already long since passed the point in the hills where the local gipsies were to meet them. Darkness caught them under the bastions of Loreto.

The Duchess looked up at that holy city with despair.

It reared out of its olive groves like a prison, framed in the hard, green spears of poisonous agave plants. Its olive groves were ghostly. The bastions were built of narrow-laid rose brick. The windows were blind. The dome and campanile brandished themselves like weapons. It was huge, unyielding, and unsafe. It was not a sanctuary, but a trap. The battlements of the cathedral apse seemed to be mounted with cannon. And it was utterly silent. There was no Virgin and no mercy there. That the Duchess felt instinctively.

Antonio touched the bridle of her palfrey. "Now," he said. His voice was a tense whisper.

She looked back at the carts, which the players had taken care of. Now the players were melting into the landscape. The carts stood abandoned on the road.

These were her household goods.

"No," said Antonio gently. "We can take nothing." One of the players rode up to him. "Come. He knows the way."

"But they will find them."

"Better they find them, than us," said Antonio. He tugged at the bridle. It was still trimmed with little tinkling bells. Taking his knife from his boot, he cut them off. They fell one by one to the road, tinkled, and lay still. That, more than anything else, impressed the Duchess with how shorn she was of any last vestige of power.

Shivering, she nudged her horse into the shadows of the road.

"Get down," ordered Antonio.

"What?"

"You cannot ride properly side-saddle. It will be rough country. Get down."

She slid from the horse, and beckoned Cariola to follow.

181

Antonio bent down, and with a quick slash of his knife, ripped up her skirt and petticoats. The Duchess flinched.

Cariola stared. Antonio threw her his knife. Obediently she followed suit. Then they mounted again, astride. The player came forward and whispered to Antonio. Then the party set off up a narrow ravine. There was no moon as yet. It would rise late. The way was difficult. When they reached the ridge it would be easier. The Duchess was dulled by fatigue. That was perhaps merciful. None of them spoke. There were only the four of them. The players had tactfully disappeared into the landscape, having their own hides to save.

The carts and wagons stood behind them, dark and forsaken in the road. There were things in them the Duchess would never see again.

As they climbed higher, Loreto spread out below them. Then they reached the ridge, and plunged into the wood that ran along its crest. The player seemed certain of the way, and they had to trust him. Their worst fear now was ambush or *banditti* unknown to Antonio.

The player was almost a dwarf. He sat on a horse too big for him, like an imp of darkness with saucer eyes, riding the nightmare through a dream. His teeth were chattering with cold. For the night became as cold as the darkness was sudden. The clammy breeze whipped into the Duchess's split skirt, and oozed against her naked flesh. She was already sore from riding astride, but did not dare to slow down. As for Cariola, she was terrified and did not know what she did. She had no choice but to follow.

It was midnight when they came to the meeting place. The Duchess blessed Antonio's obsession with gipsies now. They rode into an open clearing, but found nobody there. The moon was up, and the shadows of the trees were like the shadows of men waiting. The Duchess was bewildered. She was sure they had gone astray.

Antonio dismissed the player. In the silence the chink of coins was audible. As the player rode back towards his fellows at Loreto, Antonio stood in his stirrups and putting his fingers to his mouth, whistled like a bird of prey. The whistle echoed without an answer.

"What do we do now?" asked the Duchess.

"We wait. They will not come until they are sure the player is gone. Here we trust no one."

They waited. The horses stirred fretfully. From time to time Antonio peered about him. Then the shadows cast by the trees began to move. After all, they might have been betrayed. Why should they not be?

Antonio grunted and jumped down from his horse, disappearing into the shadows. It was as though he had vanished and left only his empty saddle. The Duchess stared at it, fascinated. Behind her, Cariola began to sob. They could hear sounds in the wood. Even the horses seemed to shy at something.

Antonio came back with some nondescript men. These were the gipsies. They were not so colourful as the gipsies of Amalfi. They were the scuttle-butt and rag-pickers of the region. But looking into their eyes, the Duchess trusted them. Antonio took her bridle.

"Dismount," he said. "And Cariola, too."

Cariola did not want to dismount. The Duchess jumped down, scarcely able to stand from so much riding. Unwillingly Cariola followed. Together they walked softly across the clearing into the safety of the trees, the gipsies leading the horses behind them. They went on for some way, and came to another clearing. There were more men waiting here. One of them brought forward a lantern.

Antonio took from him a bundle, and led the Duchess and Cariola behind a shrub.

"These are men's clothes," he said. "Change into them quickly."

The Duchess stared at him.

"They are looking for two women and a man, whoever they are. Go on."

Cariola refused. Antonio stuffed the bundle into her arms. He was angry. "These men are *banditti*," he said. "There are no women here. As one of them, you may be able to get through to Ancona. There is no other way." He turned and strode out of the rustling shrubs, leaving a lantern on the ground. Its light shone up in their faces. The Duchess and Cariola looked at each other.

Her skirt was ruined anyway. With an impatient gesture, the Duchess began to tear off her clothes. Shocked, Cariola came to help her.

Ten minutes later, and she was changed. Her poor torn dress and bodice lay on the ground beneath her. She wore hose, a doublet, soft leather knee boots which could be turned up to her thighs, spurs, and a short cloak. The clothes for some reason made her feel safer. For a moment she wondered what it was to be a man. It was like dressing up. But, as she tucked her hair under a large cap, she grew solemn again, and turned to Cariola.

"Now you," she said.

Cariola was not to be persuaded. She was genteel. Even if her life depended upon it, she could not bring herself to dress up so. It made the Duchess furious.

When Antonio returned, he was well pleased with her appearance. He smiled, examining her. With Cariola he was not pleased at all. But there was nothing to be done with her, except to disguise her in a cloak. They could not very well leave her behind, and not even the threat of abandoning her could make her change her mind. Terror had made her stubborn.

"You will be more comfortable that way," Antonio told the Duchess. He helped her vault into the saddle, and the company got under way. Her spurs seemed to drag her heels, and the small rattle the rowels made echoed like an explosion.

Quietly, led by the chief of the *banditti*, they wound their way in and out of trees and open spaces along the ridges. Once or twice they passed a dusty stream bed. It was too dark to break into a gallop. Antonio's horse stepped smartly beside her. From time to time she fell into a stupor, lolling in her saddle. Occasionally they caught a glimpse of the moon on the sea.

She did not know how long they travelled. With her legs she clutched the belly of her pony, and she dozed.

She woke abruptly. Antonio had his hand on the bridle of her horse.

"What is it?"

"Something ahead. We shall have to go carefully."

Peering into the darkness she saw some sort of reflected glow against far-distant trees.

"Where are we?"

184

"Two hours from Ancona, at the most." He shrugged his shoulders, but she could see how drawn his face was.

"It might be agents?"

"It might," he said shortly. Very cautiously he led her horse forward, as it picked its way over the rough forest floor. They were among laurels now. At the nearest touch the trees would shake like a tower of bells.

The glow became ruddier. Whatever it was, they were coming too close to it. These *banditti* knew how to move through the woods like shadows. So did their horses. But the Duchess held her breath. Then she was aware of a curious, high-pitched incessant whine, and the boles of the trees whirled with small torn shadows. She shivered.

The company halted. They could only pray that none of the horses would make any sound. The chiefs and Antonio held a muttered conference. Then Antonio rode a little ahead, slipped from his horse, and, dagger in hand, disappeared into the trees. It was an anxious few minutes until he came back.

"Well?" she asked.

"Dead drunk and snoring to the world," he said.

"Who?"

"Some bravos, by the look of them."

"After us?"

"Yes." He did not tell her he had seen Ferdinand. Apparently they had camped here for the night, and fallen asleep after too much wine. Their fire had disturbed a colony of bats. The bats shrieked and wobbled in and out of a charred tree, in and out of the flames. The air was full of the stench of them. Ferdinand was sprawled full length, next to Marcantonio. There were two others. If Ferdinand was here they were in double peril, but he saw no reason to say so.

The company moved on, carefully skirting the hollow in which the fire burned. The horses made no sound. In half an hour they were safely away.

He breathed a sigh of relief.

The Duchess was too tired to sigh. For her the rest of the journey passed in a coma, from which she was jostled only when the company came to a halt on a rise of ground. She stirred and opened her eyes.

185

It was almost dawn. The world was restive and silvery. A cock crowed. The sky was green and rose, and seemed about to shatter. Carioli was snoring on her horse. The Duchess looked around her. The *banditti* were fading away into the woods, just as her courtiers had done. It alarmed her.

"What is it?"

Antonio came up beside her. "They can come no farther," he said. "It would not be safe." He pointed ahead of him. "Look!" She looked and could see nothing. She nudged her horse on to follow Antonio's. The grove behind them was already deserted.

Below them lay Ancona and the sea. She could not believe it. The white walls of the city shone like a haven.

"It is only a quarter of a mile," said Antonio. "We are almost free."

She felt weak. "What will it be like?"

"We will be together," he said simply. "We have only to find a ship."

She understood. It did not matter where they went. Without dismounting, they touched, in sight of freedom. Somehow they had managed to break through. Yet she was a little afraid. Who would they be now? She was the Duchess of Amalfi no longer. What would they do?

"Let's race," she said. She wanted to laugh.

He glanced at her. "Well, why not?" He smiled. "We must wake Cariola, though. She must ache."

Of the aching of her own body the Duchess had become unaware. They wakened Cariola, and then set pell-mell down the slope, urging from the horses a last tired burst of speed, hit the plain in a shower of white dust, and whirled towards the city. Now the Duchess really laughed, and even on the wind, she could hear that Antonio had joined her. Money chinked in the saddle-bags, and Cariola was left a length behind.

Bosola also would be there. He had sold her jewels. With the gold from that they might take ship anywhere. In that quick silent dawn the whole world opened out, and there they were in it, together, after all.

186

It would be impossible to try to understand the Cardinal.
He did not even try to understand himself. Instead he made use
of himself, exactly as he made use of others, waiting to see
what he would do, and then taking advantage of his own
actions. At the moment, for his own reasons, he needed delay.
Therefore he made use of his finer feelings. He did so
sardonically.

This ability to make use of himself was what made him so
tricky and so difficult to defeat. For though his general
strategy may have been predictable, his specific behaviour
frequently was not. Other men are at the mercy of their whims.
His whims were at the mercy of him.

It was his custom to hand over the violent outcome of his
plots to his brother, as the Inquisition handed over the condemned to the secular arm. He was by no means pleased at
Ferdinand's departure from Rome with Bosola and Marcantonio. He knew what it meant; and to tell the truth, felt
sorry at the outcome of this latest of his plots. Besides, he
needed time, for he had preparations to make. Therefore he
sent two messengers to Ancona: one, publicly, to the Duke;
the other, privately, to Bosola. Then he departed for
Naples.

Bosola reached Ancona after the messengers, but before the
Duchess. Fear had hurtled him across the sands and the narrow
cliff roads. He knew what it was to be caught between two
masters. He could always explain to Ferdinand that he had
followed the Duchess, who had turned back. He could never
explain to the Cardinal.

Therefore, though it was the middle of the night, he went at
once to the house of the Cardinal's agent there, which was outside the walls. The Cardinal's letter awaited him. It told him
to take the Duchess prisoner, and to escort her across Italy and
back to Naples. The agent would arrange for a body of armed
men, should Ferdinand prove difficult. At Naples he would
receive further orders.

There was no question as to which master he would obey,
for even Ferdinand finally obeyed the Cardinal. It was for this

reason that when the Duchess and Antonio galloped across the plain, Bosola was waiting for them. A servant boy had called him, as soon as the figures appeared. Since no one seemed to be in pursuit, Bosola rode out to meet them.

To his surprise, they were so glad to see him that they asked for no explanation. After all, to them he meant freedom, and the exhilaration of their escape had made them as innocent as children.

It was a new experience for him to be greeted so rapturously. It made him blink. Only Cariola, when she came up with the others, stared at him sullenly. But then she was clearly crusted with fatigue.

He was relieved. It meant that he need invent nothing. He led them back to the agent's house, to wait an hour until the town gate opened. They went willingly. No doubt they wished to take cover. As they rode along, Antonio frequently glanced back at the hills. It was only by self-restraint that Bosola prevented himself from doing the same. He went to consult with the agent as soon as they arrived. He did not know how he would handle Antonio, but he must put the matter in advance before Ferdinand should arrive.

There he was interrupted abruptly by Cariola. Cariola acted as though he were not there. She was acutely embarrassed, her skirt still slit. She asked if perhaps there might not be a dress or two in the house. That was understandable. Dressed as they were, they made a peculiar company. The agent, as it turned out, was delighted to oblige, for a fee. He went upstairs and stripped his wife, to her very voluble indignation. Bosola looked towards the ceiling and grinned. The agent returned not only with his wife's best black for the Duchess, but with her second best, for Cariola.

She took them without a word, dourly. He waved her out of the room. No doubt the Duchess made a charming boy, but these clothes would suit her better. For the moment it would be best if he pretended to fall in with their plans.

An hour later, when he went down to the parlour that had been turned over to them, he found Antonio and the Duchess asleep in each other's arms, the agent's wife's dress trailing grandly over the floor, and Cariola dozing noisily in a chair.

He waked them, and they set out in high spirits for the town gate, perhaps five hundred yards away.

Antonio and the Duchess laughed and chatted merrily. The day was certainly a a splendid one. The dew still caught the sun. There was the smell of iodine in the air, and they could hear the surf.

They reached the main road, and turned towards the gate. Here, because of the shadows of the walls, it was damp and cool. There were one or two people on the road ahead of them, a peasant with his cart, a traveller. The Duchess had her documents with her. These she passed to Antonio, who intended to present them with his own forged credentials. They rode confidently under the gate. Beyond they could see the street of the town, slanting upwards towards a market place. It was like an opening into another world.

Antonio went to parley with the keeper. They scarcely noticed that there were more loiterers than usual. Antonio was gone a long time.

The Duchess became nervous. She snapped her fingers impatiently and looked about her with feigned indifference. The laughter began to go out of her eyes. The borrowed dress did not suit her. To Bosola's eye she was no longer the beauty she had been even a year ago. This early morning sun turned her complexion to chalk, and her hair was too fine not to receive more care than it had had. He hated pathos. He turned away.

Antonio came slowly out of the gate.

"We cannot enter," he said quietly.

Bosola looked instantly towards the still empty hills.

"What do you mean, we cannot enter? Is the man stupid!" The Duchess spurred her horse forward. Antonio caught the reins.

"You are banished from the territories of Ancona," he said. "By order of the Duke."

"By order of my brother, you mean." The Duchess's voice was shrill. Indeed the matter was a shock even to Bosola. He must act quickly now, or Ferdinand would be upon him. He turned his horse aside.

"None the less, we cannot enter." Antonio waved towards

189

the gate, where five guards barred the way with muskets. They were gaudy in striped German uniforms, and the muskets glittered in the pearl-grey light.

It was as though panic danced among them with a giggling face. They did not know where to look. That mocking figure was everywhere. They could neither advance nor retreat.

Off to the left a boat put out to sea. They all watched it. It was a small felucca with a red patched sail. It was probably headed for Dalmatia.

Exasperated, the Duchess tugged at the reins of her horse, and wheeled him around, so that her back was to the city, and to the boat. Antonio hesitated, and then leaped into the saddle and followed her.

Bosola noticed that Cariola was watching him. He did not care for the look in her eyes. She might say anything, if she gave way to hysteria. He suggested quickly that they take shelter from prying eyes at the agent's house, which doubled as a sort of inn. That is where they went. They could not stay there for long. The Duchess had presented herself in her own person. Word that she had arrived would quickly spread. Nor would they be allowed to stay in Ancona's territory for longer than at most an hour. It was the Cardinal's mischief, obviously.

Yet in a way it made Bosola's task easier. There would be no awkwardness now about the boat. His only task was somehow to remove Antonio. They held a conference in the parlour. In this emergency, the Duchess and Antonio seemed to accept him as a matter of course. That might make things simpler for him, or it might not.

For the moment he excused himself and went to speak once more to the agent. It was essential now to round up a body of bravos as soon as possible. They must arrive before Ferdinand and Marcantonio could intercept them.

When he returned the Duchess and Antonio were alone in the parlour. The Duchess seemed to have regained her composure. She had become deliberately impersonal.

Bosola suggested that of the two brothers the Cardinal was the more reasonable, and that Antonio should come with him to Rome. The Cardinal might give him sanctuary. The Duchess watched him while he spoke. She might even have agreed, but at that moment there was a clatter outside. Antonio went to the window to look out.

"Soldiers," he said. "Or *banditti*."

They both turned to Bosola, questioningly.

"I had them hired," explained Bosola. "You will need protection against Ferdinand. "I will go see to them."

Reluctantly he left the room, and went out into the court. The men provided by the agent were a savage bunch. Such ex-soldiers lurk in the back alleys of dingy towns, and if they do not become robbers turn their hands to any violence they are paid for.

In the room he had left Antonio was also listening to the clatter in the courtyard. "Do you believe him?" he asked.

The Duchess shook her head. "I don't know what to believe." She hesitated. "But I do not trust my brothers, either of them. They will give you no amnesty. They want you in their hands. No, you will not go to Rome."

"I will go if you wish."

Her voice rose despite herself. "I do not wish. I am still Duchess. They will not dare to touch me. They will only take me prisoner and return me to Amalfi. They want control of Amalfi. Let them have it. Bosola has the money from the sale of my jewels. You know these hills. I will send you to Milan, to beg for help there. Perhaps that will frighten them."

"There is no help in Milan."

"It will be a pretence. You can still get away. Actually wait for me at Ravello or Arosa. We do not know the people here. We know them there." She sat down. "They will kill you if you stay. In Amalfi we are in our own territory. Do you remember the gipsies?"

He nodded.

"Why should we not join them? We can get away there, somehow."

"I cannot see you a prisoner."

"I cannot see you dead," she snapped. She raised her hands in a helpless gesture. He hesitated and then kissed them.

"Very well." He made a wry face. "I cannot think of you as a prisoner."

"Go to Arosa, and you will not see me a prisoner long. Hurry. We have not much time."

He held her tightly. She scarcely felt it. She had frozen herself, in order to keep calm. Ferdinand loved her. If he found her alone he would do nothing to harm her. She had only to live patiently until they reached Amalfi. Then, somehow, she would be free. But Antonio she had to send away, for both their sakes.

She summoned Bosola. "You have the moneys from my jewels," she said. "Pay them over to Antonio."

Bosola glanced at Antonio.

"I am sending him to Milan. He will be safer there. Then we will await my brother."

Bosola stared.

The Duchess stamped her foot. "Do as I say," she ordered.

Bosola was only too willing to do so. For him it solved the problem of Antonio. Antonio rode away at once. The Duchess did not go outside to say good-bye. She could not bear to do that. But she stood at the window of the parlour, watching him canter across the plain. He was soon out of sight.

No one intercepted him. She sighed with a relief that only partially stilled terror, and turned to face the empty room. She would have been lost without Bosola. Cariola was useless. Fright had made her ill. She found Bosola soothing. Impatiently she waited for Ferdinand.

But it was not Ferdinand who came.

VIII

The Cardinal reached Naples that morning, travelling incognito. It was a nuisance to go at all, but there were times when he trusted no one but himself, and this was one of them. Fastidiously he stepped his horse through the filth of the streets, towards the convent, glanced up at its bland walls, and went inside.

It was scarcely dawn, but he knew that Sor Juana would be up. He found her sitting at her writing desk, gazing into space. She seemed subdued and disheartened, but she had a vein of iron in her that held her up, whether she would droop or not.

"Take me to the child," he said. He saw no reason to bother with preliminaries, and besides, he had been riding all night. He was too tired for either compliments or verse.

She glanced at him and then rose. Something of complicity in her manner impressed him. It had not been there before. There were times when his own creatures bored him. She had been better before she had grown afraid of him. They would never be able to talk easily again, and there were many underlings in this world, but so few people to talk to. He shrugged his shoulders as he followed her.

The dorter of the nursery was shadowy. She put her fingers to her lips, like a statue of silence, and they threaded their way through the quiet beds towards a farther door. There the child slept in its bed in a separate room.

He looked down at it with interest. "It has grown," he said. It did not look like a ducal child. But it was old enough now so that features had begun to emerge from the shapeless putty of its baby face. It occurred to him for the first time that the child was his nephew. He had not thought of that before.

He reached down and picked it up.

"What are you doing?" demanded Sor Juana. Her voice was shrill with alarm. She almost sounded like its mother, and he glanced at her with curiosity. But her face, as always, was a bland mask.

"It is no longer safe here. I am taking it away."

"It is quite safe here."

"You have a brother. Do you mean to tell me that any secret is safe from him?"

Sor Juana was silent. Something in the rustle of her garments told him she was suddenly afraid. "What is happening?" she asked.

"Nothing is happening. I gave you a trust. You violated it."

"He broke his way in here. There was nothing I could do."

That is what he wanted to know: whether she would betray Bosola or her ambitions first. "You have an all too accessible convent," he said dryly.

She looked at the sleepy bundle in his arms, whose legs dangled limply down to his sash. "What will you do with it?"

"Make him a ruling prince. He is too young to be grateful. That is perhaps just as well. Gratitude is a treacherous thing."

The Cardinal looked up at her blandly. She said nothing and dropped her eyes.

"But it needs care," said Sor Juana.

"You need not worry," he said. "You are a capable woman." He shifted the weight of the child, dandling it up and down. It was a pretty child. But it was a Sanducci. There was a sallow sharpness already visible in its eyes. He wondered what sort of person it would make, should it grow to maturity.

"You will have your convent very soon now. And who knows? Perhaps a new patron."

A little light came into her eyes. Well, why should she not have it? She would be useful there. He left her staring down at the empty miniature bed, and went back to his horse. The child was well trained. It made no sound at all. It was a nuisance to have care of it, but he could not be absolutely sure of Bosola. The man was soft inside, as soft as Sor Juana was hard.

He glanced at the Bay of Naples. The early morning light made it look viscous and dangerous. With a contented nod at its islands, he rode on. The child was his.

IX

Terror kept Cariola to a small room upstairs in the inn. Like many foolish women, she saw more than she was supposed to see. The room was dark and had only one narrow window. She lay on its bed, with her feet planted precisely together, tapered toes up, staring at the ceiling.

The arrival of the soldiers only confirmed her fears. She heard them in the courtyard, and was sure she would be murdered within the hour. She was too tired to care, but conscience gnawed at her.

There is a point beyond which fear leaves us in a certain peace. As it presses maniacally on the arteries at the sides of our head, something explodes inside us, and our head is abruptly clear. A jerky logic hacks its way through the jungle of our thoughts, clearing away the underbrush around a lost shrine. It is then we at last feel eager to sacrifice to conscience.

194

The process is involuntary. We follow it whether we would or not. Cariola got to her feet, hating the cheap rustle of her borrowed dress, and stole out into the corridor.

It was empty and silent, but the floor-boards creaked. She moved dreamily to the head of the stairs. She could see Bosola below her, whispering to a man she did not know. She drew back until they went away. Then, running slyly down the stairs, afraid of being intercepted, she slipped into the parlour.

The Duchess stood at the windows, looking out at the bravos in the court. As Cariola shut the door softly behind her, she turned.

"What is it?" she asked wearily.

"Madam, I must tell you something." Cariola looked round for Antonio, but he was not there.

The Duchess waited a moment, sighed, and then shrugged. "Very well."

"It is about Bosola."

"Well, what about Bosola?"

"He is the Cardinal's agent, Madam." As soon as she got it out Cariola felt better. Of Bosola she did not think at all. She did not even think of the Duchess. A good conscience makes us selfish, and she had removed the only bad on hers.

"Oh!" The Duchess turned back to the window. Cariola became restless. Suddenly she wondered if she had done wrong. Then the Duchess's voice came to her, small, calm and remote. "Have you known this long?"

Cariola could not answer.

The Duchess turned on her. Her eyes sparkled with anger. "Have you known this long?" she demanded, without raising her voice.

Cariola still could not answer.

"You were his mistress."

"Yes." For some reason this hurt to admit. Why did it hurt, and not the confession? Cariola did not know. She was on the verge of tears.

The Duchess smiled sadly, came over, and took Cariola's arm. "It does not matter now," she said. "But do not stay here. Go back to your room. I will call you when I need you." Her voice was flat and impersonal.

195

The door opened and Bosola came in. He looked quickly at Cariola, and then away.

The Duchess was still ominously calm. "You need not pretend any more," she told him. "I know what you are."

He looked taken aback. But the agent stood behind him. He cleared his throat.

"I have come to take you prisoner," he said.

"On whose orders? Or do you serve more than one master?"

"On the Cardinal's orders."

"And where am I to be taken?"

"To Naples."

The Duchess was relieved. Naples meant Amalfi. Indeed, being taken prisoner was little more than a safe conduct back to Amalfi. And beyond Amalfi lay Ravello and Arosa.

"How considerate of my brother to save me from my brother," said the Duchess. She turned to Cariola. "Do not stand there. Why do you not move closer to your lover?" Suddenly she smiled wanly. She had not missed the look of terror in Cariola's eyes. She felt sorry for Cariola. Perhaps the woman had meant no harm. It was only something that had happened. "There is nothing left to pack. When do we leave?"

"At once." She had no compunction in making use of him, as a safe conduct across Italy. In this age of universal betrayal, why should she not?

They left in half an hour.

The journey to Loreto had taken a month. The return journey took eight days. The Duchess rode ahead on a palfrey, at first closely guarded, then less so. Cariola rode behind. Bosola skulked at the rear of the company. The Duchess felt almost light-hearted. They had no way of knowing that Antonio was not in Milan, but posting ahead of her. She was a little hysterical, a little jubilant. She knew every cranny of Amalfi. Even if they held her close prisoner, she would be able to escape. In perhaps two weeks she would once more see Antonio.

For the rest, she was rather sadly amused, that those she had thought most loyal should prove to be least so. But the matter did not unduly bother her. If her brothers had been devious, now she would be most devious.

She had no way of knowing that Ferdinand and Marcantonio followed hungrily along the ridges, always keeping their distance, but always there. Neither had Bosola.

The trip was fatiguing. But when they came out behind Naples the Duchess felt exultant. It seemed to her that she came closer to freedom every day.

It was for this reason that she submitted to everything. No doubt the others thought her cowed. She was not cowed. She was triumphant. Somewhere south in these hills Antonio was already plotting her release, and only waiting for the signal she would somehow contrive to make.

That evening she was taken down to a boat, and boarded it gladly. The boat set out from shore, its sails unfurled. She stood at the poop, watching the Sorrentine peninsula. Amalfi lay beyond it. She paced up and down, as the boat drew into the centre of the bay.

There unexpectedly the boat ploughed straight ahead through the flaccid water, rather than turning south.

Bosola stood beside her.

"Why do we stand out to sea?" she demanded. "This is not the way to Amalfi."

"We are not going to Amalfi, Madam."

"What?"

"I have orders to take you to Ischia."

For the first and last time the Duchess lost all self-control. She clutched the rail and screamed.

Before her towered the peak of Epomeo.

NINE

There are four islands in the Bay of Naples: Capri, Procida, Vivara, and Ischia. No one ever went to Capri if he could help it. Procida was a rambling landscape with one small fishing village and a half-hearted citadel. Vivara was deserted, and lay submerged like a dead whale half awash, rolling and twisting with the tide.

Ischia, however, was another matter. It was the largest of the islands, and very fair. It was the echo of Vesuvius, a volcanic mountain that erupted when Vesuvius did not. The mountain was called Epomeo, and dominated the view. It was always green, because it caught the fogs and mists. Wisps of cloud hung round its summit, where monks had hollowed a monastery out of the living rock. Below the monastery, a third of the way down, lay a tropical rain forest five feet tall. For the rest, the island was forested with stone pines, olive trees, and oak. Its wines were famous. Its fishing villages were prosperous. Its people were stubborn, proud, and wild. But this separate and self-reliant island had one dusky feature. That feature was the Castello. It was widely feared. No one had ever escaped from there.

The towns of Ischia nestled at the foot of steep cliffs, on the Vesuvius side of the island. The Castello rose from a slab-sided rock five hundred feet off shore, connected with the mainland by a causeway. It was impregnable. It could be reached only by steep tunnels carved through the dripping, naked rock, spaced at intervals with portcullises which rattled down from the roof at an instant's warning. There was no other way into the Castello whatsoever. The cliffs were unscalable and had no toeholds and no beaches.

The castle itself was enormous, and rambled all over the top of the rock. Parts of it were already in ruins, but that made no

198

difference. The cliffs themselves were defence enough. There had once been a convent here, but now it was abolished and had fallen into decay. So had the huge church attached to it. Tunnels and dungeons ran everywhere through the naked rock. The castle itself rose above the former convent, and had been tricked out with Renaissance and Baroque decorations, to make it habitable.

Even so nobody had inhabited it for thirty years, for it was a gloomy, damp, and haunted place. It was here the Cardinal had decided to hold the Duchess, while he examined the minute indecisions of his own mind. From its windows she might look across to the mainland, if she wished. And if anything happened to her there, the world need never know exactly what.

He did not know quite why he did this, except that death is final, and she was his sister. Perhaps he wanted to shirk events. Perhaps he wanted only to inflame Ferdinand.

But the Duchess, as her little band of gaolers led her across the causeway from Ischia, thought she understood very well. The sun beat hot upon her, and though she walked proudly, with her head up, she gripped Cariola's hand. They were two women alone together now, against a man's world. The boots of the gaolers echoed like metal on the paving of the causeway. On either side the water was slabs of gelatine. You could see the black fish swimming in orderly fashion at different levels far below. The townspeople watched from the shore. The company entered the black hole in the cliff that was the entrance. Here they took donkeys, and rode quietly up through the dark, damp tunnels, lit fitfully by flares. It was like being swallowed alive.

In half an hour they emerged abruptly into an open space tumbled with weeds. Even though light shafts were let down through the rock, to air and light the tunnel every hundred yards, the sunlight out here was cruel. It made them blink, and the company was silent. The Duchess looked around her curiously. Here, she knew, she would die. She glanced up at the citadel ahead, on the topmost pinnacle of the cliff.

And yet, what mockery, the gardeners and servants were lined up on either side of the top entrance to the tunnel, along with the brightly striped and plume-hatted guards, and bowed down before her as she passed, even as the portcullis behind her rattled down into place, and the guards' pistols and crisp daggers glittered in the sun.

II

The Castello had the peculiarity that everyone in it was a prisoner, including her own guards. And this none of them seemed to realize. As men who take Orders placidly think their monastery is the world, and the world a monastery too, so do soldiers, bravos, bandits, gipsies, guards. We live in plural worlds, and think our own unique. Each man's profession is his universe. Only those who stand outside consider that pathetic. So women will never understand the vastness of even the smallest man's affairs.

And women are masochists. They see sadism through the wrong end of the telescope, and so naturally it looks small to them, just as women look small to men. And of all forms of discipline our preferences and predilections are the most inexorable. Thus Bosola.

Though the Duchess did not know it, there were other prisoners in the citadel, held far underground, or, if they were favoured and could still walk, permitted an hour's airing on the lower platforms. These Bosola visited, on the invitation of the Commandant, for military life has few amusements, and boredom finds one in the tortures of the damned. His captives had been in the citadel for two weeks. But the Commandant and his guard had been there for five years. There was little enough for them to do but toy with the prisoners. The only difference between a prisoner and a soldier is that the soldier may occasionally claim leave. It is not a difference so large as one might suppose, for freedom of action is success, and everything else is failure. Soldiers know what the world thinks of them. Therefore, in their own way, in time of peace, they bicker, gossip, and have their revenge in a series of little wars.

The Cardinal might have his nightingales, his bravos and violent men, but the Commandant rode hard on a posse of vultures. That is a harder and more exhausting game. He did not sleep easily. His name was d'Avalos. He was a rusty fifty.

He had to talk to someone and trusted no one. Therefore he made a friend of Bosola. He liked to watch. Bosola was a new specimen, who filled him with curiosity.

Bosola saw the matter differently. For the first time in his life he had others at his mercy. He almost liked that. There are times when it was a pleasure to be vile. Any man who has ever been a prisoner longs to be a guard. Children like to re-enact the crucifixion. Rejected lovers dream of murder. The tortured are fascinated by the rack. In their sleep the humbled pull down whole towns.

He watched the Duchess narrowly. Here, stripped of the trappings of authority, she was not much. Beauty cannot survive a prison pallor. Authority has shallow roots. Rip it out of its natural environment, cut off its nourishment, and it withers and dies.

Yet something kept him from tormenting her. He could not know what it was, for it was personal authority, and to him authority was never personal, nor was human dignity innate.

Her conduct made him suspicious. He could not know why she did not whine or why he could not pull her down. Her face seemed calm with hope. Often she would pace down the barren corridors, open to the sea and spotted with moss, to a broken window looking towards the blue cliffs of Sorrento. At such times her face would have a curiously withdrawn sweetness. Antonio was there.

Bosola saw only that she was untouchable. He began to hate her, just for that. He suspected she knew of some plot, and so he spied upon her. Yet he could discover nothing. In chagrin he vented his spleen upon Cariola. Her he followed, too. Her conduct puzzled him.

It puzzled Cariola no less. She had betrayed herself and him, and yet she was still here. Only as the boat put in under the citadel had she given way to panic. For the rest she felt numb. She felt condemned. Even her mistress could not give her comfort, for she had betrayed her mistress. She did not understand anything. She did not know why she had spoken out. It only meant that she had lost even Bosola. Yet part of her was still detached and reasonable. She fought down panic, knowing that should she give way there would be no one to help her. But her frightened eyes watched everything. She could not sleep. She suffocated when she tried. She became a night wanderer.

Indeed there were many things to be afraid of in that place. The guards did nothing to impede either the Duchess or herself, so long as they did not penetrate as far as the tunnel gate. So little by little she found them all out, pursed her lips, said nothing, and fled on.

The Castello served many purposes. It was an oubliette, a place to which inconvenient relatives were sent to be forgotten. In cells hewn out of the naked rock, along dusky corridors, fifteen or twenty men sat out their lives. The Duchess was lucky to be housed above them and so well.

The Commandant had shown off his charges by torchlight, and Bosola had made a point of learning their half-forgotten stories. And here, one aimless day of that endless two weeks, Cariola had wandered by accident.

Here was Count Piccola, who blubbered when he tried to speak. A nephew had coveted his garden. He was chained to the wall. There were others. The stench was peculiar. She knew now what the verb to moulder meant. It made her grateful to be kept a prisoner upstairs. Death is darkness. Life is light. She fled.

But light without freedom was horrible. She wandered again. At dusk Bosola found her in a section she had not visited, her skirts caught in the brambles of a wild artichoke, in a narrow ruined alley. This section he avoided himself. It was too noisome and too clamorous.

He went forward to rescue her. At evening the din was terrible, for it was feeding time. As his shadow darkened the end of the alley, she gasped and sobbed.

He came forward and freed her skirt.

"You should not be here."

It was the first time he had spoken to her since she had betrayed him. She wanted to keep him there. It was unfair that she should be hated only for what was her duty.

"You didn't want to do your duty. You wanted to save your own neck. Why are women so devious?" he demanded.

She drew away from him. "Are we to die?"

202

He threw back his head and laughed at her. How could he do otherwise? He grabbed her arm and shoved her ahead of him, to an opening broken away from the wall. "There. Look."

She drew back.

"Look!" he told her, and pushed her so that she half-stumbled, and caught at the ragged edge of the wall. A light came out of the hole.

Fascinated, he looked himself. He came here sometimes now, to think. He could not help it. Something drew him.

The room into which they looked had a floor twenty feet below them, and was vast. It was the old hospital. Naked men with greenish skins capered around the walls. Others, the more virile, rushed towards the centre of the room. They had scarcely a garment among them, and lived in filth. Two gaolers stood on a flight of steps, their backs to a bolted door, and threw down chunks of rancid meat. There was a stewpot steaming on the floor, a large, rusted cauldron. This was what the inmates were screaming and fighting for. It was the mad-house. Here Naples sent those too violent to keep in the city, and here they thrived, though sun and rain beat through the ruined roof above their heads.

Cariola drew back. Bosola had seen this scene before, at the convent of San Severo, with his sister. He was used to it. But unlike Sor Juana, Cariola was a woman. She evoked pity.

"Why did you show me that?" she asked. She was quiet now. It made her intelligent. "Is that why you want to kill me?"

"I do not want to kill you. I do not kill women."

"Then you will help us?"

"Help you?" He glanced back towards the hole. "Help you for what? You are despicable."

He left her and hurried away into the shade.

For a moment Cariola looked after him. Then, picking up her skirts, she hurried up through the ruins, back towards the citadel itself. She felt encouraged, and she could not bear to be alone. She went straight to the Duchess.

At least he had spoken to her. Whatever he might say, he was not so hard as he seemed. And the two women had had so little news, and were in such suspense, that that seemed news indeed. She had some vision of herself, seducing Bosola into giving them their freedom. Of the Commandant she was not even aware.

The Duchess was at the window. Not even Cariola knew that Antonio was not in Milan. Therefore she only thought her mistress was mooning by the window in the early dusk. As darkness fell the cliffs of Sorrento loomed larger, only to vanish as the stars came out. At night the Bay of Naples was haunted by the ghosts of Greek and Roman triremes, which seemed to move swiftly to and fro, under the moonlight, in the water mist.

Often, now, the Duchess must think one of those silent vessels might be real. She only had one hope, and so, perforce, she thought that hope was true.

Cariola hesitated. She did not know how to speak to her mistress now. She came over to the window and stood behind her. The Duchess sighed.

Cariola blurted out that she had seen Bosola. He was not a cruel man. He might help them. That was the substance of what she said.

"Were you in love with him?" the Duchess asked gently. "Is that why you did not speak sooner?" She sounded very far away.

Cariola was confused.

"Love is nothing to be ashamed of. And perhaps he is not to blame for what he has done. You must have been lonely sometimes. Was that it?"

"I don't know. It was so long ago. He never cared for me."

"That didn't make any difference, did it?"

Cariola was silent. To her surprise she found that it had not. She had not thought of that before.

The Duchess smiled. "We are alone now," she said. "It is foolish to quarrel. We may not have much time."

"But he might help us."

The Duchess shook her head. "No, he will not help us. Even if he could, I have nothing with which to reward him. You know that. He knows it too."

"I don't want to die!"

Night had fallen over the bay and blocked it out. The moon

was delusive and the peaks shadowy. The Duchess left the window and walked up and down the room.

"Is death so bad?" She watched Cariola narrowly and saw she was on the verge of hysterics. That would be too much. Her nerves were too frayed to deal with hysterics.

"Oh no," said Cariola, and drew back against a wall. She looked up at the Duchess beseechingly. "Do I have to die?"

"Antonio will save us if he can."

"Antonio is in Milan."

The Duchess started to speak, and then thought better of it. "He will save us if he can."

"But how do we know he is alive?" asked Cariola. Her eyes seemed to see something the Duchess could not see.

"What do you mean by that?" The Duchess whirled around and advanced towards her. "What have you and that miserable man talked about? What does he know?"

"Nothing," sobbed Cariola. "I don't know. What are we to do?"

The Duchess sighed. As gently as she could she drew Cariola into the next room and saw her to bed. The woman was shivering, and fear was not pretty. She stayed with her until she fell asleep. Then she left the room.

What Cariola had said had bothered her. She knew the confines of her prison now. Without bothering to take a light, she let herself out into the corridors. At the far end they were ruinous. There she stood in a cold breeze that had sprung up, gazing towards the mainland again. He was there somewhere. He must be.

But Cariola had only spoken her own doubt, and now it was spoken she knew she could not sleep. She went down the shallow stone stairs, and let herself out into the night. There was no one up at this hour to challenge her.

She walked down the stepped path that wound towards the chapel.

The chapel roof had fallen in. Frescoes flaked off into the rubble. In the cloister was a graveyard. The stones were set as flagstones. Disconsolately she walked over the effaced names of the nuns. Brambles and weeds overgrew the abandoned fountain in the middle.

What Cariola had said had upset her. She was confronted with the thought of death, and did not like it. For when we think of death, it is not really death we think of. Really to think of death requires a mental effort too great for us. We think only of our attitude towards it. It is the same with love, or hate, or rage. Once experienced, they make a mockery of our thoughts about them. Well, she had been in love. But no one who has died can think about death afterwards. Death has no afterwards. And though we know we have to die, few of us believe it.

Death was voluptuous. Death was erotic. Death was the ultimate embrace. The music of the age confirmed it. *Lasciate mi morire* sang the aristocracy, burst into tears, and took an orange girl to bed with them. *Io moro*. O come, come, come, come, I love you, my sunshine, my light, sang the Venetian nun Philomela Angelica. Whether she meant death, Jesus, or desire, no one could say. She gasps. She sighs. She heaves and tosses in a rumpled bed. God, Jesus, love and death were all the same.

But pacing up and down the cloister, the Duchess wondered if they were. In adolescence death rears up before us like a public monument, a lover's tomb, like that of Romeo and Juliet, the final testimony of how wonderful we were. Once dead and the world shall know.

Antonio could not be dead. But dead or alive, he beckoned to her from the farther shore, he stretched out his hands. She must join him. But maturity is more cautious. If death is the utter extinction of consciousness, how could she join him then? God has no right to take our bodies away from us. In Heaven, they say, we find another kind of joy. But why should we have to purchase it with the extinction of the only pleasure we can know? God, they said, was love, but He was also a eunuch. Love was not God. Love was Antonio.

So she paced in the darkness. She came to an opening in the wall. She went within. The darkness was three steps down. She was in a narrow crypt. Along each wall stood a series of stone chairs. Here, in past times, when the nuns were about to die, they were carried down, and sat on the chairs until they were dead. Here they mummified.

206

Each chair had a drain-hole drilled in it. This was to catch the post-mortem ichors, which then drained away through the rock into the sea. She had often heard of that. Now she saw it. She fled back into the light.

If this was death, she would not die this way. She was a Duchess. She had dignity. She would die with dignity. Death is the extinction of consciousness. So is the act of love. But in the act of love we die in each other's arms. Why should death not be so?

If he was dead, he was waiting. Then why should she not go to him? She looked around her with a smile. He was here. He would be there. She was calm. She had got back her dignity.

And besides, he was not dead. He was safe in those hills. She looked up. The stars are not constant. Man is not constant. Nothing is constant. Only the heart conceives of constancy.

III

In Naples Ferdinand had himself announced to the Cardinal. It had taken him some time to ferret his brother out, but he could not move up and down impotently along the shore. He was driven from within. He had to act. He had followed the Duchess across Italy and had seen her embark. He knew that his brother's hand was in this. He knew his brother had cheated him. Antonio, they said, was in Milan. Now it was his turn to cheat the Cardinal. Physical insanity is a tyrannous thing. It led him to confront his brother as otherwise he would not have done, for the body has its own cunning.

But as always he waited until night. Then, with Marcantonio and two guards, he stormed the *palazzo* the Cardinal occupied, made his way angrily up the stairs, and burst through the doors leading to the Cardinal's apartments.

The Cardinal was writing at a desk, by the light of a five-branch candelabrum. He looked up irritably. His ambitions had scooped him out like a melon. There was no one left inside him to be taken by surprise. But he could be annoyed.

"What have you done with her?" demanded Ferdinand.

The Cardinal saw Marcantonio and did not like him. Marcantonio had a sick swagger and big ears. He was stupid enough to be dangerous, and violence sweated his hands like a fever. "Send them away," he said.

Ferdinand told his guard to wait in the anteroom. They clomped out. Then he strode forward and planted one enormous soft-booted foot on a chair, glowering down at the Cardinal. The foot was like the paw of a St. Bernard, but a St. Bernard foaming at the mouth. The Cardinal looked at it and then at Ferdinand.

"I have not done anything with her."

"Then where is she?"

"I see no reason why I should tell you that."

"So." Ferdinand kicked aside the chair. "Do you think I don't know what you are up to? Do you think you are the only one with spies? You want Amalfi for yourself."

For a moment the Cardinal wondered if this was quite true. He did not think it was. It was merely that events had all moved one way, and he meant to have it. He had not thought of the matter personally at all. But he knew that Ferdinand was capable of irrevocable acts, and the Cardinal squirmed away from irrevocable acts. He wondered if he dare temporize.

Ferdinand smashed his fists down on the desk. "Where *is* she?" he screamed.

"She is on Ischia, at the Castello."

"And her paramour?"

"At Milan, but I do not believe it. Perhaps he is trying to rescue her." He eyed Ferdinand speculatively. Surely the man was mad. So now the thing must happen. Nor would he have Ferdinand interfere in Amalfi. Fastidiously he laid his conscience aside, took up new instruments, and looked at Ferdinand much as a surgeon would look at a patient with the stone.

"And if he succeeded, what then?" he asked softly.

"She shall not lie with him again. She shall not lie with anyone."

"Why not? She has conceived by him. She is married to him, so they say."

"Where is he?"

"I do not know."

Ferdinand prowled up and down the room. The Cardinal shifted in his chair. Ferdinand returned to the desk.

"Write me a pass to the Citadel."

"I cannot do that. You have no business there."

"Write."

"No."

A shudder came over Ferdinand. He snatched across the desk, and took the Cardinal's hand. He would not let it go. The Cardinal's eyes widened. He exerted his strength. So did Ferdinand. He tugged and twisted at the hand, bending the fingers back. He wrenched the apostolic ring off its finger, and shoved the Cardinal back into his chair. For a moment they eyed each other, suspended. Then, shouting for Marcantonio, Ferdinand hurled himself out of the room, leaving the doors flapping and ajar.

Left to himself the Cardinal rubbed his hand. He blinked. No one had dared unbidden to touch him in his life, not even his mistresses. He touched them. He looked at his finger with disbelief. He knew now what must be done with Ferdinand, and for once he would have such an act done gladly.

Suddenly, irrationally, he screamed for lights.

On the Bay of Naples it was dark. An hour later a low skiff put out towards the islands, its sails furled, its oars creeping along the water like a wounded centipede. No one aboard that vessel spoke. Marcantonio lolled on a pile of canvas, whittling at the gunnel with his knife. The moon was down. Ferdinand sat in the prow, and watched the slightly phosphorescent, green-tinged water. The apostolic ring would get him in.

Towards four the rock of the Castello rose abruptly before them. The light running surf was restless. The sky was mackerel. There was no sign of life. The boat bumped against the causeway and was still.

IV

Those in the castle rose early. They were too bored to stay in bed, and the Duchess and Cariola were too anxious.

The days of a prisoner soon become indistinguishable from each other. So do the days of a guard. Bosola found it difficult to keep busy, and longed for instructions from the mainland. No instructions came.

The Duchess's apartments he avoided. He knew he was not

welcome there, and could not bear the thought of seeing either one of them. Cariola was merely pitiable. But the Duchess upset him. He was used to being despised, but disdain was even worse. He did not sleep well. The earlier he awoke the more empty were the days. He had nothing to do until it was time to drink in the evening with the Commandant. Nor could he watch that bay on which the fishing boats hovered like predatory moths. A life without events is the worst kind of life. He had seen too much of prisons to be at ease in them.

For days now he had had the feeling that something was waiting to overtake him. Perhaps he was overtired. When he was alone, someone seemed to stand behind him. Such things cannot be dismissed merely by being named. Hallucinations are the shadows cast by strangers walking through our mind, on errands of their own.

It made him jumpy. It also made him take long walks.

Along one side of the cliff there was a narrow path. To the right the drop was sheer. To the left was a low bluff. At the end of the path was a small hexagonal chapel dedicated to St. Peter. He found himself there. Usually he did not go to such narrow places. He had a fearful impulse not to look behind him. In front of him was the closed door of the church. Irritated with himself, he looked around, and started violently.

A figure stood on the path, boldly and suddenly. It blocked the way, and ground its knuckles together, smiling hungrily. He recognized it at once. It was Marcantonio. It advanced towards him.

Bosola whirled towards the church. The door opened. Ferdinand beckoned him in. Bosola stood still. But Marcantonio came behind him and prodded him in the kidneys. He half-stumbled, and went into the church.

Marcantonio clanged the door shut behind him.

The church was small, close, and heavy with dust. Ferdinand wasted no time. Marcantonio kicked him and sent him sprawling back against the altar. Ferdinand grasped him by his doublet and shook him like a terrier, slapping him repeatedly in the face. Then he flung him back to Marcantonio. Marcantonio was clever at this sort of thing. Bosola fell chattering to the ground.

210

"Lock him in," snapped Ferdinand. The two of them went out of the church, and the key turned in the lock. Bosola was sure his ankle had been broken. He lost consciousness.

When he came to it was late morning. The light hurt his eyes. From the floor he looked around the chapel. He knew he must get out before they returned. He did not know how. He dragged himself to the ledge of the unglazed window, pulled himself up, and looked down. His ankle hurt painfully, but was only sprained. The drop was five hundred feet to the sea. He looked left and right. The building was hexagonal, so between the ledge and the end of the cliff wall was a space of about two feet. If he was careful he might be able to reach it. Half an hour later he fell in a heap on the ground next the chapel door. Urgency gave him strength. Leaning against the bluff, he reached the end of the path, and left the cul-de-sac. He was in the shadows of the castello itself now.

The light made him blink. It was so bright in that sun that it dazzled him with the effect of darkness. Lean, naked shapes seemed to flit through the trees, and there was a peculiar, sick restlessness in the air. There were murmurs, and groans, and screams, but all muted and unreal. It was as though someone had released a flock of ravenous parrots. Bosola wondered where the guards could be.

He knew that he must reach the castello. He did not know why. The impulse was irrational. Skirting the shadows, he toiled painfully uphill.

The forecourt of the castello had been elaborated fifty years before, in a Spanish taste. It was a narrow open place surmounted by an enormous Churriguerresque gateway of stone swags, ropes, rosettes, angels, and shields. Bosola slid rapidly across the open space and inside.

The great hall was immediately within. From it rose the state stair to the private apartments. He shrank back. The hall was full of gibbering, half-naked figures, dancing and screaming up and down in the shadows. Someone had let the madmen out. They had swarmed here. Some carried stones. Some bits of rusty iron.

At the head of the stairs stood the Duchess, erect and pale. The madmen tried to throw stones at her. They had not the

211

strength. The stones fell harmlessly half-way up the stair. Bosola slipped. It attracted their attention. They advanced towards him. He turned and ran.

v

The Duchess had been alone with Cariola, in the bare chamber that served them for a common room, whose windows overlooked the gate. The two women glanced swiftly at each other when they heard the uproar, and then the Duchess went to the window and looked out.

She was in time to see the madmen round the corner and pour into the castle yard. They had been kept down so long that their natural impulse was to pour towards the top.

Cariola came to the Duchess's shoulder and peered down. "What does it mean?"

The Duchess thought she knew very well what it meant. She picked up her skirts and swept out into the corridor. By the time she had reached the head of the stairs, the rabble had swept into the hall, which was paved with black and white squares of marble, once highly polished, now dull. The madmen swept across this space like demented chessmen.

Those who could see, saw her. Then they began to throw their stones. These clattered on the stairs, rocked, and rested there. The Duchess flinched. The hall was shadowy. She could not tell whether they meant her mischief or not. If they tried to mount the stairs she could not hold them back. Instinctively she knew they must not come close to her. They gibbered.

"And how do you like my entertainment?"

She whirled. Ferdinand leaned in the darkness of the landing, watching her. She went limp. "So you have come," she said.

"One might call it a charivari. A marriage chorus. You are married, aren't you?"

"What is that to you?"

"Everything," said Ferdinand. He looked down into the hall. "They sing well. Don't you think they sing well?" He whistled. It caught the attention of the madmen. Their heads turned like the frightened heads of browsing buffalo. A sigh

212

went up from them, and hesitantly, stark naked, and covered with filth, they began to mount the stairs, their vacant eyes all in a row, and somehow on the same level.

Ferdinand put two fingers in his mouth and whistled again. Marcantonio and his two bravos came out of the corridor. "Hold them back." The bravos leaped down the stairs, and began to cudgel the madmen. They did not seem to feel any pain. But they fell back, disappointed. The Duchess watched this with disbelief.

"I suppose these games appeal to you," she said.

"You should not speak to me that way." Ferdinand shoved his face close to hers and smiled. "You should beg me for your life."

"I beg no one for my life."

"Then how do you expect to keep it?"

The Duchess said nothing. But something in her face must have infuriated him. He teetered from foot to foot, and then, grasping her roughly by the arm, hurried her into the ruined darkness of the corridor, shoved open a door, and dragged her into a disused room. Part of its far wall had fallen away into the sea. There, leaning against the door, he confronted her. She could still hear the madmen, and the thwack of the bravos' staves.

"Your lover cannot help you now," he said, watching her narrowly.

"I have no lover."

He snorted, reached into his pocket, and began to draw things out. He held up his hand. There was something in it, which, as he suspended it from his fingers, wavered to and fro in the dust.

She watched it, fascinated. Her face became pale. "Where did you get that?"

It was a long white baroque pearl, set in gold. It shimmered with putrescent light, as baroque pearls do. It was the ear-ring Antonio had worn that night among the gipsies.

Ferdinand smiled. With a jerk, he sent the pearl spinning through the broken wall, out over the sea. The light caught it for an instant and then let it go.

"Antonio is dead," he said. "Very dead." He smiled at her.

213

The Duchess folded her hands gravely. "He was not my lover. He was my husband."

"Your paramour."

"We were married. I had a child by him. I wanted to have his child."

"Why do you not get down on your knees and grovel? You should be ashamed."

"Ashamed? Ashamed of what? Should I have lain with you, or that corpse you married me to, instead?

"Do you think I do not know what you have come here to do? But that will not make you forget what I have done with him. We lay together. We made love as you could never do. I would let him do anything with me. Over and over again. Whenever we could. We were young and alive. We were free. We had no use for you and what you call love."

"Be still."

"I will not be still. I would you had been there to watch. I know what you are. I know what you want. I know what you always wanted. Better than you do. I escaped from you. With him. Always with him. Shall I describe to you everything we did? Or how it felt to carry his child? It was born dead, but I carried it. I wanted to carry it. I wanted nothing of you or my brother the Cardinal. Shall I tell you how I laughed at you? How we both laughed at you? Even when you came to Amalfi, we were together. When you were in your room, he was in mine."

The Duchess advanced towards him, and he drew back. He tried to hide his face in shadow.

"No," he said.

"Yes. Always yes."

"You will pay for this."

"Of course I shall. But it happened. And you will never forget that. That will drive you mad. Perhaps you are mad already. You are impotent, and laughable, and very sad to think about. Do you not think everyone knows that? Our brother the Cardinal does what he will with you. You were born to be cheated." She watched him narrowly. She wanted it over. If Antonio was dead, why should she live?

"We cheated you. But we did not cheat each other. We lived. We still do. We always shall."

214

"With that squalid stable-boy."

"With that *man!*"

She watched his face with interest. It shifted so rapidly. Sometimes it was insane. Sometimes the face of a boy. Sometimes that of the damned. It was impossible to tell what he might do. He had not the strength to kill her. His violence was too spasmodic.

He sobbed, grabbed her, and hurried her out of the room. They came to the staircase again. Marcantonio slouched against the balustrade, watching the madmen below. Ferdinand swept her down it and out into the air. She did not know where he was taking her or why.

Marcantonio and the bravos fell in behind.

They came to the cloister and that cell in which the nuns sat to die. He shoved her in, and stood in the doorway watching her.

"There," he said. "That is what it is to die!"

She looked around her calmly. "I have seen it before. Will you have your men kill me here?"

He blinked. She looked up at him. "He is dead. If you kill me, I shall only join him."

He lurched forward and put his fingers round her throat. They were horny and hard. They pressed. She felt her head turn blue with vertigo. Then they relaxed. He fell back against the wall, stumbling against one of the nuns' seats.

She stood there, getting back her breath. "You have not the courage to kill me," she said.

"No."

"Then you must have me killed."

He turned and ran out of the cell. She lingered there for a moment. Then, slowly, she climbed back to the cloister. She felt very weak. She knew now how it felt to be at the end. Or almost at the end. He would wait for darkness. He would need others to back him up. But the thing would happen now. She felt sober, but she did not feel sorry.

Carefully she picked her way back towards the citadel, for she did not want to be alone, even though she must contrive to send Cariola away. She did not look back. If she had, she would have seen Marcantonio following her.

215

Bosola had no dignity. He had only pride. He had the appearance with no knowledge of the reality. That is what destroyed him. That is what pulled all his efforts down. Having no dignity, he could not bear to be alone.

Exclusive of the prisoners, there were perhaps thirty people in the castle. They spent an anguished morning rounding up the madmen, and then they disappeared. He knew better than to seek them out. They would not be kind. They had found him out, and so they had no use for him.

With the last madman rounded up, the rock became ominously still. A lizard ran over a stone. It was earthquake weather, with that heat that seems about to burst. Bosola was afraid. He fled down to the dungeons and the wet rock corridors. Only there, he thought, could he avoid Ferdinand and Marcantonio. He knew they would find him eventually, for Ferdinand could not rest until he had silenced his servants by making them share his own guilt. The violent would have all men be as violent as they. If they cannot manage that, they cannot rest. But at least he could evade them for a while.

At the same time he was excited. Death excited him. It made him feel voluptuous.

Underground the air was hot and dense. He poured with sweat. He seemed to wander endlessly. Yet he knew where he was going. Something drew him as it always did. He had come to the Commandant's playroom.

In his own way the Commandant was a scholarly man. Prisoners and those left much to their own devices often become so. They raise canaries, study chess, or master the Pentateuch. They read up on the history of their profession and acquire a certain pride. They become proficient and antiquarian.

He found himself, as he often did, in the torture-room. Here, to the oiled devices of an ingenious age, the Commandant had added all the machinery of the past. It had had little use, but still he kept it in repair. There was even an iron maiden, with adjustable spikes, to puncture the victim all over, to any depth one might wish.

Other devices were more practical. Some men have a passion for the mechanical. They go to the ironmonger as a woman goes to a dressmaker. A beautiful saw fascinates them as much as a yard of cut Venetian velvet fills a woman with religious awe. Swords, daggers, helmets, cuirasses, are all very well, but they are only tools. They are inert without us. But a machine, even so simple a machine as a nut and bolt, is self-contained. It can do without us, and therefore we admire it. We serve it as we would serve a god. And torture is nothing but a game with the emotions. As statues of forgotten gods still retain the awe felt by their worshippers, so do torture machines retain the screams of the overwrought. They are emotional shrines. The empty graveyard and the nursery tell us what we will be and what we were. The torture chamber tells us what we are. It is the crypt of every church.

There Bosola came, as ignorant and intuitive as an acolyte. As he bent over these machines, his face became as thoughtful and as sensitive as that of an ascetic. Cruelty makes us so. It even gives us a certain freedom. It allows us to forget the world. It makes us bigger and stronger than we are. And that, from time to time, we need to be. A lack of imagination makes all things possible.

He wandered around the room. Here was a rack. There a thumb-screw. Elsewhere the apparatus by which a man might be pressed to death. Another where he might be tortured upside down. The room was shadowy. It was carved from the rock, with holes pierced to the cliffs. What light there was came from there. He twiddled with the bolts on the thumb-screw. Next it, on the bench, lay a similar device to crush the jaw.

"You like it here."

The voice was ironic. Ferdinand stood over him. He must have slipped into the shadows unheard. Bosola had only to look up to see that he was dangerous. "Yes, it suits you very well." Ferdinand had sought the darkness too. He was working himself up. "It is almost dark up there. Come."

"What for?"

"You know why we came here."

Bosola was frightened. He could feel his fear between his

legs. This was what he was trying to avoid. He wanted no part of this.

"I know nothing," he said. "I prefer to know nothing." Despite himself his eyes grew crafty.

Ferdinand shrugged. "You will come. We need your help."

Bosola drew away. Ferdinand's eyes narrowed. "It would not be wise to disobey me."

"I will have no part of this." And he wanted no part of it. Executioners never escaped, even when those who employed them did. He shrank from any such final act. Besides, perhaps he felt pity. By choice he would have killed no one.

"No?"

Bosola shook his head.

Ferdinand's eyes glittered. He advanced towards Bosola, and Bosola backed away. Then he whirled to run.

Directly behind him stood Marcantonio, grinning in his face, holding a torch in one hand.

"Grab him," shouted Ferdinand. He was quivering like a puppy.

Marcantonio grabbed him. He was not gentle. The torch fell to the floor. Ferdinand looked around. "Put him on the rack."

The two bravos came forward. Bosola squirmed. It did him no good, and Marcantonio was laughing. There was spittle on his lips. He was happy.

They flung him down on the rack. He tussled futilely. The two bravos tied his ankles and his wrists with coarse rope. The rope bit into his flesh, but they only pulled it the tighter. Ferdinand struck his body, so it quivered and bounced in the tension of the ropes.

"You fool," he said. "Whom do you think you serve?"

Bosola did not answer. He could not.

"How many masters have you? What has the Cardinal told you?"

"Nothing."

The winch tightened. The ropes stretched in straight lines, the coarse hairs of their length standing up like wires. The pressure on his ankles pulled and tugged at his skin, and his blood seemed to turn solid at the extremities of his body.

"Are you loyal to her?"

218

Bosola was not loyal to anyone. But he was stubborn not to give in. A sort of voluptuous weakness fled through his body, untying all his nerves. It was like an orgasm and turned into one. Bosola felt nothing. He was beyond shame.

Ferdinand looked puzzled, then put his hands on his hips, and laughed. The laugh echoed in and out of the shadows. Tears ran down his face.

Marcantonio toyed with the winch. It creaked in the half-darkness.

"Her lover is dead," whispered Ferdinand. "Antonio is dead. Are you loyal to him too? Would you like to join him?"

Something happened to Bosola's face.

Ferdinand spat. "You have too many masters. I am your master now." He motioned to Marcantonio, and Bosola felt his body stretch out almost to the cracking point. Ferdinand struck the rigid legs.

Bosola groaned despite himself. "Ah, now we see. Now we listen to the weakling." Ferdinand put his finger to his nose, and peered down at Bosola. He swaggered. He posed. He laughed. "Nobody disobeys me," he said.

Bosola found it difficult to move his head. Yet in a way this was what he had always wanted, and even while he felt sick and trapped, and his mind rebelled, something inside him exulted. That made him feel more frightened than ever. If he turned his head, the pain in his arms and legs was terrible. He gazed straight up. Someone picked the torch from the floor. It was still burning. Marcantonio's head came into his field of vision. He manned the double spoked wheel that tautened the rack. It was delicately balanced. It had only to be spun a notch. Bosola felt as though his body were being boned out through his arms and legs. There was no slack now for his body to bounce at all.

"Ah," said Marcantonio. "Now you look beautiful." He gave another turn to the wheel.

Bosola screamed. It made Marcantonio laugh. The scream was involuntary and that pleased them. Ferdinand giggled nervously and bent over him.

Bosola's tongue was already thick. "Very well," he said. "I will do as you say."

219

They paid no attention to him. They had known he would do as they said. Now they were playing. Slowly Marcantonio turned the wheel again. Something inside Bosola cracked, not bone, but torn muscle.

"No," said Ferdinand. "We need him. Play with him later, if you like. But leave him there until we need him. Relax him a little bit. Not too much."

The slackening of the wheel was more sickening even than its tightening had been.

They tramped off and left him, laughing and talking to each other hysterically. The torchlight faded. It was still. Only water dripped. Bosola was thirsty. He fainted.

He came to when cold water splashed across his face. The edge of the dipper hit his chin. It was now dark.

"Now you will do as you're told," said Ferdinand. He was tense.

The bravos undid the ropes. Marcantonio hauled him up, and embraced him. "Yes, he's a good boy now," he said. For some reason he now seemed to like Bosola. He felt him all over and then handed him a knife. "He'll do."

Bosola did not dare look at Ferdinand. He wanted to kill him. He would never forgive this. But Marcantonio whistled beside him and nudged him in the ribs, pushing him on. The rock tunnel echoed to their stride. Silent, they toiled upwards towards the night. Ferdinand drew a cloak around him, and so concealed his face. Even Marcantonio seemed grim and ashamed. Men grow bashful at such times.

But if Antonio was dead, then nothing mattered. If Antonio was dead, the Duchess would want to die. So Bosola absolved his conscience. He was suffering from shock. He trembled violently. The others took it for excitement. It made him one of them. They grinned.

VII

Cariola was stunned. Though she might know better, still she believed that this imprisonment was only a mistake. Now she saw that it was not. It touched *her*.

She lost her head. She burst into floods of tears. She could not bear the thought of being left alone. She knelt by her mistress's chair. She gave way to a flood of self-indulgence. So birds deliberately fly into snares, too frightened of the hunters to want to save themselves.

The two women were in the centre of the barren room which was the inner chamber of their apartments. All splendour had shrunk to this. Threadbare tapestries had been brought from somewhere, and hung up to keep the coldness out. Instead they merely moaned on the walls. In the centre of the room stood a state bed on a dais, with four posts but no canopy. There was a chest and the field chair on which the Duchess sat. Candles burned in a tall sconce. That was all. They had not even enough underlinen to last the week.

"You must not cry," said the Duchess softly. Her eyes were turned towards the window. She was waiting. Sorrento had already been engulfed by darkness. It was only a shape beneath the stars, inert, lifeless, and without meaning now.

"But how can you forgive me?"

"There is nothing to forgive."

"But I must be forgiven." Cariola looked at her blankly. The Duchess sighed and pressed her closer. She felt very much alone.

Both women were waiting for sounds in the silence. They did not know for what sounds. Death walks down an endless corridor, but since we hear it only once we cannot transmit our knowledge of that sound. Those who die in their beds are to be envied. They are too weak to run away. So they need not pretend to a dignity no less real for being a pretence, and perhaps the more so thereby. The Duchess sat in her chair. Her real dying had been done already. Now she merely waited on the event.

Her only thought was of Antonio, a thought mixed up somehow with a landscape so real to her as to be visible. They had been happy once.

Then they heard a creaking within the building, an odd shuffling, outside, on the stairs. They imagined footsteps, even though they could not hear them. They did hear the creaking of a door.

Cariola started. "Let me die with you," she said.

221

"No. You must hide."

"But I must. What else would I do? I have always been with you. I cannot leave you now."

"Can't you?" asked the Duchess. She was scarcely listening. Poor Cariola should live. She had nothing to die for. It was not yet her time.

But Cariola was carried away. She took the Duchess's hands in her own. She begged. She implored. She wanted to die. The Duchess was touched. If it came to that, what was left for her, once her mistress was gone?

All of which Bosola heard from the anteroom. He glanced round at Marcantonio and the others, who had slipped masks over their faces. They wore Ferdinand's habit, but they were not really trying to conceal their identity. They were only hiding their faces from themselves. Ferdinand remained in the anteroom, but called back Marcantonio, and gave him a special rope, ripping away the common one that Marcantonio held in his hands. "No," he said. "She is a Duchess. Here." Then he shuddered and turned his face to the wall.

Bosola wore no mask. He scorned that. He stepped into the room, followed by the tall-booted guards, who shambled in awkwardly around him.

Cariola saw him and screamed.

"Shush," said the Duchess. "There is nothing to be afraid of." She looked at Bosola. "So, you have come to this." Keeping an eye on them, she moved languidly towards the bed. "Well, are you ashamed? Have done with it. Or are you afraid?"

Cariola began to shiver. She made no move to interfere. She shut her eyes.

"Well?" demanded the Duchess. "Why do you hesitate?"

Bosola could not move.

Marcantonio leaped forward, kicking Bosola aside, and grabbed the Duchess. The bravos uneasily fell in behind him. The Duchess involuntarily made a movement. It was enough to urge him on. He threw the rope around her neck, and pulled both ends.

When the Duchess could no longer breathe, she began to struggle. Marcantonio put his knee to her back, to steady himself, so that her body billowed outward, and pulled on each end of the rope with his coarse red fists. His face was angry and intent, and perspiration stood out on his forehead. His eyes were closed. It was impossible to tell where he was.

The whole act took perhaps three minutes. They were utterly silent. Bosola strode forward towards Marcantonio, automatically, despite himself, but it was too late. The Duchess fell limp to the bed. The rope dangled in Marcantonio's hand. It was of white silk woven with a blue thread. Such are the privileges of the aristocracy. Marcantonio opened his eyes and sighed, and looked down at the Duchess as though she had been a stranger. Then, lovingly, he began to lay her out on the bed.

Ferdinand stood in the doorway. "Get out," he cried. "Get out all of you."

Cariola screamed. Bosola turned on her savagely. She backed away. "No," she muttered. "Oh no. I don't want to die. I don't. I want to live. I want to live." She could not stop her scream. Someone had to stop it. Bosola felt his hands around her throat. They gripped tighter. She had betrayed her mistress. She had betrayed him. She had betrayed everyone. It was she who should die, not the Duchess. He lost control.

Marcantonio was by him, trying to pry him loose. Bosola let go. Cariola fell at his feet, in a tousled heap. But it was too late. She was dead. It made her suddenly pathetic.

"Now you understand," said Marcantonio softly. Bosola did not understand. Marcantonio left him. The footsteps of the bravos went away. The candle sconce had been overturned. It was dark where Bosola was. He went on staring down. Cariola was as meaningless as a dead bird found on a garden path. He backed against the wall. It was then, dimly, that he began to hear Ferdinand, choking and slobbering. Fascinated, he watched.

The Duchess lay on her bed, as Marcantonio had left her. He had even smoothed out the rumples of her skirt. The candlelight flickered over her face, making it seem to smile. She was young again and free. Ferdinand cast himself over the body.

"Amelia," he shouted. . . . "Amelia." He shook her, but she

was beyond response. It was as though that puzzled him. He gave up. "I didn't want to do it," he shrieked. "I loved you. Why don't you love me?" He squirmed and writhed on the bed. Great sobs tore out of him.

"Come back," he screamed. "I will be good. I promise."

He snuffled, and the body began to slither from the bed, almost on top of him. He cried out again, in terror, and backed away.

"You can have him back. He is not dead. I lied. You can have him. That pearl I rifled from your baggage. Go back. Do not touch me. I will never touch you again." He pushed the body back on the bed. He pleaded. He beseeched. He cried. He looked down at it, breathing heavily.

Bosola came forward.

"Close her eyes," shouted Ferdinand. "Can you not see that she stares at me? Close her eyes!" He panted, and seemed doubled up with pain. He turned on Bosola. "You did this. You and the Cardinal. You did this. Why did you do this thing?" He picked up the sconce and flung it at Bosola.

He began to shamble across the room, weeping and stumbling. Behind him lay the Duchess. "Marcantonio," he screamed. "Kill him. He has murdered my sister."

Bosola fled.

VIII

The devil was after him, demanding to be paid. He did not stop to think. Assassins would be after him, too, and the one would put him in the power of the other, either way. He flung down the staircase and into the grounds. The cold air hit him like a wall of water. He reached, somehow, stumbling and falling, the lower parade ground. Ferdinand was rousing the citadel, but that would take time.

He fled into the tunnel, past the astonished guards, but these had no time to stop him. Somewhere he heard the tolling of a bell. He saw a man on a horse, ambling up the tunnel, one of the guards, who had gone into town on his own errands. He leaped for him, tore him off the horse, and himself jumped on. He had no spurs and no whip. He wheeled the horse around and set it galloping by pinching its flesh. He dug his fingers in,

224

desperately. The horse whinneyed and hurried downhill. He passed one of the portcullises in the roof. He was almost free. Then, behind him, with an enormous clatter, the portcullis came rattling down. The metallic sound shook the tunnel.

It was another thirty yards to the exit. Dimly outlined against the night, he saw the entrance guards. One of them ran to the wall. He heard the ratchet disengage, and kneed the horse. Already startled, it jumped forward, just as the final portcullis clattered down above their heads. Bosola shinned himself forward. The sharpened points of the portcullis caught the horse's rump. It shook convulsively, its front legs flying up, and screamed. Bosola tumbled down on to the rocky ground. As he leaped up he saw the guards peering through the portcullis. The horse writhed and screamed again. Bosola half-slid and half-fell into the water, over the edge of the ramp, sank, swallowed the ocean, rose, and swam off towards a gently rocking boat. There was a light in the stern of it. The owner was still aboard. Shouts came from the entrance to the castello, but were muffled by the rock. High on the crest of the rock lights began to break out. Bosola hauled himself aboard. He still had Marcantonio's knife.

He got away. The boat swung out into the deceptive mist-shrouded bay. Bosola had no conscience now. He was running for his life, and the sight of a little of his own blood drove the boatman on. Soon they were hidden by the mist. At night that bay is no restful place. It is thronged with three thousand years of ghosts. Shapes are not what they appear to be. There is an odd humming over the water. Sometimes it almost sounds like human voices. Sometimes it sounds like something far worse.

They beached at dawn, the bottom of the boat grating sharply on the shingle of an abandoned section of the waterfront. Bosola leaped out of the boat and ran for the shadows. He headed instinctively for the convent of San Severo, hung on the nightbell, and got the porter up.

But the porter would not let him in. Sor Juana had gone.

"Gone? How could she be gone?"

The porter glowered at him through the Judas window in the gate. "She was too good for us. She has gone to found a convent in Amalfi, so they say. And good riddance." The Judas window slammed so hard that the bell jingled again.

Bosola slunk back into the shadows. He had to get away. He could go to Amalfi through the hills. No one could save him now but the Cardinal. His sister would have to intercede for him. If she would not, then he would force her to.

TEN

Sor Juana had got her wish. The Cardinal was seldom hesitant to reward those who might be of use to him later, and besides he looked upon Sor Juana as an experiment. Now she knew who was master, he was curious to see what she would do. Nor was he unmindful of his own fame. To found convents was a meritorious act.

It was true that Amalfi made her uneasy. But she did not intend to remain there for ever. At least she was free of San Severo. Her new order was approved by the Pope. She was well pleased. The foundation itself was negligible, but it would grow. She rose even earlier than usual to inspect its quarters. She longed and begged for money. She would have her cloister frescoed with the best art. At last she had something to do. And never again, in the middle of the night, need she become aware of that walled-up nun beneath her.

It was in this mood that Bosola found her.

He had no way of knowing what had happened on the island, but he was still afraid. He was glad to be out of sight of it. Nor did Amalfi make him feel any easier. He was known here. He might be recognized. He had waited to slip down from the hills, and so came to Sor Juana at dawn.

He knew it would be useless to appeal to her affection for him. She had no affections. As soon as he saw her convent, he felt it would be better to appeal to her sense of power. Others might found holy orders with two nuns and an empty room. Sor Juana's plans were more immediate and more practical.

The building lay at the back of the town. It had been abandoned for some time, but was solidly built of stone. It was now being remodelled, according to her own designs. The kitchens were to be stately, the reception rooms somewhat larger than the chapel. He flitted through the deserted building, leaving

227

footprints behind him in the plaster dust, and saw her standing in the middle of what was to be the library. The stuccoists had already been at work. It would be a noble room, sixty by thirty feet, with huge baroque wooden cases billowing out into the middle of its floor. The ceilings were to be allegorical.

She stood alone, while plaster dust danced around her, in the light from an open window. Her face was full of the wispy gloating joy of the truly bookish. It made her look young and innocent.

He stepped forward, stumbling over a peeled pole the workmen had left on the floor. It clattered away. Sor Juana looked up, and her manner was abruptly far different. "Who's there?" she called. She shielded her eyes with her hand and peered down the gallery. "Come forward."

He emerged into the patch of light.

"I have come to ask your help," he said.

She looked over his shoulder. She would not meet his eye. "Where have you come from?"

"Ischia."

For the first time she looked nervous. "What has happened?"

"The Duchess is dead."

Her face abruptly became blank. She seemed to peer around his body at the room. Somewhere a bell tolled. "We cannot talk here. The workmen will be up soon. Follow me," she said, and turned her back on him. The place was enormous. They climbed the state stairs, and came at last to the suite of rooms she had set aside for herself. He was impressed. They had the simplicity of great expense. She sat down on a chair and folded her hands.

"Now then. How did she die?"

"She was strangled."

"By you?" She looked up sharply.

"By her brother's guard." He told her about it. She listened quietly. It did not seem to disturb her. Perhaps only a threat to her convent could disturb her.

"And what do you want me to do?"

"Speak to the Cardinal. If I am under his protection, Ferdinand cannot harm me."

Her eyes widened. She did not answer at once. Instead she

228

toyed with the rosary in her lap. He did not want to hear her refuse him.

"Where is the child?" he asked.

"I will not tell you that."

"If you have it, I know who it is. Tell him I know who it is."

"I do not have it." She paused for a moment. "The Cardinal is here. He has been here for some time. But he has no use for you. There is nothing I can do."

"Are you afraid of him, too?"

She dropped her eyes, flushed slightly, seemed to grow angry, and then thought better of it.

"There has been unrest here. Someone is stirring up the bandits and the gipsies in the hills. He thought it better to come here to control them. He has the child. He will be regent."

"So he knew she would die."

"Of course he knew," she said angrily. "What is that to me?"

"You serve a good master. How does he keep you under his thumb?" he asked. For it was true. There was a new edge of fear in her eyes that he had never seen there before. She did not answer him. Somewhere in the building they heard clattering noises. Bosola became tense.

"The workmen," she explained. She stood up. "Very well. You cannot stay here. I will find some way to speak to him. But he will not help you until he has a use for you." She seemed anxious to get rid of him. "Disguise yourself and hide in the hills. You know your way there."

"Do you hope the bandits will kill me?"

She flinched. "They will not kill you," she said wearily. "You are practically one of them."

He did not believe that she would intercede, but it was the best he could do, until he found out where the Cardinal was and what his humour was. He turned and left her.

II

The safest conduct through bandits and murderers is to be one of them. Dress like the mob and keep your mouth shut, and no mob will hurt you. Destroy what they destroy, and they will love you for it. Bosola did not dare to go to the palace. In his own way he found a *lazzarone* dress, such as he had worn when he escaped from the galleys, left its owner gagged under the waterfront, and put it on. Once he had donned it, he felt stronger and safer. He rode through the early streets unnoticed and headed for the hills.

In two hours Amalfi lay below him, and he was not frightened any more, except when, far over the sea, he caught a glimpse of the dim shape of Ischia. He had done better as *lazzarone* than as a courtier. He would do better now.

Below him Amalfi seemed squalid and insignificant. He turned inland, over the uplands and the sudden ravines, peppered with trees. He had a pistol and a knife. What food he could not kill he could steal. He met no one.

Yet Sor Juana had spoken the truth. There was uneasiness and revolt in these barren hills. Something was stirring there. He could sense it all around him. People seemed to be watching him, though they had no cover from which to do so, and he saw no one. Not all the birds that abruptly shrilled out into the air sounded quite like birds. And out of the corners of his eyes he sometimes thought he saw someone draw back along the ridge.

This did not seem furtive. It seemed planned.

That night he camped under an oak tree, beside a small stream, charring a rabbit over a small fire. The dry grass rustled from time to time. A twig snapped. There was more the sense than the sound of someone moving treacherously through the underbrush. He pretended that he did not hear, but he slept lightly. His horse whinnied and he sprang up, in time to stop some lumbering shadow from leading it away. But he could not tell the features of the shadow. He lay down again.

In the morning the landscape was once more empty. He did not care for that. If someone would come forward, then he could identify himself, and so pass safe. The deeper he got into the hills the stronger the feeling of being watched became.

Then, unexpectedly, a few miles above Arosa, he came upon a small band of gipsies. As he approached several of the men took horse and rode away, but not before he had caught a glimpse of one of them. It was a gipsy bravo, tricked out like the others, but there was no mistaking that white face. It was Antonio.

Bosola trembled. If his part in the Duchess's death were known, or even if the Duchess's death were known, he would be dead himself by nightfall. He dared not alarm the gipsies. He bought a flask of wine, and then got out as quickly as he could, and worked his way backward towards the coast.

Drawing rein upon the cliffs, he saw a dark boat slowly approaching the harbour. The air was so clear that he could see every detail. He thought his own disguise adequate. Cautiously he worked his way down towards the town.

It was a boat bearing the Duchess's body back to Amalfi. It had been decided to give her a state funeral. This was to be held the next day.

The reason for that Bosola soon learned in a tavern. He learned other things as well. Someone was sending spies into the hills. Duke Ferdinand had arrived. The Cardinal was shut up in the palace. The Amalfitani were restless and terrified. They feared an insurrection from the hills, and they were without a ruler or a leader. Very seldom did the bravos and gipsies rouse themselves to sack a town, but when they did so, their violence was deadly. That night Bosola slept at the tavern.

The funeral next day was sullen and full of pomp. The authorities had heard rumour that Antonio was in the hills, and was behind the unrest. They hoped the funeral would bring him down.

Antonio did not appear.

State funerals take some time to organize, so this one had no panoply. The coffin was lowered from the ship and carried from the town to the cathedral, where a Mass was to be sung over it. The crowds along the streets said nothing. They were absolutely silent. The wheels of the catafalque made the only noise to be heard.

Bosola had slipped into the cathedral early. From the shadow of a Corinthian column, he watched the catafalque enter the square. The coffin was shouldered, tilted, and carried up the stairs, as though it had been the statue of some saint. It seemed to stare at him. Far over his head the cathedral bell tolled, and with each thunderous note a cloud of doves rose into the air

231

like shredded pieces of paper in a gust of wind. The air was full of the stench of street filth and iodine.

There was a second coffin on that catafalque. The faces of the pall-bearers ran with sweat, but it too was shouldered and started its slanting passage up the stairs. It was somewhat larger than the first, but plainer. The crowd now murmured ominously, and glanced up towards the hills.

Bosola fell back, his eyes widening. They carried Cariola past him and into the church. He could almost see her body through the sides of the coffin, and the startled look on her face, above her folded hands. Despite himself he was drawn into the cathedral after it. But by a side way, for only the Duchess's faithless courtiers were allowed inside.

This was a death of the quality. It had its own protocol. The people had no part in it.

The shadowy cathedral was tall, dim, and choked with incense. It took him a while to become accustomed to the light. Then, as though it were materializing in a haunted room, the figure of the Cardinal became visible. It was not to be told that the Duchess had been murdered. It was given out that she had caught the plague. But everybody knew. The Cardinal moved supplely through the motions of a Mass, a red wraith against the gloom. The courtiers seemed indifferent to the occasion, but they watched him. In the turn of their heads you could see that they knew who their new master was.

Then Bosola caught sight of Ferdinand. The man was standing directly before him. Bosola panicked and drew deeper into shadow. Ferdinand was unrecognizable. It was he who had brought the body here. His eyes seemed blind, and something shuffling had happened to his gait. He was dressed in black from head to foot, theatrically. On his chest he wore a medal with the Duchess's portrait. Marcantonio stood compassionately close to him, with something maternal in his stance, as though he were a nurse, or a trainer with a dancing bear. Tears streamed down Ferdinand's face, and yet he was not precisely weeping. He was only containing himself. Violence welled out of his eyes.

He broke from the crowd, rushed forward, and flung himself against the coffin. His voice was an animal bellow. The Cardinal glanced round, frowned, and waved a pale hand. Even Marcantonio seemed shocked. Then he sprang forward, with his two bravos, and pulled Ferdinand off. The sound of Ferdinand's fists against the coffin had been deafening. Ferdinand snarled.

The Cardinal seemed to hold his breath. Marcantonio spoke to Ferdinand earnestly. A crime against public decorum was the worst of all crimes. The Mass droned on. Ferdinand was led away.

Bosola was shivering. He had caught the look in the Cardinal's eyes, and knew what it meant. He slipped out of the church and went immediately to his sister's convent. If Ferdinand was here, then no one was safe. He would need sanctuary for a while. He must know if she had spoken to the Cardinal.

He was about to enter, when a porter stopped him at the door. He was denied admittance. He lost his head and shouted. It did no good. He explained that he was Sor Juana's brother. The order was specific and detailed. It was her brother who was not to be admitted. She had betrayed him. She had always wanted to, and now she had the excuse. She had her position to maintain.

He had nowhere to go, but he could not stand there and call attention to his presence in the street. Raging against her, he slunk off down a dark alley. He must wait for nightfall before he dared to leave Amalfi. With Ferdinand here, it would not be safe for him to try to storm his way in to the Cardinal. He felt sick. The loyal servant should not be rewarded thus. He was a worse fugitive even than Antonio.

Antonio at least had power in the hills. Antonio could defend himself.

He wandered round the slums of the town, working himself up. So that, at dusk, when four heavily cloaked men swept out of the town, and he recognized Marcantonio's voice, anger boiled over in him. Out of this rotten mess he decided that at least someone should escape undefiled. He himself was trapped. If die or fall he must, then he would cheat his enemies of their satisfaction. He took horse after them, with the advantage that he knew the route. He would get there first and carry a warning. He did not stop to think beyond that. Despair had swept away all his cunning, and uncovered one last remaining shred of decency. Decency, too, could be revenge.

It was the one altruistic act of his life, no matter what his motives were. But the moonlight was deceptive. He lost his way.

III

Antonio did not want to defend himself. Gipsies, too, had been at that funeral. They had ridden at once into the hills. He had learned the truth. There would be no insurrection now.

Three weeks ago he had arrived at the coast and established himself at Arosa. It had taken him a week to make contact with the gipsies and the bravos. He did not know what had happened. He had sent agents to Naples, but they had arrived too late. He learned only that the Duchess was not there. It was he who was responsible for the unrest in the hills. These men were loyal to him, and he had given them the promise of plunder. The sack of Amalfi would cover the escape of the Duchess. So much he had planned. Knowing that they would be together again had made all things possible. He had worked well.

Now she was dead.

It did not seem possible she was dead, for she was all around him. They had been happy in these hills. It was the one place where they had been happy. Her laughter was here everywhere. And lately he had felt more aware of her presence than ever, during this last day or two. He dismissed the gipsies. They waited to offer him grief, but he could not accept it. He could not accept the fact that she was dead. He did not know what to do next.

When we learn that someone we loved has died we feel much the same as in the instant when we realize someone has stolen our purse. We reach for it to pay. We turn to the one who has just died and say, What shall we do tomorrow? Neither is there. We are suddenly naked and nonplussed. But we know it is only a mistake. We shall do thus and so tomorrow anyway. Grief comes later. Like a man mortally wounded by an arrow, we go on with what we were doing before, through an emo-

234

tional no-man's-land, as though nothing had happened. Only later do we drop in our tracks. Only later are we surprised by grief.

Antonio had been walking down towards the chapel when the news came. Automatically he continued down the hill, through the meagre ruins of Arosa, past the abandoned house that was to be built for their child. Perhaps his walk became a trifle uncertain. That was all.

He heard the Duchess rustling beside him, as she would when he liberated her from Amalfi, and they ruled the gipsies in the hills, or fled the country altogether. The gipsies fell back before him. They made a space for sorrow. Then, frightened by something immobile in his manner, they began quietly to melt away back into the hills.

He did not notice. He reached the door of the chapel, pushed it ajar, and shambled inside. Then it hit him. Just as he looked around that empty, dusty room, it hit him.

The chapel was never used now. Dust lay heavy on everything. The light was dim. The church was damp. He did not notice. He sank to his knees. He did not know how long he stayed there. He was not praying. He was not thinking. He was aware only of emptiness.

The Church frowns on suicide. St. Augustine and the Egyptians saw to that. Martyrs might allow themselves to die, ascetics might torture themselves, and virgins might kill themselves to preserve their virginity, if they were Christian virgins. But to all others voluntary death was impossible. We are not allowed to incinerate ourselves. Hell is set aside to accomplish that. We must not infringe upon its prerogatives. But he did not want to kill himself. He wanted to throw himself away.

Slowly the world settled into place. He looked around him at the deserted room. Then, glancing up, his eye caught the altar-piece. He saw himself, kneeling, and the Duchess, as the Virgin, before him. She had a special way of saying, Antonio. He could hear it now. He gazed at the picture.

It was at this moment that Bosola drew rein above Arosa, was about to start down, and then drew back hastily. Four riders had appeared in the gully below him. They moved swiftly through the ruins of the town, shouting to each other, with a

235

military clatter. Then they spotted the open door of the church, jumped off their horses, and ran in.

In the chapel Antonio heard none of this. He continued to look at the painting, and anger began to stir in him. He would rouse the gipsies after all. They would sweep down on Amalfi and destroy it utterly. There would be fighting, and in the fighting he might die. Both the Sanducci were down there, so the gipsies had said. He would cut them down.

With a last wistful glance at the painting, he scrambled to his feet and turned to run out of the church. In the centre of the village there was a large gong. He would beat upon it, rouse the gipsies in the hills, and they would start at once.

He never reached it.

In the vestibule four figures jumped on him. He was not armed. He lost his footing and fell. They were quick about the business, and brutal. Something cut into him. He was bloody. He felt himself dragged along the stone floor and out into the dirt. Someone bent over his body with a knife, sobbing with rage. The figure turned, held something up, and then, lifting a spurred heel, kicked him in the face repeatedly. As he lost consciousness his last thought was of the Duchess. He thought she was standing beside him. Then he was dead.

From his hill-top Bosola saw the four riders drag the body out. He saw what they did to it. Then they leaped on their horses and galloped off. The landscape waited. Bosola shivered, but despite himself he had to ride down to make sure. Uncertainly he pushed his horse forward.

He drew to a halt before the church, but did not dismount. There was not much left of Antonio. They had kicked his skull in. That would have been Marcantonio's touch. But they had also castrated him, and Bosola knew who had done that. As he looked down something snapped inside him. He had not known before that he had loved Antonio. As he saw that raped torn thing lying beside the body, he lost all control of himself.

Automatically his spurs dug into the flanks of his horse. The horse jerked forward, almost throwing him. Cursing and sobbing, he took off after Ferdinand.

When he reached Amalfi he took refuge in a tavern. There he lay for a day and a night trying to find some means of revenge.

236

It was there the messenger found him out. That was the Cardinal's doing. For once in his life the Cardinal was angry and afraid.

IV

It would be a mistake to think that the ambitious madmen of the Renaissance were a horde of sadistic undisciplined brutes. The guards of a torture chamber enjoy what they do. Therefore they will never rise. A love of cruelty limits them. But the Commandant is above pleasures. He is an executive. Certain things must be done. He deputizes them to those best suited to the work. His genius is to know his servants thoroughly. But they are only servants. He has no part in their concerns.

Yet occasionally the machine runs wild. Even the Commandant cannot stop it. That is what had happened to the Cardinal, and certainly he did not like it. There comes a time when we must sacrifice even ourselves to our ambitions, for ambitions are omnivorous. First they eat others. Then our relatives. Then our lovers. Then us. A great man is thus always a phoenix. He rises from his own ashes into success. Therefore he is always a trifle impersonal: he has left himself behind. And if there was one flaw in the Cardinal's nature, it was that he never realized that he was not a great man.

Therefore he drove on. And Ferdinand stood in his way.

Sitting in the Piccolomini Palace, drawing up his own plans for a regency, the Cardinal was aware of every rumour. The whole palace rocked and creaked with whispers, as a building rocks and creaks before a tornado comes. And many of these rumours concerned Ferdinand.

Ferdinand had gone mad. He could overturn everything. Yet he could be removed in no ordinary way. That was troubling. But decision brings a kind of peace. The Cardinal, having reached his, felt once more serene, a little sorry, but serene. He called for a litter and had himself carried to Sor Juana's convent. He had not visited it before. He looked around him curiously, feeling faintly amused. Yet he shared her views. If religion was not gorgeous, it could scarcely be said to exist. But

237

she had spread herself too thin. Some of the plaster-work was decidedly trumpery. That would not do.

He found her in the library. It was the room that most fascinated her. Now she was in control, she need no longer pretend to be austere. The convent would also contain musical instruments and a telescope and celestial sphere. The latter was already being cast in Milan. It was to be ornate. For it was quite true, she had turned from the world, but only to the stars.

She received him rather grandly, despite the fact that her hands and habit were splattered with chalk dust. He was not impressed. He knew too much about her. For some reason her grandeurs had been more real when he had known less.

"I want you to send for your brother," he said.

Sor Juana looked taken aback. He was in a hurry and had no time for courtesies. "I know he is here," he said. "I wish to see him."

"I do not know where he is."

"He came here."

"I had him denied entrance." She was slightly nervous now. Her eyes darted away from him. But she did not lose her poise. Nothing would ever make her lose that.

It was a quality that more than any others he admired. He hated to take it away from her. He gave her one last chance. "Come," he said. "I am sure you did. But do as I say, I cannot seek him out myself."

"What will you do with him?"

The Cardinal was surprised. Again he noted that she had a stubborn mouth.

"Does it matter?"

"Perhaps," she said.

He was annoyed with her. Loyalty was a plebeian trait he would not have expected of her. It was necessary for him to use pressure. He was sorry. Their relations would now be spoiled, and he would miss them.

Though it made him sad to do so, he always made it a point to find out the truth about everyone. No one was so guileless that he had not some secret that might some day be of use. And the truth about Sor Juana now bulged to a file of documents. She was a usurer. She lent money at high interest, very skilfully and privately, but yet by now the sum must be quite large. Hence the splendour of this convent, no doubt.

He glanced around the room. "These decorations are very costly," he said.

She must have been waiting for this for years. Instantly she knew. He could sense that. "So?"

"Do you remember, years ago, that a man called Domenico Allasi came to you? You should have had him investigated with more care. He was in my employ. So were one or two others. Usury is, after all, an ecclesiastical crime. They might be forced to testify before an ecclesiastical court. Or they might not."

She did not stir. She scarcely breathed. "Have you known this long?"

"For as long as you have made money by it. You have made a great deal."

"I kept none. It is all to be spent here."

"That makes no difference." He paused. "Can you find him?"

"Yes," she said wearily. "I can find him."

Nothing stirred in her face, but he could tell she was bitter. Yet she cared nothing for the man, and even hated him. He shrugged. She puzzled him. He did not like to do these things.

He waited restlessly at the palace. He knew Bosola had some strange attachment to Antonio, even though he had helped to betray him. He thought he could count on that, but he was not sure. And the matter must be finished with despatch. He paced up and down.

Bosola was brought to him after dark, at eight.

The Cardinal looked at him with frank curiosity, and was almost unable to recognize him. Something had shattered him. He was dressed like a waterfront rowdy. He had become Niccolò Ferrante again. There was justice in that. He was not Bosola any more. It was as though he had come to the end of a long road, only to find that it did not lead to his destination. He twitched.

The Cardinal was pleased. "My brother has murdered Antonio di Bologna," he said dryly, and as soon as he had watched the effects of that, knew he had chosen the right instrument, and an instrument, moreover, that would be easy

239

to deal with afterwards. He repeated what he had said, patiently, as though dealing with a child. Something happened to Bosola's eyes.

"Shall I tell you where to find my brother?" prompted the Cardinal, and sighed with relief, eager to have the man gone. He did not like to be in his presence. He was no longer a man, but a thing.

All the same, after Bosola had gone, he found he could not sleep. For some of the things we have to do will not let us sleep, no matter how reasonable we are.

V

Ferdinand had refused to lodge with his brother. He distrusted him too much. He could bear to see no one. Therefore he had commandeered a small, disused palace not far from the Cathedral and the tomb-house attached to it, but at the rear and difficult of access through narrow lanes which admitted no light. Here he lurked with his whole company. Ostensibly he had come to Amalfi to protect his interests and to watch the Cardinal. He did neither.

The palace was a crumbling shell. Each year a little more of it settled into the earth. Scarcely a room in it had a level floor. The courtyard was too narrow. The rooms were tall, deserted, barren, and damp. They were littered with forgotten furniture. The kitchens' flues would not draw. Here he and his company camped out. A few chambers had been aired and made habitable, but the corridors were littered with fallen fresco and refuse. The great hall had been converted into a stable. The stench was bad.

What light there was came and went fitfully. Candles and torches only scorched the gloom. Beside Marcantonio, the bravos, and a few servants, there was no one in the building but a company of dwarfs in yellow suits. These had turned up from nowhere, the wreck of a travelling show, and Ferdinand had let them stay. He did not even realize they were the dwarfs in his service, whom he had dismissed half a year ago.

The dwarfs scattered everywhere. They knew every cranny of the palace. Their thin, piping derisive, laughter echoed out of unexpected places, and late at night, in a dark hall, one's torch would pick up the glitter of a pair of eyes, close to the floor, looking out at Marcantonio and the bravos like greedy mice.

Marcantonio hated them. When he came upon them like that he cast his torch in their faces. They would giggle and scramble away. But they always came back. It was almost as though they were waiting. Some cripples develop a good temper. Some do not. These were malevolent.

Marcantonio remembered who they were. He did not tell his master. These days it was impossible to tell his master anything. But he sensed why they had come, and despite himself, was afraid of them. They knew that. They watched him all the more. Like any other muscular man, he looked on deformities with loathing. They only jeered at him, and moved so quickly that he could not catch them.

Yet the dwarfs had not come to Amalfi deliberately. It was only that Ferdinand had killed one of them. They had an instinct for his fall.

Marcantonio wandered the corridors unhappily. He was a loyal dog, and these days his master would have none of him. All the same he sniffed him out. He could not help it. He was attached to him.

Ferdinand had several lurking places. His habits were predictable. Like all men who are afraid of the dark, sometimes he liked to dive into it, with his eyes open, watching avidly. But now, at Amalfi, he was more restless than ever. Since their return from Arosa, Marcantonio had been doubly uneasy. It was as though his master had become his own victim.

He went into the chapel. It was dedicated to St. Sebastian, that patron of plague victims, soldiers, and libertines. He held up his torch. Ferdinand was not there. Yet he was often in the chapel these days, and if he was not there, Marcantonio knew where he was. The bronze arrows had fallen from Sebastian's sleek marble thighs and lay on the floor. There was a rustling. One of the dwarfs appeared, handed Marcantonio an arrow, and dodged away. Marcantonio struck at him, flung the arrow after him, and turned on his heel. The dwarfs followed him. He could not see them, but he knew they were there. He ran down the stairs and out of the building. The dwarfs teetered at the entrance, unwilling to follow. They would be waiting when he came back. They seemed agitated these days.

It was raining. Marcantonio dodged the puddles and came to the darkened tomb-house. He tugged at the door and pushed his way inside. A hole yawned in the floor. The crypt had been opened.

He called aloud.

There was no answer. Looking around him at the dim and sullen marble shapes, Marcantonio started clumsily down the stairs. The crypt was fetid and warm. His light scarcely penetrated the gloom.

Ferdinand was cowering in the shadow of the Duchess's lead coffin. He held out his hands. They were bloody. He had tried to scratch at one of the seals. And he was whimpering. There was no telling how long he had lurked there in the dark. Marcantonio propped his torch against a coffin and knelt down beside him. He was very tender. He tried to put his arm around Ferdinand. Ferdinand shrank away.

"Come," said Marcantonio softly, coaxing him as a mother would coax a child.

Ferdinand merely stared. His jaw seemed unslung. He managed to speak, but what he said was unintelligible. Convulsively he turned to the coffin again and leaned his head against it, as though to cool his forehead of a fever.

Marcantonio tried to draw him up. Then, growing impatient, and knowing his master was mad, he slapped him repeatedly across the face.

No one had ever dared to touch Ferdinand before. He screamed, broke away, stumbled, and fled up the stairs. Marcantonio picked up the torch. Above him the bronze doors clanged. He did not like places like this. He did not follow his master. That would be useless. Instead he decided to put back the floor slab that covered the entrance to the crypt. It took him time.

Ferdinand fled through the dark and sticky rain, as though working his way through spider-webs. The dwarfs saw him coming, glanced at each other, and drew back out of sight. Ferdinand entered the palace and ran for cover.

The dwarfs followed him. They knew the darkness by heart. They chanted at him.

Ferdinand whirled. "Who's there?"

"We are."

Ferdinand sobbed and ran on. The darkness was a vast world. But now it felt inhabited. Things stood about in it, waiting for him. He seemed to hear the rustle of a dress. He could hear silent scurrying. He turned a corridor. He must have light. He must know these were not real shapes in the darkness.

"Marcantonio," he called out. "Marcantonio!"

Behind him there was only the giggle of the dwarfs, and the sound of the rain. The building echoed both.

There was a glimmer of light. Ferdinand ran towards it. Marcantonio was at the end of the gallery, holding a candle. Ferdinand shouted and ran forward. Again he seemed to hear a rustling skirt.

The figure became clearer. "Save me," shouted Ferdinand.

It was not Marcantonio. It was Bosola. His eyes glittered. He held a dagger in his hand. Ferdinand gasped and turned to run. Bosola followed him. The candle whipped out. It clattered to the marble floor.

Ferdinand ran for the head of the stairs. The footsteps of the two men made a hellish racket. For a moment it seemed that Ferdinand might escape. Then the yellow dwarfs moved forward. They had been waiting for something like this. Together they tackled him, hanging about his legs, and brought him tumbling down. Ferdinand screamed. All over his body he felt the tugging of innumerable tiny hands. They gripped tenaciously. He could not shake them off. Wriggling away in the dark, he lost his bearings and fell headlong down the stairs.

Bosola leaped after him. At the bottom Ferdinand lay helpless on his back. A light appeared. Bosola stabbed him repeatedly. It was as though he were killing himself. He struck with joy. The dwarfs stood in a semicircle, watching. It was they who had struck the light. They had never brought down anything so large before. It made them solemn. Ferdinand took a long time to die. Then the rustle of silk inside his brain abruptly stopped.

Bosola panted heavily. He turned, saw the dwarfs, and fled for the archway. They did not follow him. They were silent, subdued, and satisfied. They had had their revenge. Now it was time for them to move on.

Ferdinand's screams had been too loud. Bosola knew he must get out quickly. He padded into the rain and ran smack into Marcantonio. He gasped. Marcantonio had only to look at him to know what had happened. Bosola swerved aside, but one of Marcantonio's vast red hands caught at his thro t.

The Cardinal was a tidy man. He had thought of everything. A company of guards rounded the corner of the alley. They had been waiting, on orders, for just such a hue and cry. Their torches hissed and spluttered in the rain, which tinkled and spat against their cuirasses. They wrenched Bosola away from Marcantonio and took him prisoner. Then, still on the Cardinal's orders, they marched him publicly through the streets.

For the Cardinal was canny. He wanted no part in this crime. It must be identified as the act of a maniac. And the maniac must be done away with, tortured in the sight of all, and his mouth stopped for good. It was a necessary act of politics. Pity had nothing to do with it. The Amalfitani needed an outlet for their hatred. Let them have Bosola.

The soldiers had their instructions. Parade him around the town, and let the world know he was a murderer.

VI

The Amalfitani watched from behind their shutters. You could not see them. You only saw the chinks of light between the louvres. And a light rain carries sound very well.

By intention, the procession passed under the windows of the convent. Voices echoed down the well of the night. Rumour travels fast. Sor Juana watched the parade. Her brother stumbled along, his hands bound behind his back, in that ridiculous peasant costume of his. His head was bowed. He stared at the ground. That was what annoyed her most. No man should ever be bowed. He should always outstare the world.

She looked down. She had never believed in evil before.

244

Intellectual people never do. She believed in it now. It could have been the moment of her conversion, for good is always invisible. Only a glimpse of evil can convince us it is there. Then the glimpse slipped away from her. After all we live in the world. She would have helped him if she could, but she was too important now to help anyone. She did not dare. Instead she shrank back into the middle of the room.

Bosola did not want to outstare the world. He was beyond that. He only wanted it over with. Death did not bother him. It was the thought of pain he could not face. A few people gathered in the streets. Anger took fire in them, as the Cardinal had intended. They pelted him with paving stones and filth. The soldiers did nothing to prevent them. For the crowd it was a holiday. Crowds are always so.

Dully he plodded through the streets. He almost enjoyed it. He winced at the stones and filth, but he was not surprised. Some men run towards the natural goal of their lives, and some away from it. He had done the latter. It was a luxury now to meet it face to face. When they had done with him, they would let him die, and in that thought there was a sort of peace. It gave him the courage to have contempt for the crowd. For they had nothing against him. They were only expressing themselves. This ordure was what they were. It was what they loved. He had known it all along.

Beside the reality of our nightmares, the world has no reality at all. It is no pain to be tortured there, for our true pain is mental. Thus the ancient kings of Armenia must have felt, after years of fear, when at last they were driven through the jeering crowds of Rome, to decorate a triumph.

At last he found himself flung into a dungeon. There he mouldered in the dark until they came to take him out. He could have a priest if he wished, but he did not wish.

Next day he was led out into the square. He blinked in the light, but felt torpid. He did not back away. Perhaps he had been drugged. The executioner was Marcantonio, who eyed him narrowly. The Cardinal had been afraid that he might speak out, and had given orders that if he did he was to be strangled. But Bosola had no intention of speaking out. He had nothing to say, least of all to Marcantonio.

245

It did not hurt him much. He did not even cry out. The crowd was plainly disappointed. The first incision hurt, that was all. They wound his intestines on a spool. He looked on with apathetic interest. Few of us can watch ourselves die. Few of us are granted that much certainty. When they severed the other end of the bowel and tipped the wet, mucous windless into the bonfire, it was like a blessing. It was voluptuous.

Then they killed him.

Neither the Cardinal nor Sor Juana stirred out of doors that day. But that night Sor Juana completed her poem, *The Dream.* She knew now what owl. It was the only real poem she ever wrote. It was enough, with the convents she founded, to get her canonized. But it was not pious. She had seen through piety. That is why she wrote it. She would rather have been a man.

VII

At the end of the week the Cardinal presented the young Duke Raimondo to the people, and proposed the Regency. He stood on the cathedral steps, holding the little boy's sweaty palm, and then lifted him up, so that he might see his subjects.

The ovation was tremendous. The child was intelligent, and therefore frightened. The Cardinal whispered in his ear, to quiet him.

This was the last Piccolomini, a pleasant, thoughtful, handsome, charming blond with tired eyes, and the crowd, which had hated the last Duke and helped to tear the Duchess down, thought he was wonderful. So much, thought the Cardinal, for crowds.

He liked the boy. He was a docile child. And the boy liked the Cardinal, for now he did not have to study any more. He was allowed to play. Why cram his head with statecraft? His chances of ever practising it were slim enough.

Which was a pity, for the Cardinal felt drawn to the lad. He was an orphan, the last of his line, and pretty. As he looked over the shouting, applauding crowd, it occurred to the Cardinal that he, also, was the last of his line. He had not thought of that before.

He looked around him, blinking in the strong sunlight, and

found it good. It would be night soon enough. Now it was time to enjoy the day. For the devil is a dancer in darkness. We must avoid him while we can. Cheated, we learn to cheat.

"Are these really my people?" asked Don Raimondo.

The Cardinal told him yes.

"And I can do anything I like with them?"

"Some day," said the Cardinal. "Some day." And did not know why he felt so sad, or whose presence it was he missed in the crowd below him.